Striking Gold

Striking Gold

A Love in El Dorado Romance

Janine Amesta

TULE
PUBLISHING

Striking Gold
Copyright© 2023 Janine Amesta
Tule Publishing First Printing, August 2023

The Tule Publishing, Inc.

ALL RIGHTS RESERVED

First Publication by Tule Publishing 2023

Cover design by Elizabeth Mackey

No part of this book may be used or reproduced in any manner whatsoever without written permission except in the case of brief quotations embodied in critical articles and reviews.

This is a work of fiction. Names, characters, places, and incidents are products of the author's imagination or are used fictitiously. Any resemblance to actual events, locales, organizations, or persons, living or dead, is entirely coincidental.

ISBN: 978-1-959988-55-7

Dedication

To Tyler
Gold Team. White Team.
It doesn't matter as long as we end up on the same one.
And to all the overachievers out there who have felt the pressure
to always push yourself. You are enough.

Author's Note

Dear Readers,

Never forget your mental health is important. As a note about the content of this book, it touches on the past death of a parent/guardian, grief, a sick pet, complicated family relationships, and school trauma. Have no fear though as there is a happy ending waiting on the last page, including for Hermes the dog.

Chapter One

IT COULD HAVE been the perfect meet-cute.

If she were in a movie, Mia Russo was positive this afternoon would have been the romantic turning point in her life. All of the obvious clichéd beats were there inside the small-town coffee shop. She was a down-on-her-luck, twenty-five-year-old single gal. He was…well, all she knew about him was the fact he was handsome enough to inspire the chiseling of a marble statue or two. If Mia took a wild stab at a board of stereotypical occupations, she would guess…lumberjack? He wore a red-and-black plaid shirt on his healthy, broad physique, reminding her of the hunky mascot on Brawny paper towels.

At this moment, she could use a good, two-ply paper towel to soak up the lusty drool threatening to escape her mouth. Drooling over a customer would not make the best impression during her interview. It was too bad Brawny's beautiful form had to be directly in her line of sight. Did she need one more challenge in her life? This was, no doubt, the gods testing her mental fortitude.

Always-at-the-top-of-her-class Mia never pictured herself walking into Pony Expresso and asking for a job. Then again, she never imagined she'd be back in her small Northern California hometown of Placerville. A city given the nickname "Old Hangtown" when it was part of gold rush history.

Life had a funny way of slapping one across the ass when it was least expected. This exact line of thought must have passed through the minds of several ghostly occupants. In particular, those who contributed to its morbid nickname. In her situation, the trajectory of Mia's life had been wobbling on the edge for some time.

Her interviewer was a woman who looked as if she ran triathlons once a month and was around the same age as Mia—or possibly younger. *God, she better not be younger.* The thought of her future manager being younger was one more jab to Mia's already wounded ego. Plus, Natalie Gonzalez-Torres, with her wavy chestnut-colored hair and soft brown skin, looked to be one hundred percent Latina and a goddess. Mia was half Latina, half white, and neither half was close to the level of goddess. All she could do was stand awkwardly between worlds, and she was pretty sure goddesses were never awkward. Everything about this interview was unfair.

With a flip of her shiny, dark locks, Natalie perused the application in her hands, even though there wasn't much to study. Mia had spent the majority of her energy on her education. Her work resume was slim, almost to the point of nonexistent.

A month ago, when she first started looking for a job, Mia applied elsewhere, places with less of a part-time college student feel to them. But, as the rejections built, the lower and lower Mia's bar dropped. As good as her imagination was, she never expected she'd end up at a tiny coffee shop. In these positions, her education was not a benefit, more of a hindrance, but she was running out of options.

"Do you know how to run an espresso machine?" Natalie asked, giving a good impression of a sincere interview despite Mia's lack of qualifications.

"Truthfully, no," Mia responded. "But I'm a quick learner." She had always been a quick study. All she needed to do was convince Natalie of this. Her response was paired with a bright smile in the hopes it conveyed a higher level of confidence. She considered adding that if Brawny was a regular customer to Pony Expresso, she'd take all night to memorize the coffee menu.

Natalie suddenly brightened. "Oh, you went to El Dorado High? Me, too."

Mia was prepared to learn they were in the same class or Natalie graduated after. She did her best to keep her expression neutral. "Oh, yeah? Did we graduate the same year? You don't look familiar."

"I was a few years ahead of you," Natalie said as she turned the application over.

Thank god for that. The age difference shouldn't matter but it did, and these days Mia would take what she could get.

"I'm afraid the pay would only be minimum wage, but we do share tips. And it's a fun place to work. The owner of the shop is my Uncle Enrique, but he's pretty laid-back." Natalie shared this information cheerfully as though tone alone could improve the financial situation.

A sigh swept through Mia. The wage amount wasn't unexpected, but she couldn't deny the disappointment which came along with it. At least her father wasn't charging her rent while she was living at home again. Nothing said *sad* more than being a grown woman sleeping on a twin-size bed with a stuffed bear, and across from a wall dotted with old framed awards for excellence. Mia would rather avoid her childhood bedroom as much as she could and make some extra money.

"Every little bit helps," Mia replied with as much enthusiasm as she could muster.

"And we're looking for someone who can work the busy, early morning shift," Natalie told her.

"I'll work whenever you need me." Mia hoped her smile didn't appear to be a permanent fixture on her face, but she couldn't stop. Natalie may soon be under the impression she was interviewing a clown in disguise. Maybe she should see if there was a traveling circus hiring nearby. If she couldn't be a goddess, then clown would have to do.

"What's your favorite coffee or tea? What do you like to drink?"

"Oh. Um." Not having an answer ready put an instant ball of anxiety inside Mia's gut. She kicked herself for not being prepared. Of course, they would expect her to have a favorite drink. She was about to flub the most important question of all, and she tried not to flail by grabbing the first item she could read on the chalkboard menu. If she did that, an answer like *Almond Raspberry Muffin* would have burst from her mouth. It happened to be today's chalkboard suggestion, but she was almost certain this was the wrong answer.

Mia went with honesty. "I'm trying to figure that out. I haven't spent a lot of time just relaxing in a cute coffee shop like this one, and I look forward to trying new things. As well as giving your customers the same opportunity."

"I love helping people figure out their favorite drink. My uncle says I have a freaky gift where I can sometimes tell just by looking at a person." Natalie gave Mia a careful study as if she could determine her drink of choice by reading facial features like tea leaves. But after a few seconds, she cocked her head. "Hmm. Actually, nothing is really popping out at me. But I'm sure I'll figure it out eventually."

Mia didn't fault her for this failed attempt at beverage matching. It could have been her questionable goddess status causing a drink-prediction block. With Mia's tanned skin and golden brown hair, Natalie wasn't the first person to be stumped when looking at her.

"I think that's it on my end. We'll give you a call in a few days after we make a decision." The (*definitely older*) manager shook Mia's hand, and the interview came to its conclusion when Natalie answered her ringing cell, replying in Spanish to the person on the other end as she returned to the counter.

Was she really going to do this? Work in a coffee shop? It didn't seem to fit anywhere in her plans when she considered her life goals. This morning, when Mia mentioned to her father where she was interviewing, he shook his head and laughed as if it was a ridiculous joke, which it was. One big, ridiculous, dark roasted joke.

How many times had she heard her father say, *You better stick with the books, Mia, unless you want to be flipping burgers or making coffee.* She did stick with books and yet, here she was. Apparently, it wasn't a joke as much as it was a possible premonition.

Mia had a plan. Well, she had a *new* plan. Her education was extensive, first with a bachelor's in political science and then a master's in the same. After being encouraged by a favorite teacher, who praised her government studies and her involvement in Model UN, Mia's original goal was getting into politics and becoming a big-shot political manager or advisor. Add to this the countless hours she'd spent proudly helping her dad put up re-election signs, even though he often ran unopposed for Judge, and it all felt like destiny.

Since the original plan had not worked out, it was back to the drawing board. The *new and improved* plan was to get her PhD in political science. She'd become a brilliant, in high-demand doctor/professor, make tenure in less than ten years, and write a best-selling book or two. Mia would then end up as an expert contributor on CNN while touring the country to give TED talks. Okay, that last part might be nothing more than a wishful cherry on her career sundae, but the other things were sure to happen. For someone who was used to rising to the top, her plan didn't appear to be an insurmountable sundae.

Except for one problem.

Mia hated being in politics.

Being an active, informed voter? Yes, she was a big proponent of this. Being directly inside the beast? Disappointedly, it wasn't as great of a fit as she had hoped.

Her father wanted her to follow in his footsteps and practice law. He did not make his preference a secret, pushing down on the scale in hopes of convincing her of the correct path. In a single act of rebellion, completely out of character for her, Mia stuck to her guns and went against her father's wishes. The family already had a brilliant lawyer-turned-judge. Wouldn't a genius political advisor expand the family's impressive portfolio to a new arena? Unfortunately, she hadn't known then how it was all going to turn out. Perhaps if she had listened to him, there would be a timeline where she was a customer of Pony Expresso instead of a prospective employee.

This might have been her first mistake.

Her one big venture into the job world, the one listed on her thin resume, was working for a third-party mayoral campaign in Sacramento as a social media manager. The guy was an ass, and his knowledge in regards to civic duty was close to nothing.

Taking a job, any political job, might have been her second mistake.

As everyone predicted, the underdog candidate failed to win enough votes, despite his wealth and high level of arrogance, and, on election night, Mia found herself unemployed and disenchanted.

Her hopeful and expected love affair with the political world never came because it had never existed in the first place. (She came to suspect that her AP government teacher was so good, she confused enjoying his class for real interest in the subject.) In fact, Mia hated every minute of campaign work. It wasn't anything like she imagined. Her job scratched the outer surface of her shiny dream and revealed nothing but dull reality underneath. She had thought she'd be accomplishing things, helping her community, getting great people, like her father, into positions where they could do a lot. Instead, all she did was beef up the asshole's image and help scrounge the depths of people's pockets for campaign funds, which in turn were used for more publicity and more campaign money-making opportunities. Her skills and ambition meant nothing if they were only being used to help the wrong people.

But this was all the experience Mia had. And in a small, sleepy place like Old Hangtown, there weren't many paid opportunities for an expert in political science or a social media manager. Regardless, her father was sure she'd be able to land a position with a law firm as a clerk or legal assistant. Mia was more than confident she'd be able to land a job as well. But, for whatever reason, it didn't happen, not even for the position of receptionist or file clerk.

Overestimating her perceived workplace value based on education alone might have been her latest mistake.

This was how she ended up at Pony Expresso, a place chosen over the other, bigger chain coffee shop in town because it was her mother's favorite. She was now vying for the coveted position of an early morning, minimum-wage-making barista who shared her tips. Even after the interview was finished, she remained at the table on the off-chance Natalie might find herself inspired and offer her a job. This and perhaps she could bask in the presence of Brawny's handsomeness for a few minutes longer until he noticed her.

And notice her he did, because this was, after all, their destined meet-cute moment and Mia couldn't be wasting all this time and energy for nothing. Perhaps being a down-on-her-luck, future-coffee-slinging barista wasn't such a bad thing if it meant meeting her potential soulmate. Especially when the soulmate came inside a package featuring a chiseled jawline, stormy gray eyes, arms the size of tree trunks, and—

Okay. Stop. Get a hold of yourself, Mia, before figurative drool turned into literal gross, dribbling saliva.

The point was, perhaps all this job searching and bar lowering would be worth it in the end.

With their eye contact made, he smiled and leaned toward her. "Hi. I didn't mean to listen in, but I was curious what drink she was going to pick for you. It's a little disappointing she didn't come up with anything. But you did really well in your interview. I hope you get it."

She released a warm smile at his words of encouragement. "Thank you. I hope she gets back to me. I could really use the money."

Brawny shifted in his chair before his gray eyes flitted away in apparent shyness. "I know this is weird, but would you mind doing me a huge favor? I could pay you"—he made a quick survey of the contents inside his bifold leather wallet—"twenty-seven dollars." His scent wafted in her direction. It was a delicious mixture of leather wallet and pine trees. No doubt, it was the same trees he felled with the help of his massive biceps and plaid shirt.

"I guess it depends on the favor. It's the only way to determine if twenty-seven dollars is too much or too little."

"The perfect amount isn't an option?" He grinned a winning smile with dazzling, flawless teeth, and her stomach flopped around like a caught fish.

Mia attempted to play it cool, at least as much as her

stomach fish would allow. She pulled a strand of hair behind her right ear, sliding her hand down her jawline in a single, graceful motion. "You might be able to convince me that perfection is indeed a possibility."

No one was more eager than Mia to hear Brawny's exciting scheme. Her imagination whispered in her brain the various impossible, romantic situations which could occur in the near future and were inspired by too many Hallmark movies. The one she hoped for was the favor where it would be necessary to portray herself as the loving and lovable fiancée to his family, friends…or ex-girlfriend. The same ex-girlfriend, who was, of course, getting married. And his name would be Ethan or Cody or Jack. Although her nickname for him would be Brawny, of course. The daydream ended with him presenting her with a ring he purchased for twenty-seven dollars. She'd continue to wear it for sentimental reasons even after getting a major glittering upgrade.

"Great," he replied, "it's actually very simple. You see, I wanted to buy my girlfriend a special gift, but I'm not good at making decisions and the guys in the office aren't exactly helpful second opinions. It wouldn't take very long, and the jewelry store is just next door."

"Oh." If her smile faltered at all, he didn't seem to notice. Okay, well, there's a girlfriend. *Of course,* there's a girlfriend. But the Hallmark fueled imagination whirred around in her brain once again. This meet-cute could still happen. Maybe Brawny was the put-upon, lovelorn boyfriend with a materialistic, snobbish girlfriend unworthy of his affection. Later, when Bethany or Michelle or Tonya acknowledged his gift with a dismissive wave, his mind would click to the funny, delightful woman he met at Pony Expresso. Brawny would become determined to do whatever it took to find Mia again. It could happen.

"Don't you think your girlfriend would appreciate any gift regardless? I know I would if someone was nice enough to buy me jewelry."

His lips pressed together in thought. "Maybe. I would feel better having a woman's opinion at least." Okay, he said, *maybe*. Mia's impression of Tonya and her dismissive hand waving could be right on the money…maybe.

She smiled. "I think I can handle that for twenty-seven dollars."

"Great! I'm Bob, by the way."

"Mia."

Mia and Bob left the shop, their destination: El Dorado Jewelry.

The store was located on old-timey Main Street and surrounded by other Western-style, brick and plaster shop fronts. It was one of those places she had passed by enough times for it to be a familiar memory, like a sepia-colored photograph in her mind. But Mia was also surprised the store was still around. She didn't know anyone who shopped there, so it was easy to assume it never had any customers, except for the occasional tourist escaping the summer heat.

Bob opened the door for her, and Mia smiled her thanks in response. As soon as she stepped through the threshold, a wire-haired, one-eyed dog with fur the color of old snow greeted her. He appeared to be a cross between some kind of terrier and a dust bunny. His stumpy tail wagged in wild, erratic motions. It wasn't until the dog propped on her shin that she noticed he was missing one front leg. She reached to stroke the top of his bony head with a "Hello there, little guy," because that's what a Hallmark protagonist would do.

Not counting the chummy dog, the inside of the store conveyed as much personality as the straightforward name displayed on the faded, hunter green awning outside. It was filled with several glass cases, as one would expect. Still, it had nothing on its walls, nor were there fancy, glittering displays of gold and silver outside of the cases. It wouldn't be surprising to learn the store hadn't seen a gold rush of customers in some time.

"Can I help you?" she heard the single employee ask. Bob abandoned Mia's side for the man at the far end of the store, and she glanced at the nearest glass case.

The jewelry, presented on simple, black velvet display holders, took her breath away. Mia never would have imagined a boring looking store with a dull-sounding name would have such beautiful, unique pieces inside. Her favorites were the rings. Different precious metals were formed into bands, shaped to make them look like delicate twigs forged by forest nymphs. In the center were vibrant, raw gemstones.

Compared to the precision-cut gems she was used to seeing, the rawness of these stones appeared as though they were excavated straight from a mine, and placed inside a ring setting after washing away the dirt. There were several she wouldn't mind owning herself, but she wouldn't dare to dream about it on a pending Pony Expresso barista's salary plus tips.

"Mia," Bob called.

She flashed a smile and joined him. The jeweler pulled out two sets of earrings from the case and laid them on a square of black velvet fabric.

"Oh, how lovely," she sighed. One pair was silver with twig-like pendants and rose gold leaves. The other set was a pair of shiny, gold stud earrings featuring small pinecones. They were so detailed, Mia was sure the maker had gone out into the surrounding forest, found the most perfect, miniature pinecones and dipped them into gold.

In turn, she lifted and judged each set with careful consideration. Mia figured if Tonya didn't like them, maybe they would someday find their way to her. Returning the jewelry to the velvet, she smiled and pointed to the pinecone earrings. "I like these best."

"Great! I'll get them," Bob responded, pulling out a credit card while brandishing a handsome, relieved smile.

As Bob paid for Tonya's gift, Mia knelt and gave the dog an extended petting, running her fingers through his curls and offering praise on what a good boy he was.

After the transaction was complete, she followed Bob out of the store.

"Thanks again. I really do appreciate your help." He dug into the folds of his wallet.

"No, it's fine. Don't worry about it. I've decided that twenty-seven dollars is too much when I give my opinion for free all the time. You don't owe me anything."

"Are you sure?"

"Yeah. I hope your girlfriend loves her earrings."

"I'm sure she will. I wanted to get something nice because she's pregnant with our first kid."

"Aw, that's nice." She forced the words with as much cheer as she could. An unexpected stab of jealousy struck through her. Tonya clearly had a life with forward motion while Mia struggled to adjust to the backward movement in hers. She worried her life would never get started, and she'd be stuck in limbo forever. "Well, it was very nice to meet you, Bob, and congratulations. If you ever need jewelry advice again, hopefully, you'll find me making coffee at Pony Expresso."

With this, Bob walked away without a second glance back, and the meet-cute moment was not to be. Its birth and death were in the same hour, its whole existence sprung from nothing more than her imagination. Oh, well. Hallmark romances were unrealistic anyway. Mia kicked an abandoned Pony Expresso coffee cup on the sidewalk. In a moment of annoyance, she considered leaving it and stomping away. Then her better self took over, and she plucked the paper cup from the ground and tossed it into a nearby bin.

It was at this moment the sign in the jewelry store's window caught her attention. The only thing missing was sunlight breaking through the clouds and gracing it with a divine spotlight.

HELP WANTED

Perhaps the fates weren't done with her after all.

Chapter Two

WHEN THE BELL above the door jingled again, Ross Manasse glanced up.

She had returned.

As someone who was used to hiding—

Correction.

As someone who was used to *working* diligently in the rear of the shop, Ross was successful at avoiding most of the day-to-day interactions with the characters who would peruse the contents of El Dorado Jewelry. The front of the shop usually fell to his younger cousin, Luna. The same person who took pleasure in reminding him several times they weren't *characters* as much as they were *valued customers*.

But times were changing, and he needed to adjust. Ross hated adjusting. In fact, he hated adjusting more than he hated awkward interactions with valued customers. He spent the majority of his time in the workshop for a good reason. Precious metal and stones didn't require a casual exchange of pleasantries. They succumbed to his will under nothing more than calloused, experienced hands. Troublesome words weren't necessary. He preferred it this way.

Although, when it came to Mia Russo, it was pretty safe to say she fell more into the *character* category. Some things didn't change. Even so, he wasn't sure he liked this latest development to his day. Her walking into his shop the first time was a surprise. Her walking in a second time...well, now it was interesting.

"I wondered if you'd be back," Ross said as he bent to replace the silver and rose gold earrings to their original position within the glass case.

"I'm sorry?"

Ross's eyes met hers. "Did you change your mind?"

Her forehead crumpled in confusion. "Change my mind?"

"About the earrings. If so, I'm going to need your boyfriend's credit card again because of the price difference."

Mia waved her hands in front of her. "Oh! No. He's not my boyfriend."

"Fiancé? Husband? Whatever. It doesn't matter. All I care about is the credit card."

"No, I mean...none of those." She paused to take a moment before pushing ahead. "I'm not here about the earrings. I'm sure his actual girlfriend will be thrilled with them. I just met the guy in the coffee shop and he asked me to come with him for a second opinion."

Mia's eyes drifted upward, studying the ceiling panels. "Now that I say it out loud, it is...kind of weird. But I'm not surprised. Weird things always seem to happen to me."

"Okay," Ross replied, unsure of the proper response to her ramblings. "So," he said, stretching the word to fill the silence. "I take it you're here for me then?"

"What?" Mia's amber-colored gaze zipped to his, her cheeks blooming pink. She eyed the door as if calculating how long it would take to escape the shop if it became necessary.

This reaction befuddled him. "Well, I doubt you're going to reminisce with the dog."

"I...uh...I," Mia said. "I'm actually here because of your sign."

"What sign?" Ross replied, his own patience fading fast at whatever game this was.

Mia leaned, pointing to the HELP WANTED sign he'd set in the window earlier in the day. "That one."

It was his turn to stumble. "Wait. What? You're asking *me* for a job? Is this a joke?"

She crossed her arms. "Are you the owner? If you don't want people coming in asking you for a job, why'd you hang the sign?"

"Yeah, I'm the owner." Ross gave her a solid once over. "*You* have experience in jewelry retail?" He didn't bother hiding his skepticism in the question.

Mia lifted her delicate chin, drawing closer to the jewelry case, which served as a barrier between them. "I don't actually, but it doesn't mean I still couldn't do the job to your satisfaction. I'm a quick study, and I imagine jewelry, especially pieces as unique and beautiful as these, have no problem selling themselves."

Ross returned her look of bravado with a flat one of his own before reaching to retrieve a bottle of glass cleaner. He sprayed the counter, wiping away nonexistent fingerprints as if this was his biggest priority of the day and required all of his attention.

Despite his nonresponse, Mia spoke again. "Let me at

least fill out an application. I'm–"

"Mia Russo. Valedictorian. Class Treasurer. National Honor Society. National AP Scholar. Yearbook editor. Debate club. Model UN." As he rattled off the list, her eyes grew wider. "That's all I can remember right now. And, in that very impressive list, I don't think any of it qualifies as experience for working in a small jewelry store."

A brief moment of pleasure passed through him as Mia's mouth dropped open. But it would be a matter of seconds before her brain rebooted itself as she never remained silent for long. "What? How?" She shook her head. "Did we go to school together?"

Ross narrowed his eyes before returning the spray bottle to the bottom shelf. Her reaction was sincere. She didn't remember him. Hurt gave way to annoyance. He leaned against the glass case, not caring about adding a new set of fingerprints to it. "It was a long time ago."

It had been close to ten years since they last interacted, which *was* a long time. For Mia to remove his face and name from her memories, as she moved through her academically privileged life, shouldn't have been surprising. But the disappointment was startling anyway.

Ross's memory was not flawed. He knew it was Mia the moment she walked through the door of his jewelry store. It didn't matter if the braces were gone or her face narrowed, or her golden-brown hair fell in thick, soft waves instead of being pulled into an ever-present ponytail. The way her soft curves filled the short summer dress and navy blue blazer, revealing long shapely legs—

Anyway, those were the things that had changed. Her

large eyes, the color of warm, melting amber, remained the same and were still framed behind glasses. Although, presently, she was sporting chunky, black frames instead of slender silver ones. The style of the glasses didn't matter, they suited her either way. And her eyes still possessed the ability to thaw anyone's resolve. Anyone else's that is. Ross's resolve had been permafrozen.

Worse yet, the same smile was there on her lips, something he would remember today or a hundred years from now. And that single, damn dimple on her right cheek. It was burned into his memory as if it was branded with a hot poker. He used to love and hate Mia Russo's dimple because, in the old days, he would have done almost anything to see it.

But that was then. Maybe time had changed her the same way it had changed him. Life had taught him so many lessons over the last ten years, the adult version of himself was nothing like sixteen-year-old Ross. Not all changes were physical, including his late growth spurt and actual muscle definition. The teenage version had spitfire lava running through his veins. But years had cooled the heat, turning his heart into a hard, cynical stone. As a result, Ross, the man, would never succumb to anything as ridiculous as a dimple these days, even if it came in looking for a job.

At this point, Mia wasn't wielding a dimple or any of her other charms as she guided a careful perusal of his features. "What's your name?"

"Doesn't matter."

"If it doesn't matter, then why keep it a secret?" Her eyes processed the shop as if she was a detective looking for the one piece of evidence that would break The Case of the Missing Name wide open. When her search proved fruitless, she returned to his face.

Satisfied Mia was stuck, he offered a slight smile of benevolence. "I'll tell you what, if you can remember my name by the time I close today, you can have the job."

Her brow furrowed. "Are you serious?"

"Perfectly."

"Okay, I'll be right back. I'm going to talk with your neighbors."

Ross shrugged. "Go ahead. I never talk to them. They probably refer to me as the jewelry guy with the dog."

"What's your website?"

"Don't have one."

"Can I have a business card?"

"No."

Her mouth slipped into an angelic smile, her damn dimple flashing in unison as if she was auditioning for the role of innocent girl. All she was missing was the batting of eyelashes. "Come on, John."

"That's not my name."

Mia pointed one of her fingers at him while moving in the direction of the door. "You're going to lose. I'm getting this job. Nothing I like better than a challenge, Freddy."

"So, if I hire you, I lose? That doesn't make me want to hire you. This isn't a scavenger hunt. You're supposed to *remember* my name, not dig through old newspaper clippings."

She opened the door. "Okay, dig through old newspaper clippings. Got it. I actually do need a business card. How will I get a hold of you to accept my offer of employment for your place of business, Henry? Rick? Sebastian?"

"Google it."

"Oh, good idea. I'll do that now." Mia pulled her phone from her purse, typing with the voracity of a teenager as she walked past the shop window until she was gone.

Ross returned to wiping his fingerprint smudges from the glass counter. With any luck, she was out of his life again. He was alone with his thoughts, which was what he preferred. He didn't need interesting characters in his shop, even if they had tempting curves, amber eyes, and a single, provoking dimple. He didn't need that in his life or to even think about it. And he wasn't thinking about it.

One thing clearly hadn't changed: Mia was smart. A nervous finger tapped against the counter as he checked the clock. Perhaps giving her until five P.M. was a mistake. He didn't want to deal with her on a social level, let alone hire her. She had three and a half hours. He should have played it safe and given her twenty minutes.

The bell jingled, grabbing his attention. Mia poked her head in and grinned.

Shit. Twenty minutes was *still* too much time.

"Is it Rumpelstiltskin?" she asked.

"No," Ross answered, relieved.

"Dammit! I thought it was worth a shot. Okay, I'm still on this. You better not hire anyone else before five o'clock."

Then Mia was gone, possibly already forgetting him for the second time. Maybe he should be used to it. Maybe he shouldn't care. One thing for sure, he shouldn't be secretly hoping she'd remember.

Chapter Three

MIA ENTERED HER two-story family home, a structure with an overabundance of large, picture windows, hardwood pine floors, and matching decor. She found her father in the office, stationed at the computer in a leather chair, and surrounded by framed accolades. His professional achievements and community connections made her father's space an impressive career trophy room.

By middle age, the man had settled into a gruff, no-nonsense demeanor, someone who was used to being in a position of unquestioned authority. While most found his formidable presence intimidating, Mia had no problem treating him as she would a lovable bear.

"Hey, Dad."

Her father glanced at her from over the top of his reading glasses. "Hey, honey. How was the interview? Did they offer you the manager position?"

She gave him a squeeze across his broad shoulders and a quick kiss to his balding head, where the wispy moss of hair formed into a perfect horseshoe. "Oh, yeah, the interview."

"You didn't go?" he asked, his attention split as he read something on the monitor. "What have you been doing all this time?"

"No, I went. It was fine. The girl who interviewed me was really nice. Maybe I can make a new friend while I'm at it."

Her father shook his head. "I think getting the job might be the more important thing here."

Mia let out a soft laugh. "Maybe for you. You're not the one with an extra friendship bracelet kicking around in your purse. But she said she'd get back to me if I had the job."

She shot him a quick glance before pushing ahead. "Afterward, I ended up at the jewelry store next door." She chose to omit the other details, such as being persuaded to follow a stranger because of handsomeness and twenty-seven dollar bait. The last thing she needed was a lecture from her overprotective father on something which had turned out to be not a big deal. Plus, a dad lecture was bound to waste the valuable and diminishing time remaining for her detective work.

"Why were you at a jewelry store?"

She picked some lint from her sleeve. "Oh. Uh. It doesn't matter. Have you been to El Dorado Jewelry before?"

"Do I look like I visit a lot of jewelry stores?"

"I don't know. I assumed you may have picked up a bauble or two for Mom when you got in trouble for one thing or another."

Her father harrumphed at the suggestion.

Mia pushed ahead. "Anyway, long story short because who has time for pesky, boring details, I need to figure out the name of the guy who owns the place. I tried looking on Google, and it says it was owned by a guy named Victor Lanza. But he's dead, and the only other name I can find connected to the business is Luna Lanza."

"You were there. Why didn't you just ask?"

She groaned while crossing her arms and using the desk as support. "He won't tell me. Apparently, he knows who I am, and he said if I could remember who he is, he'd give me a job at the jewelry store."

With this additional information, her father swiveled his chair, his cool blue eyes searching her as his face turned serious. "What? Who is this guy?"

"That's what I'm trying to figure out, Judge. Don't you have any connections at the courthouse that can help me? I only have until five P.M."

"No. It's a courthouse, not the police department. Also, I shouldn't have to tell you how unethical it would be for me to call in a favor like that. And even if it was something I could do, I wouldn't use connections to get you a job at a jewelry store. Forget this guy. He sounds like a creep. Why would you want to work there, anyway?"

"I don't exactly want to work in a coffee shop either. At least the jewelry store would be less stressful. Plus, I'd be surrounded by beautiful jewels all day and next door to my future BFF. Why wouldn't I want that?"

Her father's focus returned to the computer. "You're better than this, Mia."

"Stop it. If you aren't helping me, then I'll just investigate on my own. Do you know where my old yearbooks are?"

"If they're not in your room, maybe check the craft room."

Mia knew they weren't in her childhood bedroom.

When she'd moved back a month ago, she went through everything to adult-ify the room. She removed the old poster of Einstein sticking out his tongue, the pastel, ruffled curtains, and most of the stuffed animals. Without much ceremony, the items were plunked into cardboard boxes and made to live out their future existence inside the Russo garage.

The craft room became the next logical place to look. But she stopped at the closed door. It wasn't just a craft room. It was her mother's craft room. She had died suddenly of a heart attack while Mia was away at college. For the remaining Russo family members, it was easier to keep the door closed. They could pretend her mother was still on the other side of it, forever crafting undisturbed. Mia didn't want to experience the dull pain of grief today and instead made a beeline for the garage. The distraction of a silly mystery was more welcomed than the harsh reality of unfinished quilts.

After shifting a few items around, she uncovered a box with the words *Mia's books* written in black Sharpie. She broke the tape, scanned its contents, and was excited to find her senior yearbook. The jewelry job would be hers within the hour.

She lugged the heavy box to her room and pulled out the book. It had been a long time since she looked through it—not since she had received it and asked fellow classmates to sign its pages before they parted for the final time. There were more memories of putting the yearbook together than of her fellow Cougars.

In a word, her experience in high school had been…fine.

She had friends, and plenty of acquaintances, but never really belonged to any one clique or another. Mia never cared about things like that. She was too busy trying to race to the top of the GPA. The fact she was able to move quite easily between groups, due to her quick wit and diplomatic charm, was another reason why the instructor of her AP government class, Mr. Cleavers, put the bug in her ear that she would do well in the political world.

Even so, high school was a means to an end of getting into a prestigious college and a fantastic career. Being labeled as *smart* was a simple byproduct of this arrangement, and one Mia wore as an invisible badge stitched onto her identity.

At the time, this was enough. Mr. Cleavers, along with all Mia's teachers, was proud of her academic accomplishments. The other smart kids respected her scholarly game. And her mother made scrapbooks to honor her daughter's achievements.

But none of these compared to what she got from her father. Honorable Judge Russo was Mia's real-life Atticus Finch. Her disillusionment may have occurred with politicians, but her father was the real deal. Prudent. Just. Ethical. These were accurate descriptions of the judge, because the accolades decorating his office were well earned. If she did right by him, then there was no doubt she was doing right by the highest of standards. His approval was the most significant achievement she could ever receive, and she had planned to show him that she could take on the political world at the highest level and win. With that idea dead, she settled for showing him she could become Dr. Mia Russo, and he had happily endorsed her plan of applying to doctoral programs.

Flipping through the yearbook pages, Mia soon located her own picture: the dorky girl in glasses with a smile which occupied fifty percent of her face. A single response floated to her mind. *Yikes*. Was it possible to burn every copy of her class's El Dorado High School yearbook? Who needed a reminder of her past awkwardness?

Although Rumpelstiltskin had no problem recognizing her, making it obvious some of her physical awkwardness remained to this day. This was made worse by the fact that, with a tall, athletic frame and hair anyone would classify as *good*, the man was the opposite of a troll monster. Sure, he wasn't as broad and muscled as Brawny, but with the sleeves of his gray shirt pushed up, she couldn't help noticing his forearms, the same ones which leaned impatiently against the glass jewelry cabinet. She was a sucker for sexy forearms and this might have been the best pair she'd ever seen in real life. Her ex-boyfriend, Thomas, definitely didn't have the strong, capable forearms with a slight crisscrossing of veins like the jeweler. She couldn't help wondering what the rest of him looked like.

While mentally fanning herself, Mia made the snap decision to invest in a full makeover as soon as the jewelry store position was hers. Rumpelstiltskin wouldn't know what hit him when she strolled in looking like…well, not a supermodel. Who was she kidding? She'd at least need the biological beauty building blocks to pull this off and her smile still took up fifty percent of her face. It was best if she remained realistic and instead dreamed about being an amazing, upscale version of herself. Anyway, it didn't matter. Her only goal was causing Rumpelstiltskin's jaw to smack on the display cabinet. This would, fingers crossed, leave a big enough mark, his sexy forearms would have to reach for the glass cleaner again.

"It's two-ply," she would say while suavely tossing a roll of paper towels at the flabbergasted jeweler.

Or something like that.

Under the photo were her high school achievements. Her finger swiped down the list. Mr. Mystery Man got it almost complete, but there was one he hadn't listed. *Most Likely to Succeed.* It was a good thing people in high school weren't keeping close tabs on her because they'd *most likely* ask her to give the title to someone more worthy.

Sitting in her childhood bedroom, Mia couldn't view her life and see any part she would call a success. For now, it was easier to put off her future with more education, something she never had any problem succeeding in. Though she hated a career in politics, her life (and her parents' money) had already invested a lot into it—into her. Mia didn't want to risk another misstep, a worse one.

But she wasn't here to mull over her successes or lack thereof. Mia's challenge was to discover Rumpelstiltskin's true identity. She hadn't noticed him during her first venture into the store. She was too occupied with visions of beautiful jewelry and the handsome man in the plaid shirt. But during their subsequent conversation, she had ample time to take in his appearance which should help her now as she scanned the images of past classmates.

Mia's impression? He was someone serious and reserved,

like the well-worn, long-sleeve gray shirt he wore. He didn't have the personality of a typical salesman. If he was like this in high school, it could be why she didn't remember him. There was a quietness about him. They might not have interacted much at all.

His eyes, on the other hand, were another matter. They were probably a deep brown but had the dark glint of obsidian, and they managed to blaze into hers with the intensity of the sun. Mia didn't want to make a habit of staring into his gaze too long for fear he'd pick her apart and figure out her inner workings, which were nobody's business but her own. There was something about his eyes that might have been familiar, but it was all locked behind a thick haze. Or maybe it was because she couldn't connect the eyes with the body.

His jawline was peppered with the black dots of a perpetual five o'clock shadow. This same jaw was locked into place as if his skull was carved from a single block of oak. This block was topped with a thick mane of hair as dark as his eyes, raven black.

But there was nothing extraordinary about his appearance, nothing to help Mia in her current goal. A three-inch-long scar, lazy eye, or a broken nose would have made this challenge too easy. It also would have been nice if the apparent chip on his shoulder or sexy forearms could have been captured by the school's photographer. She closed her eyes, and tried to imagine what a younger version of the man would look like, but couldn't get past the intensity of his dark eyes. The whole thing was incredibly aggravating.

She sighed and continued flipping through the pages.

She searched under the name Lanza. Nothing. Next, each photo was studied with a detective's attention to detail, looking for anyone who fit his physical description. She wasn't able to narrow it down to a definitive person. She had to admit, he seemed confident in his dare, as if there was no chance of her discovering his identity, same as the real Rumpelstiltskin. Maybe he had been in an accident, and they reconstructed the majority of his face. (If so, he should be on billboards because the surgeon did an extraordinary job.) Or perhaps they didn't go to school together, and he was a creep who kept tabs on her all these years. Even if this was simply a riddle created by a bored, nameless jeweler, Mia didn't like to lose.

"How's your weird search going?" her father asked from the doorway.

"Not good. I'm beginning to think the whole thing was a figment of my imagination. Maybe I'll walk down Main Street again, and the jewelry shop won't even be there. I'll pull a nearby person aside and say, 'What happened to El Dorado Jewelry?' and they'll tell me it burned down thirty years ago and Victor Lanza still haunts the area, like an old prospector's ghost."

"Sure." Her father, the skeptic, was unimpressed with her creative story.

"Oh, I just came up with an idea!" Mia said. She pushed the yearbook off her lap, retrieving her cell from where it sat on the bed. She found the store listing and hit call.

After a few rings, a deep, gruff voice as fan-worthy as his forearms, spoke. "El Dorado Jewelry."

"Hello, I'm interested in purchasing some of your finest

rings," she said in her most affected, rich lady voice. "With whom am I speaking to, young man?"

There was a slight pause on the other end before the voice replied, "Nice try, Mia."

"Dammit! Is it Victor Jr.?"

"No." And he hung up.

Chapter Four

THE TIME ON the clock read four forty-five P.M. That was it. The day was practically finished. Ross might as well flip the OPEN sign to—

The bell jingled. *Goddammit.*

He stalked from the small office, expecting to find bad news in the form of a young woman with a single dimple.

"Hey, Ross!" Luna, his younger, spitfire cousin with mahogany-brown hair stood inside the shop, much to his relief.

"Oh, thank god. It's just you, Lulu." A hand went to his chest to calm his racing heart.

"Luna. How many times do I have to tell you? A twenty-one-year-old, sophisticated woman going off to college is not called Lulu. Who were you expecting?"

"No one."

She raised an eyebrow. "Okay, weirdo."

Ross untied the straps of his leather work apron, slipping it off. Growing up under the same roof made Luna more sister than cousin. She was extroverted, making her the opposite of him. But their differences, and four-year age gap, didn't prevent their closeness.

He studied her as she applied balm to her lips. "What are you doing here, anyway? I'm closing up soon, and I'll be at the house to help you pack up your car—"

"I'm already packed," she said before tossing the lip balm into her purse.

"What? You should have waited. You don't know how to pack a car to its max efficiency."

"And yet, I still managed to get everything in regardless. Strange." She rolled her eyes.

"Are you really so eager to get away from home? I mean, I know it's a dump and all—" His words stopped when Luna sniffed. "What's wrong?"

"That dump has been my home for...what? Twenty years?" Her voice fractured. "You would have laughed at me. I spent an hour today crying over how much I'll miss the cracked window pane in my bedroom. How can I be so sentimental about something so silly?"

Ross pulled his cousin into a hug, rubbing her back. "You're right. That is something silly to get sentimental over. I hope missing *me*, an actual person, generated at least two hours of crying. When did you find time to squeeze in packing? I bet your car organization job is shit."

Luna sputtered a laugh in between weepy tears, but Ross understood what she was going through. His sarcastic words masked his own depression, which settled across his soul from the reality his kid cousin was leaving him for better things, like being accepted to Chico State. This caused Ross to go through a fair amount of eye-rolling sentimentality as well. He'd miss her taking ownership of the bathroom counter with numerous hair and face products. Or their countless thermostat battles at the childhood house they shared. Or the constant tug-of-war over how El Dorado

Jewelry should be run. There were too many silly, ridiculous things to count.

But spirited Luna couldn't be held back forever no matter how much he wanted it. She'd already delayed her ambitions long enough to help him with the shop. Ross should be used to being left behind, but his cousin had been in his life since her birth. He adopted the protective big brother role when Ross's aunt departed for better things shortly after Luna's fourth birthday. Whatever those *better things* were, Luna wasn't included. The cousins were connected in their financially poor, unconventional upbringing, both of them parentless being raised by their grandfather. Ross worried this new distance could affect their connection and perhaps she wouldn't want to come back at all. Why would she when it was possible to do so much better?

"You know," he started, "I can close the store for a few days and make the drive with you if you want."

At this moment, he'd take anything to stave off the inevitable change that arrived with the force of an emotional train. It seemed as though it was yesterday when Luna had shared the news about getting into a university. They had celebrated the rare moment of good luck without a thought to the bittersweet parting soon to follow. It was too bad Ross couldn't spend an hour crying over a cracked window pane as freely as his cousin. Instead, he'd rather avoid the situation and lose himself in his work.

Luna leaned away from him, giving Ross a flat expression. "And what would Grandpa Victor-for-victory say about you closing up the store?"

Thinking about their grandfather, a man who had died

several years prior, brought another layer of sadness to Ross's heart. He pulled himself out of it for her sake and smiled. "He'd say, *That Lulu got her act together and is going to college? My god. Ross, drive your cousin and make sure she actually gets there and doesn't take a detour to go party instead.*"

She laughed. "Okay, you might be right, but that means he'd still be working in the store."

Luna followed him into his office, stopping to pet Hermes, who was snoring on the carpet. Ross began his standard closing practices at the desk while she watched him.

"Speaking of which, have you found a store replacement for me yet?"

He kept his focus on the computer, not wanting to reveal anything in his demeanor. "I've had a few inquiries."

"Anyone good?"

"There's a woman named..." He shuffled through a stack of papers on his desk in an attempt to refresh his memory and found the application from an older Indian-American woman. "Ah, here it is. Aanya Pujari. I'm considering hiring her. She worked in a jewelry store in Sacramento. I guess she's not enjoying retirement as much as she thought she would. She's nice."

"Well, she sounds like a good choice," Luna agreed. "And maybe let her actually do the sales work, so you can concentrate on what you're good at."

"Being good looking?" Ross gave her a wink.

She wrinkled her nose. "Gross. In what world? I know you're not referring to the one we're living in now."

"Uh-huh," was Ross's dry response. He gave her a glance before clearing his throat. "I actually had a person from school stop in for the job."

"Oh, yeah? Anyone I would remember?"

"Nope." Ross powered off his computer. "Just someone who used to tutor me."

"You mean someone who *tried* to tutor you."

He gave Luna a small grin. "I guess. This person was the smartest student in school. It would make sense to pair them with the biggest educational disaster in the district."

"Shut up. You know I hate it when you talk like that." She examined his face. "You didn't want to help out an old friend asking for a job?"

"She's not an old friend," Ross corrected quickly. He had to prevent Luna from getting the wrong idea—or any idea. Her hobby was conclusion jumping, and this situation didn't require any.

"Ooh, a girl," she responded with a cocky grin of her own.

Goddammit.

"Is she cute?"

He blew out an impatient sigh. "I don't know, and I don't care. Working with her would get on my last nerve."

"So, she *is* cute?"

"It doesn't matter if she's cute or not, because I don't care. I'm not going to hire her."

"Are you going to miss working with me?"

"No, working with you gets on my nerves, too. You're doing me a favor going off to college. Good riddance."

"When everyone bugs you, it's probably you," she said.

"Hermes doesn't bug me." Ross nodded to the sleeping dog on the carpet.

"Poor Aanya doesn't know what she's walking into."

Luna bent to claim the dog, cuddling Hermes to her chest. They made their way to the shop door after Ross locked the office behind him.

"Can I take Hermes with me?"

"No." Ross couldn't lose his pet as well. That might make him openly sob.

"What a mean man," she said into the dog's floppy ear. "He's definitely going to miss me when I leave tonight."

"Tonight? I thought… I thought you weren't leaving until tomorrow. I don't like the idea of you driving when it's dark. Are you sure you don't want me to go with you, Lulu?"

"Luna. And it's not dark yet. Plus, if you take me, we might never get there. You have the worst sense of direction in the whole world. It's just…I'm already packed. I thought we could get a quick bite to eat at the diner down the street and then I could leave. I'm ready."

But Ross wasn't ready. Not even a little. His jaw tightened as he stared at his younger cousin hugging Hermes, and a lump invaded his throat. Adjusting to a home with a single occupant was still a punishment, even while believing Luna deserved this opportunity—for her, for him, for the business. This was what he had to focus on.

"You'll take care of my store, right? I'm counting on it to help pay for my degree."

"*Our* store, smartass. It's only in your name as a technicality." They smiled at each other. Having the old standard argument one final time was fitting. It was Ross's store as much as hers, but he didn't have a stellar history and therefore technicalities were a reality.

Luna's hazel eyes glossed with new tears. "You're going to be fine, Ross. And don't worry. I'll be back." She gave him a wry grin. "If you're really going to miss being annoyed you should consider hiring your cute friend. Maybe being driven wild will be good for you."

"Well, there was a chance I would have. But, unfortunately for her, she just ran out of time." And with smug satisfaction, tinged with some unexplained disappointment, Ross flipped the OPEN sign to CLOSED.

Chapter Five

FAILURE SUCKED. BUT working in a coffee shop actually wasn't that bad. Yes, Pony Expresso had busy mornings due to caffeine-addicted locals and tourists, but the task of making coffee was simple. Of course, there were days when Mia's feet hurt, or she had to deal with the occasional crabby customer B.C. (before coffee). But even on the busiest, worst mornings, it was better than working for a political campaign. Plus, Natalie made for a fun coworker as she attempted to guess people's drinks before they ordered. (Amazingly, she was right more than wrong.) Mia came to the conclusion that burger flipping and coffee pouring wasn't the worst fate to befall a person. Not that she would tell her father this.

If there was one thing she excelled at, it was learning, and she'd use the opportunity to learn as much as she could about the coffee business. Macchiato, cappuccino, latte, Americano, cafe crema. After a week at Pony Expresso, she understood what these words meant instead of them being random coffee names for hot beverage snobs.

To a busy and ambitious student, coffee was coffee. When she needed caffeine, Mia didn't want to waste time and energy on the particulars. The same had been true when she worked long, late hours for the Sacramento campaign. Perhaps this was her chance, as she stated during her job interview, to decide what she liked, instead of settling for whatever was easy, convenient, or handed to her.

She was in the groove, blocking out the usual coffeehouse chatter inside the shop. Her mind was focused on making an Americano. After pouring the espresso shot into the hot water, she popped the plastic lid on the paper to-go cup and slipped on the cardboard sleeve. She raised the cup to eye level, giving her clear sight of the name scratched in black Sharpie.

"Ross!" Mia called.

All of a sudden, a treasure trove of memories flooded into her mind.

There he was, standing in front of her, his hand reaching for the cup.

"Ross Manasse," she said, meeting his gaze. *Good lord.* Ross Manasse was the owner of the sexy forearms? He had definitely grown since the last time she'd seen him and what he'd grown into was all man.

His dark eyes reflected surprise before one side of his mouth kicked up in a slight smile. "I see you made a full recovery from your tragic case of amnesia."

And she had. She remembered…

THE HIGH SCHOOL counselor, Ms. Burgos, a scattered woman with wild, curly hair, visited Mia's AP English class. "Hello. Hi, everyone," she said, disrupting the small group discussions around the room. "We're starting a new program of peer tutoring, which pairs an outstanding student with one who might need a little extra help. I know a lot of you are busy with extracurricular activities. But we're only asking for a one or two day a week commitment after school. This would definitely be something that would look great on college applications. If you're interested, please come up and put your name on the list."

Mia joined a handful of students as she made her way to the sign-up clipboard. Ms. Burgos gave her arm a light squeeze. "Mia, I'm so glad you decided to sign up. Can you stop by my office real quick during lunch?"

"Okay," she agreed.

It was then the counselor told her about Ross Manasse. While being in the same grade, Mia wasn't sure they had ever shared a classroom together. They existed side-by-side, but on a different plane of academic experiences, separated by classroom walls.

"Ross is a nice kid, you see, but…" Ms. Burgos twisted a rubber band around her finger as she pondered the next words with careful consideration, "…well, he's always struggled. He probably should have been tested way back to see if he was better suited for other…more specialized classes. From talking to his teachers, it's amazing Ross got this far. He just barely manages to get through. He lives with his grandfather, so I'm not sure he's getting the family support he needs at home. With all the students I have on my list, he'd probably be the most challenging one to take on, which is why I'd like him to go to you."

"I don't mind." Mia's chest had inflated at being singled

out. Even if Ross still failed his classes, her own pristine record wouldn't suffer. But maybe Ross could succeed more than Ms. Burgos thought possible. Mia could have even received some prestigious award if she was able to take a struggling student and transform him into an honor roll one. An educational *Pygmalion*. It could happen.

They were scheduled to meet in the library on Tuesdays and Thursdays after school. Mia had jumped into her role as a brilliant peer tutor, ready to polish the piece of coal into a dazzling diamond. She had been taken aback to discover Ross had come into the program less than enthused. His dark eyes glinted with churlishness, and his mouth had been set in a straight line. Lanky, raven-haired Ross had been sullen, quiet, and not about to do his part in making Mia the star tutor the school would be referencing for decades. An uncooperative participant had not been part of her plan, but she had no doubt he would soon get with the program. Instead, Ross slumped in the library chair, crossing his arms as he stared at everything except her.

She pushed ahead, undeterred. "What do you want to work on? What book is your class reading? Or do you want to work on history? I'm really good with history and government type stuff."

Ross shrugged, the image of teenage aloofness.

At this point, it became clear, tutoring Ross was going to be more difficult than she had imagined. After much encouragement, she was able to coax out his ragged copy of *The Odyssey* from his ripped, faded backpack. But Ross slid his long, spindly arms across the table, laying his head on top of them.

"Oh, you guys are still on this book? I read it last year. What do you think of it so far?"

Keeping his head down, a silent shrug was his only reply.

"Do you want to read some of it together?" she asked.

"How about you read it to me? I'm too tired today."

This was how it went for the next few sessions. She was pulling teeth to get anything more than single-word responses from Ross. Mia considered returning to the counselor and telling her this wasn't a challenge, it was impossible. She dreaded their tutoring sessions as much as Ross did. Instead of her enthusiasm rubbing off on him, his own gloominess had latched itself onto her.

One morning, Mia told her father that Ross graduating high school would be a miracle. Especially if he treated all his schoolwork in the same unmotivated manner. She had asked her father for his opinion, because he'd never steered her wrong before.

"You are the brightest, most tenacious kid I know. You don't have to expect miracles, but if tutoring gives this kid a little bit of hope, that not everyone has given up on him, then that will still be an amazing accomplishment. Maybe that's the real reason you're there. Sometimes that's all it takes."

Mia had contemplated her father's wise words. In the end, she decided to give it one final push.

"Hey, Rosso!" she exclaimed at their next meeting, pairing it with a good-natured grin.

"That's not my name," Ross said in his usual depressed tone before slumping into the plastic chair beside her and dropping his battered backpack on the floor.

"Yeah, but, see, my last name is Russo, and your name is Ross, so we could be like Russo and Rosso."

His grave eyes held hers unimpressed.

"Hey, do you like cookies? My mom made some Mexican Italian wedding cookies for the holidays coming up, and I brought some to share." She burrowed into her bag for the bundle of cookies she'd snagged from the counter that morning.

"You know you're not supposed to eat in the library, right?"

"Come on, Rosso. You wouldn't rat out your partner, Russo, would you?"

He didn't reply, but his eyes dropped to the small balls of baked goods covered in powdered sugar with a healthy smattering of rainbow sprinkles on top. Mia offered him one which he accepted in his palm. He tossed it into his mouth, and it was gone in seconds.

"Why are they *Mexican* Italian?" Ross asked.

"My mom came up with it because it's like me. I'm both. Also, I'm very sweet, which I'm sure you've already noticed."

He didn't react but his eyes scanned her face. She was used to it. When people couldn't quite place her into an easy box, they'd study her like they were trying to figure out which of her features belonged to which group. After fielding strangers' questions like *What are you?* over the years, Mia tried to take it in stride. She was who she was, and, for the most part, it didn't have much relevance in her normal day-to-day life.

"So your mom…" he started.

"She's Mexican-American. My dad, he's a judge, is Ital-

Lord Jesus,
We worship You in the blessed Sacrament. Bless our work of reviving a true and lasting devotion to You in the Sacrament of Your Body and Blood. Help us bring others to perceive with the eyes of faith, Your Real Presence in the Holy Eucharist. Enlighten the minds of Your people and set our hearts on fire with love for You, O Jesus.
Fill us with the desire to receive You often in Holy Communion. Amen

Sr. Ann Norton, C.R.

What is missing is YOU

ian-American." Her father's parents had immigrated from a Northern Italian village near the Switzerland border after World War II. Her mom's family had been in California since the 1930s.

"Do you speak Spanish?"

Mia's cheeks warmed. It was embarrassing that she was half Mexican-American and yet wasn't fluent in Spanish. English had always been the primary language at home. She rarely heard her mother speak Spanish except sometimes when talking to her grandma. Mia's lack of bilingualism was one more thing which made her feel less like a real Latina.

She covered her uncomfortableness with a smile. "Just what I've learned in Spanish class. ¿Tú hablas español?"

"I'm white."

"Why does that matter? I think it's funny you didn't ask me if I spoke Italian."

His expression turned introspective before his lips pulled into something softer than a frown. "Do you speak Italian?"

"Just what I learned from my grandma and it's mostly swear words. What are you, besides *just* white?"

His dark eyes dropped as he picked at the table's edge. "I don't know. Italian, Spanish, French. I guess a little of everything."

"Aw, so you're like me then, an American melting pot special number one." She grinned. "Maybe someone should put together an Italian Spanish French cookie. But these cookies are pretty good, right, Rosso?"

He eyed her, taking another one from her hand. "They're alright."

"Do you ever smile?" she asked.

His brow merged together. "What?"

She leaned her head against a hand, popping another cookie in her mouth. "I was just wondering if you ever smile."

He pulled his lips apart in a fake, toothy smile as if he were a robot attempting his first experiment at showing human emotion.

Mia almost spat out her cookie in a snort as she dropped her head into her arms, laughter shaking her core and crumbs spilling from her lips.

Ross's expression melted into a deep frown.

When the laughter subsided, she touched his arm. "Sorry, but you're a lot less of an angsty, bad boy when you have purple sprinkles stuck in your teeth. How's mine?" Mia provided a broad smile for his inspection.

This time his mouth pulled at the corners in a genuine smile. "Yeah, I guess you're a lot less of a know-it-all, nerd-girl when you have sprinkles stuck in your braces."

She giggled, bringing her finger to her lips. "Shh! You're going to get us into trouble."

He met her eyes shyly. "Thanks for the cookies, Russo."

"You're welcome, Rosso."

Things improved enough for Mia to stick with it, but it wasn't always easy. A brooding Ross flared up enough times that she suspected his reading and writing skills were lacking more than he was willing to admit. She issued gentle corrections, but she could sense simmering frustration behind the wall.

But their time together wasn't all homework. There were moments of chatting about school, friends, or whatever else was going on. When a hesitant Ross shared a paper, marked with a red *C-*, Mia hugged him as if he'd been accepted into Stanford. They also spent a fair amount of time teasing each other and laughing. She began to see Ross as a true friend and hoped he saw her as the same. When their sessions elicited angry glares and librarian hushes, she suggested they move the operation to her house.

From that point, her mom would pick them up and take them to Mia's house for tutoring and dinner. Afterward, Mia accompanied her mother in dropping Ross off at his home, a tired, brick-red ranch-style house on the outskirts of town.

Their time together lasted for about four months with Ross becoming a regular part of her weekly schedule. Until he wasn't. One day, Ross didn't appear at their meeting spot beside the bike rack. He also didn't respond to her texts. She tried to convince her dad to take her to Ross's home to see if he was sick. Her father refused, not wanting her to get sick if this was the case. Regardless, she worried about her friend.

The next day, she was informed by the school counselor Ross wouldn't be back at school for some time, and Mia could have another person to tutor if she wanted.

"What happened to him?" Mia asked.

"I can't talk about it. Do you want someone else to tutor?"

"No, I'll wait for Ross to come back."

She was more surprised when her father told her she wasn't allowed to tutor Ross anymore and to stay away from him.

"Why?"

"He got into trouble. I don't want you around him."

It was irrational, but Mia worried that she was somehow at fault. What if Ross was eating inside the library because she previously flaunted the rule and now he was in trouble? She pushed down a flutter of anxiety. "Did I—Was it something that happened at school? Did he get in trouble because of me?"

The judge's stern face softened as he slipped an arm around her, rubbing a shoulder. "No. Why would you think that? He's not a good kid, honey."

"But—"

"I talked to the school. I know you try really hard, but I think tutoring this kid might be beyond your capabilities."

Her gut dropped off a cliff. "Is that what they said?"

"We all agreed, including Ross—"

"Ross doesn't want me?" It didn't make any sense. He had never given her a clue. But, then again, at their last session, they tried to go over an English assignment and Ross had been especially surly. Maybe he had gone to the school to complain. She wasn't enough. He didn't want her. She'd failed. Her cheeks blazed hot and tears stung the corner of her eyes.

The judge released an impatient breath. "I told you he got into trouble. Look, how would you feel if the person you put in all this time with, turned around and cheated? Some people are just cheaters and there isn't anything you can do about it. The last thing we want is for his failings to reflect back on you. Stay away from him. You just have to trust me."

Her father, her Atticus Finch, was someone Mia trusted with her whole heart, who gave her the best advice, who was always truthful with her. Ross cheated? Was it on something that they had worked on together? Was this why he didn't want to work with her anymore? Because cheating was easier? Mia pushed herself and studied nonstop and didn't have much of a social life outside of school. She was working toward something better and Ross could just turn around and take the easy way. The more she thought about it, the angrier the whole situation made her. He didn't want her? Well, maybe she didn't want to waste her time on him either.

Several months later, Ross returned to school for a short time before he was gone again for good. But she didn't care because she had her own future success to worry about and she wasn't going to waste her help on someone who didn't want it.

BUT ALL THAT happened nearly ten years ago. Ross was right. It was a long time, and they were no longer kids. As Mia stared at the man across the counter, she couldn't miss the remnant of adolescence there: the reservation, the quietness, the dark, grave eyes. It was him.

"Rosso." The old nickname floated from her lips on a breath.

The intensity of his eyes warmed to slow-burning embers, still capable of heating her insides. "Hey, Russo."

He gave her a slight smile as a hand claimed the Americano on the counter, but she hadn't removed her own hand and his fingers brushed over hers. The coffeehouse chatter melted away in the background and she could remember how it used to be between them. When they would tease each other, or he made her giggle, or he'd shyly share a small moment of success. It was those tiny moments that made her heart swell, and she could forget all the bad feelings that followed later.

But she didn't know Ross. Not anymore. After an initial glow of pleasure swept through Mia, her thoughts shifted in a different direction. Ross grew up without any of the expectations and pressure she had. If the school had been cruel enough to have a title for someone like Ross, it may have been *Most Likely to Fail*.

Except Ross hadn't failed. In fact, there was a store. He was a businessman. Ross had found success. In her own desperation, Mia had asked him for a job. Heat crept over her ears at the shame and embarrassment. He knew her secret. She was far from being the success everyone thought she would be. She had not been a cheater, but she had also not found prosperity.

Mia could have said a lot of things to Ross. She could have said it was great he was doing well. She could have asked how he became a jeweler? Did he ever leave Placerville? Go, see, have exciting experiences since they last talked? How was his family? Did he remember eating her mother's Mexican Italian wedding cookies with her in the library? She could have said any number of innocent, pleasant things.

But her mind was so focused on the negative. He hadn't wanted her. He had cheated. His life had turned out fine—more than fine. Whatever she had contributed during their sessions had meant nothing. And she was about to hand this successful businessman his morning coffee.

"Did you ever graduate?" *Oh, god!* Did she really just blurt that out? It was a bitter question, and instantly followed by regret. Her teeth clamped onto her bottom lip to keep from saying anything more.

The dark embers, which had been so warm before, cooled as if doused by a bucket of ice water. Mia swallowed hard, waiting for the response she deserved.

"Miracles happen. Even for someone who's dyslexic." He took his coffee and walked away.

Dammit.

Chapter Six

D YSLEXIA. DYS MEANING *lack of.* Lexicon meaning *language*.

Ross stared at the handwritten name on the Pony Expresso coffee cup, and with it came the familiar feeling of frustration and shame. He tossed it into his office's trash can.

In a different period of human history, before writing was an ordinary skill, Ross would have been no different than any other laborer, farmer, or peasant. But in the modern era of texting, the internet, and books, Ross *was* different. For a long time, he lacked the skill and, therefore, spent much of his life avoiding it. This was as easy as dodging raindrops during a monsoon.

He learned about a town in New Zealand while watching a documentary late one night. It held the record for having the longest name in the world: *Taumatawhakatangihangakoauauotamateaturipukakapikimaungahoronukupokaiwhenuakitanatahu*. The part of the documentary which stuck with him was when the film crew asked random people to pronounce the name typed on a piece of paper. The subjects laughed at themselves stuttering, stumbling, and attempting to pronounce the town's name until it was nothing but a collection of random sounds without any connection to the real thing. It was during this moment when it clicked for Ross. This was precisely what reading was like for him.

Ross had been diagnosed with the *dyseidetic* type of dyslexia when he was twenty years old. He was relieved to learn there was a real reason reading and spelling was difficult for him. His brain's difficulty in visualizing and recognizing words wasn't him being lazy or lacking intelligence.

Soon after his diagnosis, he made a commitment and for weeks had practiced spelling the name *Taumatawhakatangihangakoauauotamateaturipukakapikimaungahoronukupokaiwhenuakitanatahu*. He may be dyslexic and tripped over words such as *from* and *that*, but there would be one fucking word he'd be able to replicate better than most non-dyslexics.

Try harder, Ross. He had said this phrase to himself as much as the various adults in his academic life had said it to him. The implication being, if he gave more effort and brainpower to his task, he would, at some point, achieve success. All he wanted was to stop living in a dense fog of words and disappointment. This never became truer than when Mia became his tutor.

Ross had knowledge of the dimpled nerd-girl before they'd been paired together to spend countless hours going over his school work. It was a frequent occurrence for her to be trotted to the front of school assemblies to receive one award or another. At some point, he stopped paying attention to these award ceremonies because they rarely pertained to him. To him, assemblies were nothing but a welcomed reprieve from the stress in the classroom.

Throughout his school life, he had received a single accolade. The name *Ross Manasse* echoed within the walls of his grade-school auditorium. He marched to the front, smiled, and waved at his grandpa, who sat in the stands and marked the momentous occasion with a flash from an old digital camera.

His teacher had handed him a black-and-white printed page and exclaimed, "Congratulations, Ross. Good job, buddy!" He marveled at the green, fuzzy caterpillar sticker his teacher had placed at the top right corner of the paper. This was the singular thing of interest for Ross, but he knew what the award was for. Perfect attendance in first grade. His small rib cage expanded with pride, knowing his grandfather was proud as he beamed a smile in his direction.

In third grade, he was called on to read a passage from a book. Ross dragged himself from his chair and made the long, arduous trek to the whiteboard, a sense of dread building in his stomach. As he fixed his eyes upon the page, he shifted his weight from one leg to the other.

"Come on, Ross. We don't have all day," Mr. Hayes said.

"A...h-ho...home—"

"House," the teacher corrected. "It's *A house*. Not *A home*. Try harder, Ross. Focus."

He couldn't finish the short paragraph without Mr. Hayes issuing more corrections as he went along. The rest of the students tittered around him in amusement, and Ross's cheeks grew hot with embarrassment. The small Placerville classroom could have been struck with an earthquake, a fissure opening in the Earth at the exact spot where he stood, and it would have been a godsend.

"Alright, settle down," Mr. Hayes interrupted, scolding the class. "Jeez, we're going to be here all day. Why don't you take a seat, pal. We'll give someone else a chance."

Ross trudged to his desk, glad his moment of punishment was at an end, but he had been overwhelmed with a feeling of shame. He spread his arms across the surface of his desk and sank his face into one bony, undeveloped bicep.

"Mr. Manasse, I hope you're not napping back there. You're not even following along in the book with the rest of the class. I don't want to have another discussion with your grandfather about this. You need to focus."

This was how a typical school year went for Ross. Each year became harder and harder to get by even with his creative ways of getting out of public readings or his attempts to be invisible inside the classroom. In return, his teachers invented new ways to suggest laziness or sighed their disappointment at his stubbornness to try. And this happened when they still cared and believed there was some potential in him. When the adults gave up on him, there was nothing but silence.

The school counselor reached out to his grandfather, telling him something needed to change, or Ross would be held back.

"I don't care! I'm not doing it!" Ross had shouted, slamming his backpack into the seat of a dining room chair.

"Ross," his grandfather said in a quiet, gentle voice, his shoulders hunched from his work.

"No, I'm not doing it. I'll try harder. Okay? Please don't make me do this." A smart girl discovering his embarrassing truth was the unseen height of degradation. Mia would laugh at him, which was the worst fate of all.

But, despite his fears, that hadn't happened. Mia had been kind. Her desire to help him seemed genuine. On top of this, she wanted to be his friend, and Ross wanted the same.

There was at least one person out there who hadn't given up on him.

Until she did.

Chapter Seven

"WHAT ARE YOU reading?" Natalie asked during a slow period inside Pony Expresso one day.

Mia glanced at her boss before slipping her phone into an apron pocket. "Sorry. A friend of mine sent me something she thought I would find interesting. I plan on getting my doctorate in political science, and it was an article regarding how education is used as a social hurdle for controlling the political—"

"El agua de Jamaica," Natalie shouted like it was the answer to a game show.

"I'm sorry?"

"Agua de Jamaica. It's been bothering me ever since your interview. You seemed so familiar, and I finally figured it out. Was your mom Lori? Laura?"

"Laura."

Natalie clapped her palms together. "I knew it! I can totally see it. She used to come in a lot because I would always make a fresh batch of the drink during the summer. She loved it."

"Is that the hibiscus tea?" She remembered her mom ordering it whenever they went to one of the local taquerias.

"Yeah. I should really bring it back. I don't know why I

stopped making it. Looking at you just reminded me of it though. My god, I can't believe how much you look like Laura."

Mia scratched at the countertop, feeling uncomfortable. She wasn't in the mood to reminisce on the subject of her mom today.

Not noticing any awkwardness, Natalie continued while wrapping her long locks into a sloppy bun. "Yeah, she and her friends would go to the Pine Pattern Quilt Shop down the street and come here afterward for fabric talk. It was like a weekly thing. Now that I think about it, I haven't seen them around as much. But if they come in, I'll point them out to you. I bet they'd love to talk to you. I was sorry to hear about your mom."

Mia pushed down the lump in her throat while wiping a cloth across the espresso machine. "Yeah. Thanks."

"She was so nice. Always really sweet and loved my agua de Jamaica. During the holidays she'd always bring me a batch of polvorones. Do you also quilt?"

"No."

Natalie released a light sigh. "Your mom definitely loved her fabric. I always imagined your house was bursting with it, like coming out of the windows kind of thing."

This made Mia laugh. Yes, her mom definitely had an impressive fabric stash, one which was organized by color and labeled on shelves. "Thankfully, it wasn't that bad, but my dad got mad one time when he discovered that an old couch in the garage was actually made from bins of fabric. My mom had stacked up large plastic bins together in the shape of a couch and draped a cover over it."

Natalie burst out laughing. "God! I totally believe it. Your mom was hilarious and pretty smart."

"She could be sneaky when it was necessary." While Mia had been uncomfortable at the beginning, laughing with Natalie about her mom's fabric problem made the whole topic suddenly not so heavy. In fact, it was kind of nice.

"Well, I can tell you're just like her," Natalie said, breaking through her thoughts. "Not only do you look alike, but you're also just as nice as her. I'm sure your mom would have gotten a kick out of you working here."

This observation had a sobering effect on Mia. First of all, she wasn't sure if her mom, like her dad, would feel let down that her pride-and-joy daughter wasn't doing more in her life. And, secondly, Mia wasn't sure she was nice at all. Especially after what happened the previous week and what she had said to Ross. Her mom would have been disappointed in her lack of kindness. Whatever positive feelings he had from them spending time together was probably tarnished forever, and she didn't blame him. She spent a considerable amount of time replaying Ross's expression as it went from warm to cool.

She hated that no matter where she went in the world, there would be a person who held such a poor opinion of her.

She could fix this. She had to.

"You have got to be kidding me. This damn dog is back again. Go on. Get out."

Mia glanced up from cleaning and spotted her boss waving her hands in an attempt to rid them of the three-legged dog, who had parked its curly-haired ass in the middle of the small coffee shop. The dog's one eye gawked at the counter as if he was one more customer, who needed extra time reading the chalkboard menu.

"Isn't that the jewelry store dog?"

"Yeah. That jewelry guy has a habit of leaving the shop door open on nice days, and I made the mistake of giving this scruff-muffin a stale bagel once. Now he thinks he can come over here for treats whenever he wants." Natalie blew out a frustrated breath and tried communicating with the dog again. "*Gooooo hoooome!*" She motioned in the jewelry store's direction in wild, exaggerated movements as if she and the dog were involved in a game of charades.

Mia laughed. "Does it help to say it louder?"

Natalie dropped her arms in a frustrated smack. "I don't know. I'm not even sure the dog can hear me or maybe he doesn't want to hear me."

"Well, I'm off for the day. How about if I lure the dog back to the jewelry store on my way out?"

"Yes, please."

This could be the opportunity Mia was waiting for. The animal appearing in the coffee shop was like coming across a lucky penny. What dog owner wouldn't be grateful when a lost, beloved pet was returned to them? This would for sure put her character back in good standing. She snatched one of the day-old bran muffins. "Hey, Lucky Penny! Who wants a treat?"

Despite his questionable hearing, the dog understood the idea of treats. He turned in tight circles while barking in bursts, the noise becoming an ear-piercing percussion as it bounced off the shop's walls. His stumpy tail wagged with such velocity, it would have flown off if it wasn't attached to his rear.

Natalie covered her ears. "Somehow you've managed to make it worse. You should take the dog home with you and disguise it as an old couch inside the garage. I'm sure it's what your mom would have wanted."

Mia laughed before jogging through the door. "Come here, little pupster. I know you want it," she exclaimed with a deceptive sweetness. The dog scampered after her, his pink tongue rolling from his mouth. He followed behind as she guided him to the jewelry store, hot on the trail of bran muffin bait.

As Natalie predicted, the door to the shop was propped open. Mia fixed a bright smile on her face as she coaxed the dog inside. "Hello!"

When she turned around, it wasn't Ross standing at the counter but an older woman with a low center of gravity, not one hard edge visible, and a colorful blouse. The woman smiled at her with a twinkle in her eyes. "Hello there." Her focus shifted from Mia to the off-white dog. "Oh, Hermes, there you are. I wondered where you went. You're going to get me into trouble."

Mia made a quick recovery, adopting a friendly expression. "He made his way to the coffee shop in search of food." She tossed the scrappy dog the remaining muffin, which he caught and devoured. Small crumbs flew from his mouth onto the shop's worn carpet, and Hermes went to work, licking it without an ounce of shame. "Is he yours?"

"No. He belongs to the owner. I've only been working here for a short time. I'm Aanya."

"Mia. Obviously, I work at Pony Expresso." She pointed to the company name printed on her black T-shirt.

"Can I interest you in some jewelry? Even a barista could use a sparkle or two. And all our beautiful pieces are locally crafted and unique." Aanya's warm personality made her a better salesman than Ross. Mia liked her right away.

"I could use a bit more sparkle, and I do love the jewelry here, but I'm afraid I only have some of my tip money on me." She dug into the pocket of her half apron, pulling out a handful of wadded bills. "What kind of sparkle can fourteen dollars get me? And do I get a discount for saving the dog from a life on the streets? Placerville can be pretty tough out there for both little dogs and poor baristas."

The older lady laughed. "If it was up to me, I'd give you the Hermes Recovery Discount, but I don't think the boss would like it. He's very serious and doesn't price anything here for fourteen dollars."

"I guess I'll keep saving my tips then."

"Well, thank you for bringing Hermes back. I'll try and keep a better eye on him so he does not bother the coffee shop again."

"I...uh...was actually hoping to see Ross. Do you know if he'll be back soon?" Mia asked.

"Oh, he's here."

Before Mia could say anything further, Aanya shouted over her shoulder at the closed office door as though she was his mother calling him from his bedroom. "Ross? There's a young lady who's asking to see you!" Aanya's dark brown eyes continued glittering with amusement.

There was no escape. She would have to go through with

it and in front of El Dorado Jewelry's new mom. This was going to be awkward. But, after her tactless comment, it seemed fitting her punishment was to be additional embarrassment.

Ross poked his head out, his eye coming to rest on her with the intense scrutiny she hated. "Can I help you, Mia?"

She couldn't sense anything but a noncommittal, business tone from Ross's question, but Mia heard an underlying impatience at being pulled away from his work to deal with her. He wasn't even coming all the way out of his office for this discussion.

She became nervous, swiping a strand of hair behind her ear. "I—I brought your dog back."

His face fell into confusion. "I didn't know he was gone."

"Um, yep. He came down for a coffee and muffin, which he had. Muffin, I mean, not coffee. I wouldn't give a dog coffee. Coffee is probably not the best thing for dogs, and Lucky, here, probably doesn't need any other uh…issues."

"Lucky?"

"Sorry, I meant, Hermes." She tapped a clammy hand against her thigh. "Maybe a more appropriate name would have been Ares, the god of war. The dog looks like a warrior. He'd at least look adorable with a small eye patch. Hermes was the messenger to the gods, protector of travelers…patron of literature…trickster—well, lots of things. Hermes the god that is, not Hermes the dog."

Her eyes dropped to the animal in question, who sat at her feet. Hermes wagged his tail in apparent encouragement, being the one occupant in the shop ignorant at how much

Mia was botching this and rambling. *Ugh!* Why did she ramble so much? If there was a title for most-likely-to-ramble-when-nervous, it would be hers for sure.

"Uh-huh," was Ross's response after an awkward moment. "Well, thanks for bringing him back." And his head disappeared into his office.

"Wait," she said.

But the door shut with a click, providing his final reply.

She rushed to the office. She didn't care what happened, but there would be an apology. Her mother would have insisted on it and was probably tapping her foot in heaven because it hadn't been done sooner.

"I'm sorry. The office is for employees only," Aanya said.

"It's okay. I'm an old friend." Mia gave a quick tap on the door before letting herself inside. The office was packed to the edges with old banker boxes as though Ross had inherited at least a decade's worth of paperwork from the previous owner. They lined the walls and surrounded his desk like a cardboard fortress.

"What the hell are you doing? You don't belong here. And you may be an old friend, but you're not necessarily a current one." Ross's voice was flat, edged by slight exasperation.

"Okay, I know I deserve that," Mia replied to his back as he hunched over the sturdy, well-worn desk. His fingers worked on the mechanisms of a digital camera. She sank into the other office chair available after moving a box from it. She took a deep breath, sent a thought to her mom, and calmed herself. "Ross, I'm sorry."

The words stopped his current activity, but he remained

fixed in his position.

"What I said in the coffee shop... It was rude. I shouldn't have said it, and I'm really sorry that I did."

After an uncomfortable pause, Ross said, "Okay."

"So, maybe we can try being friends? I promise to pick up your tab the next time you come in. Anything you want will be on me."

"Thank you for apologizing, but I really need to get some work done." He returned to his previous task with the camera.

Mia tried not to feel the sting of rejection. She couldn't blame him. Why was she absurd enough to push it, asking him to be her friend as if they were still kids in high school? She came to apologize, not force the man into a friendship. She wasn't here to make friends anyway. Her stay in Placerville was nothing but a short detour.

At the same time, this current situation didn't feel satisfying enough. Her character was still in the negative and it didn't seem quite fair. She was willing to forget about Ross cheating on his schoolwork behind her back. That was a long time ago and they were just kids. Life was now different for both of them. But leaving it like this, when Ross clearly didn't like her, it made her feel unsettled. Not being able to fix this and being hated was a horrible punishment for Mia. Luckily, she had won over Ross Manasse before, and she could do it again. This time, though, she'd have to do it without her mother's cookies.

"What are you working on?" she forced out in a bright tone.

He sighed, giving her a quick glance. "I let a customer

trade his camera for an engagement ring. I might as well get some images for our website if I can figure out how to use it."

"I thought you didn't have a website."

"We don't. But my cousin is all for it, so I'm willing to try."

There was a selection of jewelry laid across the desk's wooden surface. A glitter of inspiration sparked her insides like a flame on a dynamite's fuse line. This was Mia's *in*, her wedding cookie. Ross may not want the friendship she offered, but he might be willing to accept her help instead. She could prove her value to him again and to herself. This type of help was what Mia was good at, the type she thought she'd be doing in the political world. "You're not going to take pictures on your desk, are you?"

"I don't know. I'm not there yet."

"Can I see what kind of camera you have?"

A disapproval line formed between his eyebrows but, after a moment, he surrendered the camera to her grasp before crossing his arms. His grumpy barrier was as established as the old banker boxes stacked inside his office. Mia offered a smile as she took it, pushing her confidence to the forefront as if his emotional wall didn't bother her. She grew up with the judge. Grouchiness didn't scare her.

She turned the camera in her hands as if handling a rare jewel. For being a used camera, it was in near perfect shape. She would have loved to have this camera for herself, and it kindled an awakening to take the type of photos she always dreamed of. "It's a Samsung NX1."

"Great. Thanks for your help, but I already *read* that for

myself."

Mia ignored the sarcasm and lifted the camera body to squint through the viewfinder. She then scrolled through the camera settings and menu options. "How much did the ring cost?"

"What ring?"

"The engagement ring, in exchange for the camera."

"Five hundred."

"You got the better end of the deal. Well, I don't recommend taking the images here. There's not enough light. You could crank up the ISO. Or use a wider aperture, but this might shorten your depth of field. That's not a bad thing, especially for some interesting jewelry shots, but it may take a novice a little while to figure it out. I also don't think you should use your desk as the background, because there's not going to be enough contrast for the jewelry to stand out. Having a website isn't going to matter if the visuals aren't going to blow customers away. Were you planning on creating the website yourself?"

Ross's eyes narrowed as he studied her. "Luna, my cousin, was going to work on it between her studies."

"You guys might also want to consider e-commerce sites, such as Etsy, especially since your pieces are handcrafted and unique. You can probably get a lot more eyes on your jewelry and make some decent sales from that and social media, rather than solely relying on a traditional website."

"I'm sure we'll figure it out."

"I can help," Mia blurted.

"No, thanks."

"I'm serious. I worked for a political campaign—"

"Yeah, I get it. You're very smart. But I think I have more experience selling jewelry than you do, and I'm pretty sure it's different than a political campaign."

"But I was the social media manager, and I really know my way around a camera. Can I please do something to make up for being an asshole?"

Ross held out his hand. Mia hoped he was offering a handshake to say she earned the job as a temporary jewelry photographer. Instead, his facial expression excluded any of the joy which should come with an offer. Fingers beckoned for the return of his expensive camera. "I'll just take the coffee. It's safer."

"But—"

"I don't need your help, Mia. And, most of all, I don't want it."

Disappointed, she returned the camera to him, her confidence deflating along with it.

"Thank you." Ross swiveled in his office chair away from her, setting the camera on the desk. "If you don't mind, I need to get back to work."

Mia stood, making her way to the door. "Okay." There was one last thing she needed to say. "I'm happy you're doing so well, Ross. I mean that."

"Great. Thanks."

Wedding cookies weren't going to fix this.

Chapter Eight

IT WASN'T UNUSUAL for Ross to jog on the El Dorado Trailhead on his days off, but since Luna had departed, it had been a few weeks. Aanya did well enough to run the shop alone, and a break was in order. Ross and Hermes jogged past the towering pine and oak trees, the twisted manzanitas, tall grasses, and pink sweet pea vines. It was still early, and the sun's rays were already beginning to warm the air around them. It was fall, but nature still had a few warm days left.

As he made his way along the trail, he lost himself to the music playing through his earbuds. These days he preferred any kind of background noise. If he had complete silence, his disobedient mind turned to thoughts he had no interest in entertaining.

He couldn't stop pondering Mia's offer since the day she invaded his office. Ross wasn't sure if he was a stubborn ass or if his refusal made him smart. He'd like to believe it was the latter. He could at least admit that she had more knowledge on marketing than him. At least, this was the impression she gave. When she shifted into nerd-girl mode, she exuded a natural confidence, and he could never be sure about anything.

The truth was, Ross could use a different perspective since he preferred being in his workshop instead of trying to figure out how to create a website and make everything look good. Also, Aanya didn't seem to be technologically advanced, and Luna was busy with her classes. But it was a continual blow to his ego when he found himself depending on someone else for help.

Plus, there was a small voice inside insisting it would be a mistake working with Mia, even at arm's length. He couldn't stop his mind from engaging in thoughts about how touchable she looked sitting in his office. Like he could hold her and become lost within the softness of her skin and hair and—

These types of thoughts were worse. He didn't want them. Mia would stay in her world and he'd stay in his. This was how it should be.

Anyway, it didn't matter how nice she appeared—he couldn't trust her. Not again.

Ross was halfway on his return trip when he threw a glance at Hermes. Most of the time, even with three legs, one eye, and no hearing, Hermes did fine keeping up with Ross. But the dog was struggling today. His mouth lulled wide, his tongue close to scraping the pavement as the sides of his small body heaved with exertion. Ross jogged in place, giving Hermes a chance to catch his breath.

"Come on, boy. You can do it."

Despite the encouragement, the dog made it a few more steps before lying in the middle of the trail.

"Okay, let's take a break. I know it's been a while since we had a run. We're both a little out of shape." He approached Hermes, pooling cool liquid into his palm from his water canister for the thirsty dog.

Hermes wasn't the only one getting overheated. Ross removed his earbuds before taking a long drink himself and pulling off his T-shirt with the idea of fanning the fabric over the dog.

"Oomph! Ow."

Ross turned his head toward the off-trail wilderness and saw a body slumped chest first on the ground about fifty feet away. He squinted through the shadowy tree line, and the identity of the person grew clearer. "Mia?"

She remained collapsed in the dirt. Her head eased in his direction as if she could escape detection if she moved slow enough.

"Mia, I can obviously see you."

With this, she plastered on a sheepish smile, pushing herself to her knees. "Oh, hi, Ross! Isn't this an accidental coincidence?"

"Huh?" He walked to her. "Are you okay?"

"I tripped over a damn log." She glared at the offending log as though its sole purpose was to knock Mia to the ground. She adjusted her glasses, blowing a chunk of hair from her face. She stood but almost fell again when weight was placed on her left leg. "Ow! Oh my god!" Hobbling her way to the same villainous log, she took a seat, her hand reaching to her ankle.

Her eyes lifted to him, but the gaze never rose higher than his chest. This was when he realized he was still shirtless. Growing self-conscious, he slipped the T-shirt back over his head and resisted saying the words, *Eyes up here, Russo.*

Snapping from her daze, Mia blushed, and her focus shifted to her ankle.

"Are you hurt?" he asked. His instinct was to scoop her into his arms and take her to safety. Instead, he shoved his hands into the pockets of his joggers. Carrying her was the opposite of maintaining distance and, therefore, not an option.

"I think I just twisted it weird."

Ross kneeled, taking her ankle in one hand and her bare calf in the other. It was like touching silk, but he tried to push the thought from his mind and keep his hand from sliding the rest of the way up her leg. He studied her while rotating her foot, being careful not to add too much pressure with his grip. "Does this hurt?"

She sucked in a quick breath, biting the corner of a full bottom lip. "Yeah, a little. But I don't think it's broken. I think my ego is more injured than my ankle."

He forced his eyes to her shoe. "What are you doing over here?"

"I just wanted to go on a walk and take pictures. You know, take a break and get out."

He cocked his head after noticing her hands were empty. "Take pictures? Without a camera?"

"Oh, no, I-I was using my phone. Can you do me a favor and hand it to me? It's right there in the dirt. I was…looking at a picture on my phone and tripped over the log."

Reluctantly, Ross unlatched his hands from her leg and retrieved her phone, handing it to her. "Why are you over here, though? If you stay on the trail, you don't have to worry about things like tripping over logs."

"I like going off-trail."

He found her simplistic response, along with her chipper attitude, annoying. It was so typical of Mia. She got to breeze through life as if her cheerfulness and positivity were enough to keep the rain clouds away. It was clear, no one had ever proven anything different to her. He took a deep breath. "It's not very practical. What if you're out here, by yourself, you trip over a log, and break your leg?"

"I don't know. I guess I would cry and then call someone on my phone to help me."

"Did you even bring any water on this solo hike of yours?"

"No, but—"

"Do you have bear spray?"

Her eyebrows rose. "Bear spray?"

"Black bears have been known to come down to this area. So you break your leg, have no water, and then have nothing to protect yourself against a bear."

Mia blinked. "Good lord, Ross. You wasted no time in imagining such a dire situation for me."

"Maybe the next time you think about doing something like this, you'll decide to come a bit more prepared."

Her brows returned to their original positions as she watched him, pushing her glasses closer to her face with a single finger. "Here's another situation for you. What if—and this is a *huge* what if because, obviously, you're much more logical about this whole hiking thing than I am. But what if I'm out on a nice sunny day, I take some pictures with my phone, and I trip over a log, slightly twisting my ankle, but then you happen along and help me?"

"Or there could be a hungry bear."

"I guess that's also possible. But between your imagined situation and my situation, which one actually happened?"

Ross's mouth opened to reply, but not a single word escaped. The dimple indented her right cheek as a confident smile spread across her face. *God damn her.* "It must be so nice that you can afford to be careless and get away with it."

Her bright smile slid away, and, with it, a dollop of guilt plopped onto Ross's conscience. Despite the situation, he regretted being the cause of the disappearing dimple. Some of the ice surrounding his heart broke off in a snowflake-sized chunk.

He sighed. "Come on. Let me help you." He offered a hand, pulling her to her feet, and wrapped a supportive arm around her waist. She felt small within his grasp and he again fought the urge to scoop her up. Mia clasped the top of his shoulder and, with his assistance, limped to the trail.

At a slow pace, they made their way on the path with Hermes lagging not far behind. Ross gave Mia a sideways glance and cleared his throat. "How's your mom, by the way?"

She kept her eyes locked on the surrounding brush, using her free hand to pull a strand of hair behind her ear. "Oh, she…passed away a few years ago."

A moment of awkward silence passed.

"Sorry to hear that." He tightened his grip around her. More fractures developed in the icy glacier barricading his heart. "I always liked Laura. She made the best lasagna and was always nice to me."

Mia's eyes darted to him, and she gave him a small smile.

"She liked you. We all liked you, Ross."

He scoffed. "Your father definitely did not like me."

Despite the pathetic hitch in her step, she grinned. "Okay, but that might be a case of not liking his precious daughter spending so much time with a teenage you. Not that Dad had anything to worry about."

Ross wasn't sure if this last comment was a dig at his unfortunate situation in high school. "Why do you say that?"

"Uh, do I need to bring out a copy of my last school photo to remind you what a dorky late bloomer I was? It's not like I had anyone beating down my door to hang out with me. At least, not someone who wasn't being forced to by the school counselor."

Ross had a precise memory of what sixteen-year-old Mia looked like, and he smiled to himself.

Mia slid a glance to him, her mouth dropping. "Oh god, you remember. Please stop. It's so embarrassing."

"And now?"

"And now what?"

"Are they beating down your door?" Looking at the woman limping beside him, he couldn't deny Mia was pretty. She was never ugly, but time had enhanced what she already had. Her chipper attitude, the same one he found so aggravating ten minutes earlier, had the ability to light her face, her eyes, her everything. She glowed with it and it didn't matter if it was present day or ten years ago, he still had this unexplainable urge to press her to his body as though her warmth could be absorbed into his soul. Who wouldn't see Mia Russo and greedily want her all to themselves? She had always possessed this quality. It's what made her so attractive. This wasn't even taking into account the amber eyes, the adorable faded freckles, or the damn dimple. He wouldn't be surprised to learn there were all kinds of guys asking for "opinions" as an excuse to talk to her, including the grizzled, behemoth she came into the jewelry shop with that first time.

She shook her head while rolling her eyes. "Oh, sure. In fact, there are swarms of them around the house all the time. Why do you think I have to escape to the solitude of the woods? It's the cute nerd thing I'm doing these days."

"I thought it was to take photos."

"That's right," she replied.

"On your phone."

"Well, it's currently the only camera I have. Here I'll show you." Mia pulled her phone from her pocket, scrolling through the screen. The image she shared was a beautiful shot of a great oak tree with gnarled, twisting branches. The golden light from the sun pierced through the gaps as if the tree was ordained by Apollo himself.

"It's nice," he agreed.

"And this was done with just my phone. Imagine what I could do if I had a camera like yours."

"Why don't you buy a nice camera?"

Her shoulders pumped in a light shrug. "It's just a hobby and not a priority right now."

They arrived at the trailhead parking lot.

"Did you drive?" Ross asked.

"Yeah, I'm right over there." She pointed to the white compact while digging into a pocket for her keys.

Arriving at her car, his arm dropped away. Ross scowled

at the emptiness he felt in letting her go. He would do best to remember that Mia didn't belong in the space at his side.

Her eyes scanned his face. "Do you hate me?"

"I just helped you all the way back to your car. Would I have done that if I hated you?"

"Or you're just a good guy."

"I don't hate you. You're kind of impossible to hate. I'm sure I wasn't the only one in high school who tried and failed."

Mia appeared to consider this. "I think you should take a page from Hermes. He clearly likes me." She motioned to the curly-haired dog, who had clear adoration shooting from his eyes. Ross considered his pet's loyalty to be wishy-washy at best.

"First of all, Hermes is not discerning in who he likes. And I can't just pick up like ten years haven't passed between us."

"I know," she relented quietly. But her lips scrunched together in thought. "I just feel weird asking you for a favor under the circumstances."

A short laugh escaped from Ross. "I'm sure you'll try it anyway." He'd give her credit; she had a lot of nerve.

Her expression, painted with sweetness and innocence, turned its charm toward him like a spotlight. "Rosso—"

"That's not going to sway me one way or the other."

"Ross." Her voice became gentle. "Do you think I could possibly borrow your camera?"

"Why?"

"I'm going to work on the social media accounts and website for Pony Expresso, and I want to use a nicer camera for some images."

"This sounds like something I'll regret." He didn't realize he'd stepped closer until Mia's backside bumped up against the car.

But her upturned, sunny face remained confident and fixed in place, meeting him head on. "What do you think can possibly happen?"

"I don't know, but it feels like some kind of trap."

"Come on, Rosso. It's your old pal Russo." She gave him a light tap on a bicep as if they were old, chummy friends again. Her amber eyes melted another chunk off the old glacier.

He released a record-setting groan. "Look, how about you borrow it for your coffee shop thing and then maybe you can take a few pictures for me."

A bright smile cracked across her face. "Deal!"

"I just want to make it clear here that I'm helping you out. It's not the other way around."

She adopted a serious expression, but delight slipped through at the edges. "I can live with that. Although, technically, it's more like a favor-for-favor thing, but you did rescue me from becoming a black bear appetizer so I'm willing to overlook it."

Ross didn't know what he was getting into, but when her cheek crease turned into a full-fledged dimple he knew he was in trouble.

Damn that dimple.

Chapter Nine

"WHAT THE HELL am I doing?" Mia asked.

"Getting paper towels for the bathroom dispenser. At least, that's what you said you were going to do."

Mia flipped around to find Natalie standing behind her in the storage closet's threshold. "Uh. Yeah, you're totally right." She snatched the appropriate box.

"You've been very distracted today. Is everything okay with you?" Natalie's expression turned into concern.

"Yeah, everything's great." She did her best to push out a convincing smile. "I, uh, just get a little absent-minded sometimes."

Natalie laughed. "I do catch you staring off into space, especially when it's slow. It's like your body is here, but your mind is somewhere else."

"Oh, it's just the usual school stuff and trying to think of creative names for my future books I plan on writing." Her hand flicked through the air as though this dilemma was standard Mia behavior and, maybe, it was.

At least that was a better answer than starting a conversation with, *Well, you see, there's this good-looking, grumpy jeweler.* This type of answer wasn't very adult and Mia was an adult…At least, she was *adult-lite*, which meant she was technically an adult but she didn't necessarily always feel like one. She still had a habit of looking around the room for someone who was more adult than her. Since Natalie was a few years older, and in a management position, it meant she was the designated *real* adult here, and Mia would rather impress her than appear like a silly teenager with silly teenager thoughts.

Natalie snorted. "Yeah, sure. Maybe you're thinking about book stuff or maybe it's daydreams of the *sexy* kind."

Her face must have revealed something, because Natalie snapped a closed fist under her chin, indicating she was all ears.

"Girl, you are hiding something juicy."

"No, I'm not." She snatched some more random cleaning supplies, until her arms were overloaded before leaving the supply closet.

"Just where do you think you're going?"

"To take care of the bathroom, because I'm an adult and I'm doing my adult job." This statement would have been more impressive if it had been said with more eloquence—and also if she hadn't dropped a roll of toilet paper, and accidentally kicked it across the floor.

Natalie's laughter trailed behind her. "Uh-huh. I bet you're going in there to do more of that daydreaming."

Mia shut herself in the bathroom and took a moment to lean against the door and stare at herself in the mirror. Okay, maybe Natalie was also adult-lite, but she didn't seem to care. The young manager never had to impress anyone. Natalie, in true goddess fashion, was confident enough.

She didn't know where her need to impress came from.

Sure, her parents pushed her, (sometimes they pushed her hard), but there was always this fear that if she didn't do well, it meant something was wrong—with her in particular. She couldn't remember not ever having this fear embedded within her gut as if it was another protective instinct like fight or flight. Mia *had* to be smart and clever and make organized plans in a mental notebook on how to accomplish her ambitious goals. For people to realize that she struggled was too much exposure. She was positive this would be sunlight on an unprotected film strip, and the image could be ruined beyond repair.

But, seriously, to get back to her original issue—What the hell was she doing?

Placerville was a detour, a pit stop, a temporary place to make a little money. What was the point of making friends, both at Pony Expresso or at El Dorado Jewelry, when it would be a blip compared to the larger picture? She'd narrowed down her top PhD programs, looking at mostly the East coast, and setting her sights on places such as George Washington University in DC or MIT in Cambridge. But because she wanted to put her "new" plan into action as soon as possible, Mia was open to other places, and already in the process of gathering the necessary letters of recommendations.

At the same time, she had trouble letting things go. Running into Ross the other morning was indeed an accidental coincidence. She hadn't lied. Mia wasn't a creepy stalker, which was why she'd dashed off-trail when she spotted him. And then she *really* spotted him. When Ross pulled his gray T-shirt off, revealing that his attractive forearms were simply a preview for the rest of him, her mind was desperate to convert the vision into slow motion to savor every drool-worthy moment. His runner's body was tight and lean with a perfect formation of dark chest hair dipping down to his—

And that's when the log sprung up in the middle of her walking path.

Even now, her groans reverberated between the bathroom walls. It was so embarrassing, and she tried to convince him she was doing a "cute nerd" thing. *Dream on, dork.* Why did she have to be so awkward?

She didn't remember it being this way with her ex-boyfriend, Tom, but maybe because he was a little stiff himself. If he hadn't been so set against long-distance relationships, perhaps they would be an equally awkward couple to this day. With their breakup passing its one-year anniversary, Mia now realized Thomas made the right call. She never got the same chest flutters with her ex, and him moving all the way to Boston didn't bother her as much as it should have.

"Are you leaving?" Natalie asked when Mia was finished restocking and cleaning the bathroom.

"Yup. I'll see you tomorrow, boss."

"Bye-bye, daydreamer."

Mia wrapped her sweatered arms a little closer to her body as she stepped into the chilly late September air. A ping of excitement buzzed through her stomach. Despite the embarrassing situation, one bright spot did emerge. Ross was going to let her borrow his fancy camera. Her fingers itched to adjust the f-stop and play with shutter speed. It didn't matter if she was taking photos of coffee or jewelry.

Even though Ross didn't want to be friends with her, and in the grand scheme she shouldn't care, there was some invisible force drawing her to him, wanting to win him over, wanting it to be like the old days when everything in her life felt sure-footed and concrete. That was why she was walking in the direction of the jewelry store after work. Well, that and the prospect of playing with his fancy camera, of course.

"Hey, Aanya," she said upon entering the shop. Hermes wagged his tail but remained glued to his bed. Mia bent to scratch along the top of the dog's skull.

"Hello again," Aanya replied. "Have you gotten enough tips to go jewelry shopping yet?"

Mia met Aanya at one of the display cases and leaned against the top, gazing at the lovely jewelry within. "Not yet. But I already picked which one I want. That ring with the pearl." She tapped the glass, pointing to the most beautiful ring she could imagine, a ring for a forest fairy queen. Like much of the jewelry, the band itself looked like a twisting twig of glistening gold with a soft pink pearl at its woodsy center.

"You can try it on."

"Oh, you don't have to open up the case just for me. I'm sure it'll be a while before I can afford to touch it."

Aanya had her keys in hand and removed the ring from the black velvet display holder. The tiny tag at the bottom of the band read three hundred and fifty dollars, because, of course, Mia had expensive taste. It was too big for her ring finger, and she slipped it on the one beside it. At a nearby window, the sun highlighted the rosy, glistening undertones of the ring. "It is stunning. Who makes these? Is it an elf from the nearby woods?"

Aanya chuckled. "Close. The boss."

Mia's gaze flicked to the older woman. "Ross makes these?"

"Uh-huh."

"Wow. I mean, he's really good." And she meant it. There was something about his solid, firm fingers molding metal and stone into beautiful pieces that made for an attractive visual. Her thoughts again went to his bare torso on the hot, dusty trail, and warmth bloomed within her veins. Mia couldn't deny that talent and ability were seductive qualities.

She jumped when the door to the back room opened. The subject of her current fantasy walked out, rubbing a hand through his dark, disheveled hair. A gray, plastic magnifier rested at the edge of Ross's hairline, and he wore a leather apron. The apron was captivating in its old-school craftsmanship lines and its worn, distressed edges. Mia didn't need to press her nose to the apron to know what specific smell it would emit, all raw earth and hard work. She could imagine it being both comforting and familiar. Like she wasn't already in trouble with enticing forearms, a bare torso, and perfectly tousled hair. He had to go ahead and throw a sexy leather apron onto the kindling. Her infatuation with everything related to him was on the verge of combustion.

She fixed a bright smile on her face. "Hey, Ross, can I borrow this ring for…well, forever? I'll give you a nice shout-out on my Instagram page."

He approached, taking her hand in a light grip, and held

it up as though inspecting his work. "We accept cash or credit cards. Social media exposure is not an accepted form of payment, but nice try."

"Ross."

He met her eyes. "What?"

"You make beautiful jewelry."

They held each other's gaze for a moment, Mia's breath catching inside her lungs, before Ross slowly slid the ring off her finger. "And it's priced accordingly." He returned the ring to Aanya. "I assume you're here to collect the camera."

The door to the shop opened, and a middle-aged couple walked in. Aanya, with real customers, welcomed them and moved away from Ross and Mia after locking the ring inside its case.

"Come on," Ross said to Mia, who followed him to his office. "How's the ankle?"

"It's fine."

At the office threshold, he paused and called for Hermes. The dog lifted his head but remained in his spot, resuming his nap.

"Is he okay?" Mia asked.

"Yeah, he's fine."

They entered the office with Ross shutting the door behind them. On the other side of his desk, he reached to the floor, retrieving a black bag. The camera was on his desk, and he went through the process of packing it inside the bag.

"You know, I was thinking," Mia started. "I know our deal was for me to take your jewelry images—"

"Are you changing the terms of our agreement already, Russo?"

She smiled. It gave her a warm feeling when Ross used the old nickname. "Well, it wouldn't be that hard for me to help set up some social media or an e-commerce account and get those started. It'll make it possible to reach a larger market and give people from all over the country or world a chance to own your pieces. I don't mind giving Aanya a few pointers on writing some posts and using hashtags, that—"

"I *can* write."

"N-no, I-I wasn't…" Mia's face flushed, her fingers slipping a strand of hair behind her ear. She was here to make progress between them, not make things worse with misunderstandings. "That's not what I was implying. Really."

With the camera packed, he released it into her possession, his expression muted.

"Thank you." She took the bag but sank into the chair, going through it and making a note of its contents.

Ross leaned against his desk, watching her while crossing his arms. "So, what exactly were you implying then?"

Mia used the camera bag as a distraction, giving herself a moment to think about the best way to proceed without aggravating the chip on his shoulder. With a deep breath, she reset the moment. "First, let me ask you something. When you think about coming into work, what is it you look forward to doing the most?"

"What do you mean?"

"Which part of working here is the most fun for you?"

Ross shrugged. "I guess working in the back, creating."

"Making the jewelry."

"Yeah, I guess. Where are you going with this?"

"Okay, then. That's what I was implying. My impression

of you is that you're a behind-the-scenes kind of guy. You create and then let your creations speak for themselves. You're most likely not happy working on the sales floor. And you don't seem to be excited about taking your store to the online world. You need to do the things you're good at and find other people to do the things you're not good at. In fact, you've already done it. Aanya was a good hire. Not as good as me, but we'll let bygones be bygones for now."

He rolled his eyes. "When have you ever let a bygone go by?"

Mia enjoyed prodding him and grinned. "As I was saying, she's a better salesman. She's friendly, people like her, so you use it to your advantage, and that becomes the voice you want customers to hear. Unless you feel your cousin is that person. And then you have me." She waved a confident hand toward herself. "A brilliant person who has exceptional taste in jewelry and is also willing to help you with what I'm good at, and I *am* good at this stuff. Use it to your advantage while you can. That doesn't make you weak, it makes you smart."

Ross didn't say anything at first, taking his time to study her. As usual, Mia grew nervous at his intense scrutiny. Sure, she could put on a good show, but she didn't want him gaining real insight and noticing her foundation had a few holes of insecurity in it.

"Did he win?"

"Did who win?" she asked.

"The candidate of the political campaign you worked on."

"Well, I'm living back home and working in a coffee shop, so that's your answer right there. But he was an asshole and less intelligent than a box of white chalk. *You* are neither of those things."

Ross dropped his arms. "Let's start with the pictures and see where it goes from there."

Mia stood, slipped the camera strap on her shoulder, and made her way to the door. "Ross, do you know what the difference is between selling a politician and selling jewelry? I don't have to use any fancy camera tricks or wordplay to make the jewelry look good. You've already done the work for me."

Chapter Ten

"ARE YOU AN expert in accounting yet?" Ross asked, relaxing on his living room couch with a beer in one hand, and his cell in the other. Hermes rested his head on Ross's lap.

"I'm an expert in learning about how much I really don't know." Luna sighed in frustration on the other end of the phone line. "I don't know what I'm doing, Ross, and I feel overwhelmed. Maybe I can't do this, after all. Every day, I just want to flee and start over somewhere new, like Alaska."

"You just need to give it a chance, and you'll find your rhythm."

"You sound like Grandpa."

"Well, the man definitely had his own rhythm, but so does everyone else in this family, me especially. I was overwhelmed by school, and I still made it out on the other side. You haven't been struggling long enough to give up yet."

"How's it going at the store? I can't believe how much I miss it. There must be something wrong with me."

Ross shook his head at his cousin's dramatics. "The store is fine. Still standing. Nothing's changed."

"Do I get anything else? Come on, Ross, give me something. I don't care how small and insignificant it is."

Ross took a drink from his beer as he gave her request consideration. "Let's see. Aanya's working out well. She's not getting on my nerves yet. Although she has a bad habit of humming, and I don't recognize any of the tunes. I try to spend as much time as possible in the office or in the workshop."

"Hmm. I think Aanya may have stumbled onto something really great here. This is a good tip for keeping you from scaring off the customers. Thanks, Aanya!"

"Damn, that's all I need is a store full of hummers," he said, laughing in response. "Oh, here's something. You remember I told you about the woman who I went to school with?"

"The cute one?"

Ross let his silence be his answer for a moment. "I don't remember saying whether she was cute or not."

It would be a lot easier dealing with Mia if she *wasn't* cute. Resenting her ability to charm him would certainly make things more convenient, but he didn't always have the energy, let alone the willpower for it. Those amber eyes and single dimple could melt away a man's resolve—or rather another man's resolve. Not his.

"But you didn't deny it," Luna pointed out. "I think that makes it obvious."

"Should I continue?"

"Still not denying it, but, yes."

"She's going to take some images for us to use online. She used to do social media work or something for some political campaign and is trying to push El Dorado Jewelry into the modern world."

"Oh my god, Ross. Isn't this exactly what I've been saying to you for a while now? Good luck to her getting through your stubborn head."

"Well, it might be slowly working its way through. Mia just has a way of explaining things. It makes, whatever she wants, sound like the most obvious, logical choice. I guess her ability to persuade people shouldn't be surprising. She was a star on the debate team, after all."

He shook his head, eyes lifting to the ceiling. "She's probably one of the smartest people I've ever known. Yet, half the time, I want to strangle her." Ross imagined Mia pushing her glasses along the bridge of her nose with a finger while providing an in-depth, know-it-all explanation on how he could handle a strangulation situation better. Of course, in true Mia fashion, she'd be perfect and correct. Her lecturing him was both infuriating and possibly a turn-on.

"I think that's exactly the type of person you need in your life. I like it," Luna said, bursting through the fantasy playing in his head.

"You would." Unfortunately, so would he. At least he had some resentment to keep him grounded.

"Well, keep me in the loop. This is one thing in your life that I actually find interesting. Everything else is boring. Seriously, go out and make some friends or something instead of sitting at home with your dog, drinking beer, and watching documentaries."

"I'm worried about Hermes." Ross's gaze dropped to the dog in his lap, who watched him with one solitary brown eye.

"What's wrong with him?"

"He's been very low energy lately, not eating very much and he's starting to feel really skinny. He just seems different."

Luna released a long sigh. "Ross, who knows how old that dog is? He's probably just winding down."

This wasn't reassuring at all. Ross had a sinking sensation in his gut, and the feeling was all-too familiar. "I'm taking him to the vet tomorrow just to be sure."

"I remember when that dog first appeared at the jewelry store, and you were so annoyed you tried to push poor Hermes out. Now, look at you. I'm sure the vet is going to tell you the dog is too spoiled and has given up on walking. He probably expects you just to carry him around in a baby chest carrier thingy and be hand-fed fresh steak."

A smile tugged on his lips at the idea. "Do you think he would fit in one of those?"

She laughed. "I'm sure Hermes is fine. Just keep in touch and let me know how it goes."

"I will. And don't give up, Lulu."

"You too, Ross."

Chapter Eleven

"Tea for Aanya," Mia called from the Pony Expresso counter. "Oh, Aanya, hello! How are you?"

"I'm good now that I have my tea." The older lady took her drink with a sweet smile.

"I've been busy lately, but I was planning on stopping by after work to maybe start taking some images in the store. Can you let Ross know? Maybe he'll be less cranky if he's prepared."

Aanya frowned. "I don't think today would be a great day. Ross took a call earlier, and poor Hermes has cancer. He's been sitting in his office with the dog all day. Maybe you should talk to him."

"God, that's horrible. Yeah, thanks for letting me know."

Mia hadn't known Hermes for long, but a heavy sadness settled in her heart for the El Dorado Jewelry family. After work, she walked to the jewelry store to pay the dog and his owner a visit.

Aanya's eyes raised at her arrival, and she pointed to his office door. Mia tapped on it, opening it when she heard, "Yeah?" from the other side.

Ross leaned his head against his knuckles as he read something on the computer. The other chair had been pulled close and turned into a pedestal, the dog's bed placed in the center. It was clear Hermes had ascended to the status of royalty in the small jewelry shop, which was understandable.

"Hey," Mia said.

Ross blinked in surprise as she placed an Americano on his desk.

"Aanya told me the news about Hermes. I brought you a coffee and Hermes his favorite muffin," Mia said, giving the animal gentle pets. Hermes opened his eye, and she offered him a muffin chunk. The dog sniffed the food but turned away uninterested. Mia's heart broke for him, and she returned to petting. "It's okay. We'll save it for later." She turned her focus to Ross. "How are you doing?"

His finger fiddled with the plastic edge of the coffee lid. "It took me three tries to spell canine lymphoma before Google could actually figure out what I meant."

"Did you find what you were looking for?"

"Yeah, I've been reading up on it." He studied her as she continued petting the sick dog. "You don't know how frustrating everything is. And when something like this happens, it just makes my process that much harder. I already have to read every word twice to make sure what I think I'm reading is actually what's there. By the time I get to the end of the sentence, I've already forgotten how the beginning started." He focused on the screen, leaning against a bent arm on his desk.

"If you're tired, I can read a section out loud. Give yourself a break, Ross. Anyone would have trouble processing information under these circumstances."

He didn't move. "I don't need any help."

"Okay."

Mia focused her attention on the dog instead, running her fingers through his soft curls.

"What stage did the vet say the cancer was at?" she asked after Ross's chair turned to her again.

He rubbed the bridge of his nose. "Stage three. She did mention we could try chemotherapy, but without treatment, he might only last a few weeks or so."

"Are you considering treating him then?"

She noticed his muscles working across the tight set in his jaw. "I'm using every extra penny now helping my cousin with college. The vet is estimating around forty-five hundred dollars for treatment, and there are no guarantees it's going to work." His eyes shifted from Mia to his dog. "I don't know if I can do it, and I feel like a bad person. But I have to make an appointment for Hermes soon either way."

"Hey," Mia said, waiting until Ross met her eyes again. She leaned across the desk in an attempt to be closer, placing a hand across one of his forearms. "You're not a bad person. Hermes is lucky to have someone like you to look out for him. Do you want me to go with you to the appointment? I don't mind."

"No." Ross shifted away from her, returning his focus to the computer. "Thanks for the coffee. Can you leave?"

"Ross—"

"I can handle things myself, Mia. I don't need your help."

All the progress they'd made was sliding backwards and Mia didn't want to let go. All she wanted to do was hug the man. Ross looked like he needed it. "Okay. I know you can handle it. I wasn't offering because you needed help. I was offering because I thought you needed a friend."

Ross didn't look at her. When his iron jaw locked into place, her heart began to deflate. "Well, that isn't necessary either."

Chapter Twelve

LIFE WAS A greedy, hungry tapeworm.
Ross once asked Aanya if she had any family in town. She proceeded to relay the Pujari family genealogy to him, or, more accurately, the immediate family, which included four grown children and their spouses. The family was full of engineers, doctors, teachers. In fact, one of her sons was an English teacher at Ross's old high school and, according to Aanya, he was recently awarded Teacher of the Year. She talked about her family with a lot of pride.

He found other people's families intriguing. As someone aware of his own unorthodox family unit since grade school, Ross was curious about normal family dynamics. The one taste he got of the real thing was during those few months he went to Mia's home after school. Alongside tutoring and dinner, Ross could imagine he was part of the Russo family. How would his life have been different if he had it from the start? Or was his life always fated to fall in the same way?

Ross found it odd when people used the word *blessed* to describe their life or family. He had never felt blessed in his life. The figurative tapeworm, like its real-life parasitic counterpart, took from its host with no mercy. Perhaps he hadn't noticed he was already a carved out, empty shell. The tapeworm made him leery about accepting anything, or anyone else in his life. Especially if there was a chance it might also be taken away at some point.

Ross's tapeworm started taking from him at three years old, when his own parents were killed in a car accident. It took his sense of self-worth in grade school as he fell further behind academically. In high school, he temporarily lost his actual freedom. A few years ago, it took his only adult compass, his grandpa.

Today his tapeworm was taking Hermes.

When he first met Hermes, the dog was already down to three legs and one eye. Ross had exited the workshop with an expensive watch newly repaired. Hermes was napping on the worn, blue carpet of El Dorado Jewelry, beside the propped door, as if it was his designated spot. The dog was a rejected, dingy quartz on the deserted shore of blue-gray pebbles.

"There's a dog in the store," he informed his cousin while using a soft cloth to polish the watch face.

"Hmm?" Luna said, giving the smallest attempt to glance at him before returning her focus to her phone. "Oh, I know."

"Let's try this again. *Why* is there a dog in the store?"

"The door's open, and he was hot and tired. He's not hurting anything. If it doesn't bother me, why should it bother you?"

"He could be hurting our business. I mean, look at that mangy thing. He's filthy, probably covered in ticks, and— What the hell happened to his leg?"

"I don't know. It was missing when he came in," Luna responded while continuing to scroll through her phone.

"Well, he's not staying here. Either find his owner or call the shelter."

The stray dog lifted his head and watched them as though realizing his future was the exact topic of conversation between the two humans. He turned one big, soulful eye in Ross's direction and wagged his stubby tail in hopefulness. Ross refused to succumb to anything as pathetic as a single, soulful eye—even if it came in looking for a nap.

"Oh, come on, Ross. Look at that guy. He clearly doesn't belong to anyone, and he's really sweet. Why couldn't we have a little shop dog?" His cousin captured his gaze with her own large, pitiful eyes. The universe was determined to turn this fight against him.

Ross pushed his resolution deeper. "Because I don't want a shop dog. What if customers won't come in because they're allergic or scared of dogs?"

Luna rolled her eyes. "You don't hear me complaining about how many customers we've lost because you're out front. Seriously, stay in the back and leave the dog and me alone."

Her reaction wasn't surprising. His cousin had a soft spot for furry creatures, whether it was a three-legged dog or orphaned kittens. The responsibility fell to Ross to be the cold-hearted villain. He walked to the dirty, white dog and encouraged movement by pressing the tip of his shoe against a furry rump. "Get out, dog. Go find somewhere else to take a nap."

The dog gave him one more sad plea with his brown eye, before easing into a standing position, yawning, and making his way outside. With the animal kicked out, Ross reentered and shut the door behind him. But the door wasn't able to obstruct the dejected gaze coming from the other side of the glass.

"Why are you such a mean man?" Luna's hands had locked onto her hips.

"I'm not mean. Someone has to be the adult around here. And how about you stay off your phone and do some work, Lulu?" He handed her the watch, and she stuck out her tongue. With his heartless task completed, Ross returned to his workshop.

Later that afternoon, he departed the rear entrance with a bag of garbage destined for the alley dumpster. No one was more surprised than him to find the grungy dog, sitting beside the door as if expecting Ross to make an appearance. Hermes panted and wagged his tail as though greeting a long-lost friend.

"Go home," Ross said while the dog trotted alongside him, acting as if the bag of trash was filled with bits of meat instead of discarded chunks of plaster.

After he took care of his chore, Ross made his return trip, determined to ignore the animal. A sharp bark pierced the air. Ross's mistake was turning around. Hermes made his final argument with his one eye and an optimistic wag of his tail.

Ross groaned, dropping his head. "Alright. Come on." The dog understood what these words meant and scampered through the door.

Hermes took a spot on a discarded rag at the edge of the workshop. He turned around a few times on the small scrap of fabric before settling with a contented breath. Hermes was home.

Today, the three-legged dog with the one solitary eye rested his final moments in Ross's lap. His hand stroked the length of Hermes's bony, frail body. "You're a good boy," he assured his dog while rubbing an edge of his sleeve across his own damp eyes.

"Mr. Manasse?"

A vet technician in pastel purple scrubs stood at the exam room entrance. She gave the pair a sympathetic smile. "You can bring Hermes in now."

Ross swallowed the lump in his throat. It felt like the size of a boulder.

The tapeworm was an evil bastard, but Ross wasn't ready to surrender. Not this time.

"I've changed my mind," he said. "I want to talk to the doctor about doing the treatment."

Chapter Thirteen

"DO YOU NOT want me in there disturbing Hermes or something? I'll be quiet." Mia said. There had to be some reason he was refusing to let her into his workshop.

"No. He's at the vet doing a treatment. I just... I don't think anyone is going to find it interesting," Ross stated for the second time in the last ten minutes.

She gave a slight shrug. "Well, maybe I'm the only one, but I'd love to see how it's actually done. What if you give me a tour, and if I get some nice pictures out of it, what does it hurt? I think you're wrong, though. I think lots of people are interested in the behind-the-scenes type of images and seeing how things are made. You're an artist, Ross. Show people how you make your art." Mia had arrived this morning with the camera in tow. She had the bright idea of taking some images, which focused on the heart of the business rather than the jewelry alone. Getting access to the El Dorado office had been a breeze compared to what she was fighting today. Gaining passage to the workshop, Ross's main domain in the rear of the store, made it seem as if Mia was asking to tour Fort Knox.

Ross's eyes shifted between the workshop door and her as though he was weighing the pros and cons of her proposal.

Resistance only made her more determined. What was he protecting?

Mia changed tactics. "Can I ask you something? How'd you get into this business?"

"It belonged to my grandfather."

"Was that Victor?" she asked.

"Yeah. I've been working here since I was a kid, helping on the weekends and during school breaks. When I wasn't interested in anything else, he taught me how to make jewelry."

"I like that story." Mia smiled because it was true. It was so hard to get anything from Ross, a tiny nugget of personal information was like striking the motherlode. "I'm working for you, remember? I'm not doing an exposé or anything. The images are for you and the shop, so anything you don't like, you don't have to use. Do you have any pictures of your grandpa making jewelry?" Mia certainly wished she had taken photos of her mother quilting.

Ross's brow furrowed. "I don't think so."

"Don't you wish you had something like that? You're adding to the history here, and it might be nice to chronicle your work. It'll also give you something to show your own grandkids someday."

Ross's lips pressed together in a frown. "I wish you wouldn't work so hard at getting me to change my mind."

Despite his sullen expression, she laughed. "I'm flattered that you think I'm always working hard."

"Which is why I don't want to make things too easy for you."

"You know I love a challenge."

A delicate cough from Aanya drew their attention and the store employee suddenly shifted her eyes to something outside the window.

"Anyway, I think we should just focus on the jewelry out here. You don't need to see the junk in the workshop," he said.

"What exactly are you afraid of, Rosso?"

"Maybe you're a spy?"

She raised an eyebrow. "A spy who works at a coffee shop? How long does it take to learn all this stuff? Can I really pick it up in an afternoon?"

"No, it takes years."

Mia lifted her hands. "Then what are you worried about?"

He stood in silence before releasing a breath in defeat. "Alright, come on."

The front of the shop represented the glittering, perfect by-products of Ross's work. But the workshop encompassed a sense of the authentic, dedicated craftsmanship that went into producing the sparkling jewelry. It was utilitarian and grimy. The tools and well-worn machines appeared as if they had been around for generations. It was the dirty guts of the store, the old but reliable engine that made it all possible. Mia was fascinated. She was in a new, unfamiliar world with Ross as her guide, and she loved everything about it.

He stood there as she took it all in, his fingers fumbling along the lines of the magnifier headgear in his hands.

"What do you call yourself? Do you have a more specific name other than jeweler?" Mia asked.

"Jeweler usually refers to the person at the front of the

store, the salesperson. The person doing the work in the back is a bench jeweler." His weight shifted from one foot to the other. "I don't know what I'm supposed to be doing."

"What would you be doing if I wasn't here?"

"Working."

"Okay, then do that. I'll try and stay out of your way and not bug you too much."

"I'm just not used to someone else being back here with me. I'm usually alone."

"I'm not planning on moving in, Ross. I'm just hanging out for the afternoon. Just be yourself. Wait a minute." Mia reached up and swept her fingers through his hair, fixing the one section which had become mussed when he removed his headgear earlier. Since she was here anyway, she might as well straighten the neck strap of his apron, her fingers brushing along the heated skin of his neck. "Okay, now you can be yourself."

"Are you done?"

"I don't have to be." There went Mia's mouth again, but this time she didn't care. Why not have a little fun? To be honest, she didn't want to be done and her mind raced for additional excuses. At this close proximity, she could capture the full scent of his leather apron and spicy body wash. Her fingers itched to trace along the lines of his arm, from the top of his bicep to his strong fingers. His sleeves were pushed up again, tempting her.

"I'm sure it's good enough if you're looking to get a bench jeweler in his natural habitat. It's not like I'm a model." The top of his cheeks took on a rosy shade though, his gaze dropping.

"Obviously." Mia threw him a cheeky grin, enjoying the game of teasing him. Maybe Ross wasn't a model in the traditional sense, but he was in every sense she liked.

He narrowed his eyes. "Okay, I'm just going to work at my bench."

"Great!" She turned her attention to her camera, adjusting the settings, and took a couple of test photos before fine-tuning again. When she aimed the camera on Ross, he was seated on a stool at his work table with a small brown block between his hands. Mia focused her lens on this, his steady fingers working the block with the finesse and care of a surgeon, the veins on his exposed forearms flicking with subtle movements. She didn't know what he was doing, but it was hypnotizing nonetheless.

Mia clicked a few frames with the camera. "What are you making?"

"A ring."

"You carve a ring by hand?"

"I do. There are bench jewelers who use fancy computer programs like CAD, which allows you to design jewelry in 3D. It works with a special printer to create the ring model out of the carving wax. But I can't afford one of those yet, so I still create the model by hand." Ross's voice was as low and as soothing as the repetitive motion his work instilled.

"Why do you make it out of wax?" she asked.

"It's used to create the cast."

"How does that work?" She scrolled through her images before continuing to take more photos.

He stopped his work and studied her. "Are you really interested in this?"

"Yes, of course. I wish I had the talent to create beautiful things with my hands. I was always interested in taking some type of art or pottery or even a woodworking class in school just to try it. But I was pushed to take something else, something that would look more impressive to colleges."

"How did you learn photography then?"

"It's mostly what I picked up while doing the yearbook stuff. The advisor was good at photography, so I was always bothering her to show me how to do things and then I learned on my own through trial and error."

"Okay, well, I create the ring out of wax, and then it goes on a wax platform like this one." He retrieved a ring model from the corner of his work desk and displayed it. The brown wax ring was attached to a stick on a base. He stood, going to a different station. "Then I take my wax ring, place it in one of these metal cylinders, and pour a special plaster into it. This dome comes down to vacuum out any air bubbles because when I create a mold, I only want the ring, not bubbles."

"I think my heart might be bubbling." Mia wasn't sure what it was but listening to Ross describe the technical side of his work, stirred something within her. As if he wasn't already attractive enough, he had to transform before her eyes into Professor Ross, and she liked it a lot.

He ignored her, stepping to the next station. "Then I put the cylinder in this cooler for a few hours, because it needs to harden. Once that happens, I can melt the wax out—"

"And you get a cast?" she guessed, unable to hide the excitement in her voice. Was it possible to sign up for additional private lessons? This was the most fun she had in a while.

He seemed surprised at her reaction. "There isn't going to be a test on this, Mia. Is this what you were like in the classroom?"

"Maybe. But please continue. I love this."

"Anyway, whatever metal I'm using, such as gold, gets heated in the crucible with a torch, and I place the plaster cast in this holder. Once the gold is completely melted, I turn on the drum, it spins around, and uses centrifugal force to push the melted metal into the cast."

"Wow. A guy who can casually throw out some Newtonian mechanics like it's nothing? Be still my heart." Mia grinned, trying not to fan herself with a hand. Professor Ross might be becoming her favorite Ross.

"What?"

"Centrifugal force."

A noticeable shade of pink colored his cheeks, and he cleared his throat, his eyes dropping to the ground. "Oh. Anyway. Then water breaks up the plaster. You get the ring. It gets sanded, set with stones, and polished. That's the general path from start to finish." The end of his jewelry tour rushed through his lips in a blur. Ross returned to his chair, taking the carving wax in his hands once again.

She cocked her head. "I noticed your gems look different compared to traditional jewelry."

"Yeah, I leave them raw, not cutting them. There are exact specifications for cutting gems, and my grandpa was a fast cutter. Me, not so much, although I can do it. But he was definitely better at it than me. On the other hand, I kind of like them raw and natural, instead of conforming them to the ideal standards of perfection."

"Me too." She resumed taking photos. "I would sign up for another one of your TED talks again."

"You don't have to pretend so much, Mia," he muttered, his attention absorbed in his work.

"What do you mean?"

Ross gave her a sideways glance. "You don't have to act like you find all this interesting. Don't patronize me."

Mia lowered the camera, meeting his eyes. "I—Why do you think that?"

He abandoned his work, leaning forward on his bench. "Let's just say you have a teacher's pet vibe. You're a people-pleaser."

Her body stiffened at the criticism. It wasn't the first time someone called her out on this, but it was hard to hear nonetheless. "Well, maybe you're right. But I was rude to you before at the coffee shop, and I didn't like it."

"A t least you were honest."

She adjusted her glasses while crossing her legs. "Just because I'm saying something positive doesn't make it less honest, Ross. Maybe I'm a people-pleaser, and maybe you have trouble accepting people thinking nice things about you. Both of these things can be true. But I don't think it's fair to assume I'm saying things I don't actually believe."

"Where you're concerned, I'm not sure what's true."

"What's that supposed to mean?" Mia was confused on where this sudden verbal aggressiveness was coming from. What happened to the old Ross? The quiet one? The thoughtful one? Was it one more thing she missed seeing the first time around, like missing the fact Ross could be the type of person who'd cheat on his schoolwork?

He took a pause as if regaining his control. "This." His finger flicked between them. "What this is, is a favor for a favor. Nothing more. I don't need a friend. I don't need you to soothe my ego. And most of all, I don't need your help. If you get a sudden urge to help someone, stick to helping people who want it, like that guy you met at the coffee shop who needed help picking out a pair of earrings."

Mia's arms laced tightly across her chest. "Well, I can believe you don't have any friends considering how you treat an old one."

"Did you really think we were friends?"

This stopped her. Was this true? Were they never friends? Her jaw tightened as hurt spiraled inside her torso. "I had friends in high school, but I also had people who were nice to me because they wanted to be in my group for whatever project was being assigned. Probably because, no matter what I had to do, I would deliver the grade, even if it meant taking everything on myself. You never used me like that, so, yes, I thought of you as a friend."

His lips stretched into a straight line, appearing unimpressed as he shrugged a single shoulder. "Well, maybe you saw friendship, but I saw myself being forced to interact with you. I certainly didn't have any choice in the matter. But if you believe that makes a friendship, then that's on you."

Mia studied his dark eyes, which revealed no emotion besides a cool distance. "It may have started out that way, but—" The second part of her sentence disintegrated in the air between them.

He took in her defensiveness. "Maybe now we can get

some real honesty. Did you feel sorry for me? Was I a pet project for you? Someone for you to rescue?"

In high school, and present day, Mia had felt a lot of things in regards to Ross, and not all of them were good, including jealousy, frustration, and aggravation. She would even throw in attraction if she was truthful about it. These days, she spent far too many daydream moments remembering his well-defined, naked torso on the dusty trail path.

Her cheeks heated, and Ross acknowledged it with a nod. "Maybe there's some truth to it then. It must be hard for someone like you, someone who will do anything to deliver the grade, to have dealt with such a lost cause."

Her emotions shifted from embarrassment to anger. Mia leaned closer, her eyes locking onto his. "Maybe I was a silly, naïve girl back then, and maybe I still have my moments, but I've never treated you with pity, Ross Manasse. And, yes, I did think of you as my friend back then, and perhaps it's foolish to think I can be friends with you now. But currently, you're being an absolute asshole for no reason. You clearly have more respect for your raw gems and their imperfect but beautiful existence, than you do for yourself or for me."

With this, she set the camera on a table and abandoned the workshop, slamming the door behind her. He succeeded in bringing her down to the dark. She'd failed once again.

Chapter Fourteen

Ross's workshop fell into a quiet, but unsettling, solitude after Mia stormed out. It had never been emptier than it was at this moment. His day had been off-balance ever since he got up early this morning to take Hermes to the vet. Then she appeared in El Dorado Jewelry with the camera bag slung over her shoulder, and her dimple breaking through without an ounce of restraint.

Mia was nothing but an invader in this space. It was a rare occasion for Luna to enter his workshop. The area belonged to Ross, his grandfather, and, to an extent, Hermes. But his grandfather was gone, and Hermes was doing his first chemotherapy treatment. His world was on a skewed plane, and Ross didn't like the wobbling that occurred under his feet whenever she was around. He missed the silent, steady workday he used to be able to depend on, without any attention, dimples, or Mia buttering him up with kind words. None of it was natural, not to Ross.

He glanced at Hermes's empty shop bed. The shabby sage-green cushion cratered in the center as if the dog's spirit was taking a phantom nap. Ross missed his dog. He missed his grandfather. He missed Luna. Mia's chattiness and forced friendliness did nothing to change this.

He scanned the workshop to find some remnants of his grandfather here. The one thing Ross could look at was the leather apron he wore. This was the dearest physical token remaining.

Mia was correct about one thing. Ross wished there was some visual memento of Victor doing what he loved, instead of depending on his own memory, something more faded with each passing day. When did Ross become so sentimental? He was sure when his world was no longer tilting, everything would slip back into its original position.

Ross abandoned his carving wax, taking a seat on the stool, which had been occupied by Mia ten minutes earlier. He supposed her exit, and the abandoned camera on the table, was her way of telling him she was done, she'd given up on the lost cause once again. At last, she understood the reality of the situation. He did not need her. He did not want her. Sure, Ross preferred not being so blunt and his gut dropped at the clear hurt reflected in Mia's face, but whatever connection existed between them before meant nothing in the present. Ross would not be affected by her. He ignored the jump in his heartbeat due to her nearness or when her fingers swept through his hair or adjusted the strap around his neck. He'd also ignore how much his body yearned to fit within her soft curves, to dip his face into the gentle swoop of her neck, and feel her arms wrap around him in an encompassing hug. To accept a real connection meant letting his guard down. Ross had to ignore it because his guard was his *only* protection, and he didn't need to be taken care of. Not by her. Not by anyone.

He took the camera and twisted the top dial to preview

mode. His finger clicked the shuttle button as Ross went through her images, the most recent being the photos she took in his workshop. He never considered his occupation to be anything extraordinary. It was his job, and, like him, nothing special. But, through her images, he discovered a way to see himself as Mia saw him, to see through her lens in every literal sense. There were a few wider shots, showing him immersed in his work in quiet composure. His posture, a bowed head and hunched shoulders, snapped Ross's memory to Victor. Through some unknown sorcery, Mia had gifted him something which seemed impossible. The camera transformed itself into an apparatus of an oracle. He was given a vision of past and present, seeing both himself and a younger version of his grandfather. Ross shook his head at the ridiculous conclusion his brain envisioned. He *was* getting too sentimental.

The majority of Mia's images fell into the category of the close-ups, with a focus on the hard to notice details. Her photography captured his dirty hands, the tools in the pocket of his apron, the wax models which were at one point deemed unworthy. Ross could admit, she had an excellent eye. Her pictures were good.

Ross didn't need her. He and Luna and Hermes had managed fine this whole time. The little jewelry store could continue to ramble in quiet existence because he'd make it work. It's not as though the store was about to go out of business. But, if Ross was honest, he wasn't sure how long he could afford to let it ramble, or if it was time for him to consider the future.

For the first time in his life, Ross was stuck at the helm

of El Dorado Jewelry alone. He had an employee to pay for. Luna was counting on him to bring in money for her education and future. Plus, he had Hermes's lymphoma treatment to fund. If Ross thought about it for too long, the tidal wave of financial responsibility threatened to overcome him. It was time to face facts. Pride was not enough to live on. And it was nothing but his pride pushing Mia away, to prove he wasn't weak. Although his bitter words this afternoon may have shown the opposite.

A few days later, he entered Pony Expresso. The coffee shop was empty, and Mia's eyes were on him as he made his way to the counter. There was no dimple in greeting. "What can I get for you?" She kept her eyes on the register, slipping a strand of hair behind her ear.

Ross removed the camera bag from his shoulder, placed it on the counter, and slid it across to her. She tracked the movement before lifting her gaze to him.

"I want to continue with our deal," was all he said.

Her eyes dropped to the black bag as his hands held its edges, but she didn't move. It was as though all life inside the small coffee shop had stopped, awkward silence filling every space.

She shifted, still avoiding him. "I don't think—"

"Mia." He waited until her eyes met his own. "What I said before—I'm sorry. I was having a rough... I shouldn't have taken it out on you. I'm sorry for what I said." It had been a long time since Ross had been this sorry. He suddenly didn't want to disappoint her or for her to give up on him. "Can we try again? Please."

Mia's lips turned into a slight smile. "Okay." She took

possession of the camera bag, her fingers brushing his for a moment before he released it to her with a feeling of relief sweeping through him.

The following evening, she entered Ross's store with the camera bag, tripod, and a box full of odds and ends. He locked the door and followed her to a glass display case where she set down her items and equipment. Investigating the contents of the box, he found two small lights, sticks, rocks, moss, and other random things. It appeared Mia may have gathered them on a nature hike in the surrounding area.

"What is all this stuff?" he asked.

"Oh, I just grabbed a few things I found walking around the neighborhood yesterday. You never know what props might help make the image and the jewelry…well, *pop*, so, I just brought a bunch of things, and we'll see what works."

She removed some large white panels with a roll of duct tape. "I wanted to make a cheap lightbox, so I made this with some foam board and tissue paper. I just need to put these panels together really quick." She placed two of the panels side-by-side and began taping them together.

"You have your own lights?" He removed rickety, cheap, metal lamps from the box. "Are you sure these are safe? They look like an accident waiting to happen."

She glanced at them. "Oh, yeah, I've already used them before at the coffee shop. If you're really concerned, you can bring out the shop's fire extinguisher and have it on hand. But they work great and, with the lightbox, I can diffuse the light more evenly. I actually picked up those lights and the tripod at one of the antique stores, the one across the street. Have you ever been there?"

"You mean the junk shop."

"It's not *all* junk. It's a treasure hunt. And the guy who works there was really nice. He had some cool political memorabilia that I guess is something he personally collects. I listened to him talk about it for forty-five minutes."

Ross's brow shifted in confusion. "Why?"

"Because I found it interesting. I like to listen to people talk about things that get them excited, and I learn something new. You can watch when someone gets energized about a topic. They get a little gleam in their eye. I always look for the gleam." She returned to taping, her hair falling across her shoulder. "You had a gleam when you were talking about making jewelry in your workshop."

"I don't think so. I don't think my eyes have ever gleamed."

"Oh, I remember them gleaming a few times in high school, Rosso." She slid him a coy smile, with the dimple making a marked appearance. "I know for sure there's still a gleam in there."

Ross shoved his hands in his pockets while rocking on his heels. He couldn't escape a need to steady himself whenever she was around. "You were saying something about the antique store."

"Oh, yes. Anyway, we had a really nice conversation, and while I was there, I found these table lights and the tripod. He gave it all to me for ten bucks."

"That was very generous of him."

"Wasn't it? He's definitely a more generous shop owner than you." Mia propped the handmade, standing lightbox on the table. A falling leaf could probably knock the whole thing over. "There. What do you think?"

What did he think? Ross wasn't sure. Mia being here seemed to be both a mistake and the best decision he'd made in a while. While the first was a given, the latter went against his instincts. "I think if you can get some decent images with this setup, it's going to be a miracle."

The coy smile returned. "Yeah? Maybe we should make it a bet then, make it interesting. If I can get some decent pictures, I get jewelry."

"Yeah, this bet is already way too expensive. What could you possibly offer on your side to be worth jewelry?"

"You're already getting a bargain with my level of expertise and photography skills. What are you afraid of, Rosso?"

Ross studied her for a moment. As usual, he wasn't sure how much of her was pure bravado. "You seem way too confident. I have a feeling you know you'd win this bet."

She shrugged her shoulders. "Like I said, the guy at the antique store is way more generous than you."

She set the lights on either side of the makeshift lightbox. "Voila! I think that'll work. Can you bring me some of the jewelry you want pictures of?"

He unlocked the display cabinet and removed a few pieces to start with. He handed her a pair of silver earrings. The thin, precious metal dangles, woven together like a rushing river.

She put an old wooden board with pale blue, distressed paint in the center of her lightbox. A tuft of brittle, vibrant green moss was placed on top. The earrings hooked into the moss, setting them upright.

Mia tinkered with the camera settings. "In high school, I

bought a vintage camera at a yard sale for seven dollars. I was so excited, I moved stuff out of my bedroom closet. I had the idea that I'd create a darkroom to develop my own film."

"What happened?" As much as he tried to quash his curiosity, he couldn't help it. Mia always had the ability to draw him into conversation, like a grumpy moth to a dimpled flame.

"Well, let's just say my parents insisted I start using my closet as a real closet again. Especially after the curtain rod got ripped from the wall. For some reason, it couldn't handle being used as a makeshift clothing rack. They definitely were not on board with the idea." She sighed. "Just as well. I never got any film for the camera. But I'm still disappointed I never got to use it."

"You can still buy film for those?"

"Oh, sure. Not anywhere around here, of course, but there are photography places around LA where you can buy film. And there's this magical place called"—she paused for dramatic effect—"the Internet." A single hand, with fingers spread apart, swept through the air as though she was explaining the existence of Mount Olympus. "Also, it's where cat videos, memes, and jewelry store websites go to live. You should look into it."

"Shut up, Russo." But a grin escaped his lips, rendering his words less potent.

For an hour, Ross assisted in handing her jewelry to be photographed. He grew fascinated watching her work. She kept her thick, golden-brown hair locked behind her ears as she hunched over, becoming level with her subject. Mia didn't say much. She was so focused, the corners of her mouth would shift and pull at different angles. In between, she'd make minuscule adjustments to the jewelry, fixating on the smallest detail before snapping more images. Her movements were confident and graceful, like the rest of her. While she was completely focused, he allowed his gaze to linger lazily across her back, following the gentle slope of Mia's neck, down the length of her spine until his eyes reached the luscious curve of her—

"You know I was thinking," she said, breaking through the silence and causing Ross to flinch at the sudden interruption of his daydreams. "We should take some images of the jewelry on someone. People like to see what it looks like on an actual person, especially if they're purchasing online."

"Is that something you can do?" he asked.

"Not very easily. If your cousin's around, we could use her as a model."

"Maybe if she comes for a visit, but it probably won't be until the holidays."

"She's not nearby?"

"No, she's going to school in Chico," Ross responded.

"Oh, well, the holidays aren't too far away. I also think it would be nice if we had some couples photos."

"Couples photos?"

"You know, images of madly in-love couples, where someone has just received beautiful jewelry from their true love."

"Why?"

"Because you're not just selling jewelry. You're selling romance, love, happiness, all the Valentine's Day clichés. In this business, I would think you'd have to embrace the clichés. And people like pretty pictures, it allows them to imagine it could be them."

As far as Ross was concerned, he was selling jewelry, not romantic promises. The last thing in the world he worried about was giving people the feeling of romance, not when the emotion was so far removed from his day-to-day existence. While he'd had various relationships over the years, he had never been in love and never expected anyone to fall in love with him.

"Did you want to see?" Mia's voice broke into his thoughts.

"See what?" He was confused. Was she still talking about romance?

She gave him an odd look. "The images I took. What else could there be?"

"Oh. Yeah, okay." He moved closer, viewing the camera's display screen over her shoulder as she flicked through the images. Considering Mia arrived with a box filled with garbage, Ross was impressed. Though it was hard to concentrate when he kept noticing the gold and red hue variations playing across the strands in her hair.

"I still need to do some work to adjust lighting and coloring, but I think the box did a pretty good job." Her vibrant eyes lifted to his. "What do you think?"

"Yeah, they're fine," he managed to grumble. Her eyes stayed with him as if expecting something more. She would be disappointed. He didn't have anything else as all additional thoughts scattered from his brain.

"And what do you think about my couples photo idea?"

He shifted, moving to a safer distance. It was easier dealing with Mia when she was further away. An acceptable range would be one where it was necessary to shout at each other through cupped hands. Perhaps then, he'd be less tempted to release the hair being held captive by her ear. "I don't know," he replied. "I really don't think all that's necessary. I'm sure what you've done is good enough."

"Can I just try a test photo? Maybe it might convince you."

"What?"

"It'll be real quick, Ross. Come on. You and me." She drew nearer in eagerness.

He backed into one of the display cases, the corner jabbing him in the ass. "Ow. I-I don't think that's a good idea. Besides, we've already agreed I'm not a model."

"Well, neither am I, and we both know you're better looking than I am."

Ross's eyes snapped to hers at the compliment. The control he wanted to maintain in this situation was squeezing between his fingers. He became desperate to yank it out of arm's reach. "That's obviously not true."

She flashed a grin. "Aw, you think I'm better looking? That's so sweet."

Shit.

"No, that's not what I was say—"

"So, I'm not good looking? What *are* you trying to say?" Her grin was replaced with a frown.

"Dammit, Mia. Fine, we'll take the damn photo." A judgmental finger pointed at her. "Stop trying to manipulate me. I know you're doing this on purpose."

"If you mean purposely trying to get a photo, then you're

right. I told you I wanted a photo." She raised the legs on her tripod, getting it in position. "Okay, go stand over there where we have the most space. And stand, so your profile is to the camera. Do me a favor and put your left hand on your right bicep."

This was silly. Ross followed her directions with as much *grudge* as was possible when doing something begrudgingly. A smart girl like Mia was sure to get the hint. If she was expecting him to smile for a lousy picture, she was going to be disappointed for the second time this evening.

"Your *other* left hand, Ross. You need to flip sides."

He sighed, switching to the correct position. How was Mia able to talk him into doing things he didn't want to do? He was glad she used her powers of persuasion for good rather than evil. In the past, there had been, no doubt, people who would have considered Ross a bad influence. In a shocking twist of irony, Ross never had agency over a single person. And he wouldn't mind having some, especially when it came to her.

"Can we just get this over with, please?" he asked, unable to keep the impatience from invading his question.

"You cooperate, and it'll be over before you know it." She peered through the viewfinder, adjusting the lens. "Okay, here's what's going to happen. Oh, you can put your hand down now. I just needed it to focus." She walked to the display counter, and her fingers danced across the selection of jewelry before choosing a ring and slipping it on.

"I'm going to set the timer, and then come over to you to put my hand on your arm, so it's, hopefully, the focus of the image." She turned one of the metal lights around to shine on Ross, placing one of the lightbox panels in front to defuse it. Mia repeated this action on the opposite end with the second light. "We'll be in the image, but slightly out of focus. I think as long as you don't seem as grumpy as you look right now, it'll turn out pretty good."

"I'm not smiling."

"As long as you can *not* smile *and* also not look crabby, I'll take it. The camera shutter will go off a few times because I have it on the setting where it'll take a few images in quick succession. Got it?"

"Yeah, I got it. Let's get it over with."

Mia approached, and, in what was getting to be a bad habit, her fingers swept through Ross's hair as though this would also sweep away the cobwebs surrounding his heart. Those dusty webs weren't going anywhere but they may have swayed a fraction in the breeze. She then brushed the top of his shoulders as if to rid his gray sweater of invisible lint or wrinkles or whatever damn thing her eyes could see. Did it even matter when she had already stated he was going to be *slightly out of focus*.

"How about me? Do I look okay?" Mia's body stilled, giving him the time to study her.

Ross did the one thing he'd wanted to do all evening. He released the lock of hair from behind her ear.

"Really? That's it?"

"Yeah," he said. To be honest, he didn't know what he should have found wrong with her. Except for that one time she had been sprawled on the ground during her off-trail hike, he couldn't remember a moment that she wasn't adorably put together. And even at that moment, with a streak of dirt smudged across her chin, she still managed to be endearing.

Mia returned to the camera and pushed a few more buttons before saying, "Okay, ready, set, go," before rushing toward him. Their bodies collided in her haste and she almost tipped over. On instinct, he wrapped his hand around her waist to catch her.

"Oops." She braced herself by placing her hand flat on his chest. "Sorry about that." She blushed but maintained her position, and he kept his hand at her waist. She put the jeweled hand on his right bicep, the spot she marked earlier.

"Are you sure you set the timer?" he asked.

"Sorry, it goes off in about thirty seconds. I always misjudge how long that actually is, which is why I raced over here, and now we get to stand here, awkwardly waiting for it to go off."

He could sense her eyes on him.

"Ross, can you look at me?"

He didn't want to. It would be a mistake. But Ross sucked in his courage, rotating his face to her. Somewhere in the background, the camera's shutter clicked several times, but she didn't move, and neither did he.

Besides the one or two "friend hugs" he'd received from her many years ago, she'd never been so close. It wasn't as if sixteen-year-old Ross hadn't craved this type of contact. It may have passed through his thoughts once, twice...or possibly a hundred times. He had lost count.

Her ever watchful gaze tracked the length of his face: his brow, eyes, nose, and mouth. It was as if she was studying for a future quiz. Mia appeared to be committing every detail of him to memory. Perhaps she was preparing for a situation where another ten years passed and needed to make sure her brain didn't forget this time.

From his convenient vantage point, he was able to take his own notes on her features. This was, after all, Ross's super strength: the visuals. He noticed the soft, faded vestige of freckles across her nose. The way her elegant brows came together. Her thick lashes framing her warm eyes behind glasses. And, yes, his eyes landed on the lines of her lips. It wouldn't take much effort for him to—but it would be a mistake. He swallowed and returned to her eyes. But her lowered lids seemed to indicate she was also calculating the geometric angle and physical effort necessary to come closer.

"Mia?" he said.

"Hmm?"

"The camera went off."

She blinked, snapping to sensibility. "What?" She pulled away, leaving a cold void in her place. "Sorry. It was a long day of working at the coffee shop and then doing this. I may have just fallen into a daze, and I-I was trying to find that gleam."

She busied herself with the camera and packed her stuff.

"So, that's it, then?" he asked.

"Uh-huh. Yup. I think it's enough for now." Mia tossed items into her box as if she couldn't wait to escape. "I'll let you know when I have some finished images for you. And I'll just take the SD card so you can have your camera back."

"You don't need it for the coffee shop?"

"Nope. I've stockpiled lots of photos, so they should be good on social media posts for a while." She slipped her hair behind her ear again. "Anyway, thanks for letting me borrow it." Her eyes caught the ring glistening on her hand. "Oh, here's your ring." She jerked it off, placing it on the counter, but her fingers fumbled the landing, and the ring clattered against the glass. "Sorry." Mia pocketed the camera's SD card and claimed her box of supplies.

"Mia?"

"Yeah?"

He took the silver, rushing-river earrings and held them to her. She glanced at them before meeting his eyes, clearly unsure of what her response should be. He offered them again. "Go ahead. You won the bet."

She released a soft breath. "Really?" Returning the box to the counter, she took the earrings with a timid hand as though expecting him to snatch the jewelry away without warning. With the earrings in her possession, she released a wide smile, one which lit her whole face. A deep dimple marked her right cheek as she threaded the hooks through pierced lobes. She spotted her reflection in a mirror, moving her hair away so she could examine the dangling, sparkling earrings. "I love them. They're beautiful. Thank you."

"I hope this makes me better than the junk man across the street."

Mia reclaimed her cardboard box, resting it against a hip, as he walked her to the door. "Oh, yeah, you're way better than Gary. Maybe if I do some more images for you, I can get a necklace to match."

"Don't push your luck, Russo."

Chapter Fifteen

"I HAVE TO tell you that I'm not getting an Americano vibe from you. But here you go." Natalie set the cup of coffee beside Mia's laptop.

She took a sip, making a face. *Yuck. Definitely don't like that.* Maybe if she added more sugar, it would help.

Natalie took a seat across from her, with her own cup of hot tea. "I knew it. To tell the truth, you seem more like a person who likes something on the sweeter side. And why are you here on your day off, M? Are you working on your school submissions or something?"

No. No, Mia wasn't. A stab of guilt sliced through her gut. This was the single reason why she was at the coffee shop. She was already getting enough of the same question at home from her father.

Are you sending out your applications? and *How's the smarty-pants PhD thing coming along?* became frequent questions from the judge.

It didn't matter if she spent evenings working on a research proposal or examining the published papers of department faculty at different campuses. Any hint she was working on something else, such as the photos for Pony Expresso or El Dorado Jewelry, was met with a heavy sigh from her dad. This was usually followed by, "You're getting distracted. You need to stay focused. Do you really need to be doing that when you have other important things to do?"

He was right. The judge was always right. But, at the same time, Mia wondered when she'd be allowed to get distracted. There was a part of her beginning to feel it wasn't fair. She knew how to get things done. She'd been getting things done her whole life. But there was always this implication that if she ever let herself slip, *get distracted*, she would never climb out again. She'd be slinging coffee for the rest of her life.

If Mia was at Pony Expresso, she could work on anything she wanted without judgment. At least this was the theory until Natalie asked her the same question.

"I was, but I'm taking a break and working on some images for the jewelry store. Look at this. Doesn't it take your breath away?" Mia rotated her laptop, giving Natalie access to the screen. It was one of Ross's rings, the pearl one, her favorite, perched on a stack of gray river rocks. It was gorgeous. Someone scrolling through a page of images couldn't help but stop at this one.

"Wow. I had no idea that was the kind of jewelry he had over there."

Mia smiled, a soft flutter floated within her chest. "Oh yeah. It's amazing. I love everything he does."

Natalie studied Mia, her soft brown eyes catching the light with a mischievous twinkle. "Uh-huh. Is there something going on between you and the jewelry guy?"

Mia returned the laptop to its original position and swiped dust off the keyboard with her sleeve, attempting to appear casual. "What? No. We went to school together. We're just old friends."

Although, considering the number of times she replayed the jewelry store scene, the one where she pressed against his firm body, maybe being old friends didn't feel satisfying enough. There was something there. A buzz. A spark. She wondered if Ross could sense it as well. He must have. That one single moment where everything stilled around them, her breath caught, and she could have leaned into—

Her father was correct. She was getting distracted.

Mia flicked a look at Natalie. "Why do you think something's going on between us?"

"Come on. I've been doing this for a while. I know the regulars. They come in like clockwork. As long as we've been shop neighbors, that man has never been a regular. That's definitely not the case anymore."

Mia's cheeks warmed. Was it true? Was he coming in almost every day because of her? Or was it a delayed caffeine addiction kicking in, and the timing was coincidental?

Stop getting distracted, Mia. This was ridiculous. She wasn't the awkward, bespectacled teenager anymore. She was an adult. She'd gone to college. She'd had a boyfriend. Granted Thomas wasn't like Ross but she was pretty sure no one was. Ross was someone special—*Ugh. Stop!* He was special alright. Special in his ability to peel away the layers and reveal the silly girl underneath.

Placerville was a pit stop. It would be beneficial for her to remember.

Anyway, Ross didn't like her. At times he appeared to barely tolerate her. He saw who Mia was, who she had always been, and he wasn't impressed. Forbidden fruit. This was what the attraction was. She was not meant to have Ross because she was moving on. Distraction with a capital D wasn't enough. The whole word needed to be capitalized with several exclamation points thrown in.

This was the only way to explain her desire to leap in front of El Dorado's windows, shouting, "Pay attention to me! See me! Like me!" It was part people-pleaser, part thirsty nerd, and full-on pathetic. Mia devolved to where she was ten years ago but, this time, with twenty percent more lonely loser included.

"You doing anything fun this weekend?" Natalie asked while removing the wrapper from a hard candy mint she pulled from her pocket. "Anything that isn't schoolwork or photography work being done inside your place of coffee work?"

"Photography is fun. And I like being here at this time. It's quiet. I like to imagine this was my mom's regular table." The table was in the quietest corner, framed by sizable potted fiddle leaf trees and cute local artwork featuring girls reading classic literature. Mia could see her mom sitting here and inspecting her latest fabric purchases.

"I take it then you're *not* doing anything fun."

"And what's the president of the fun patrol doing this weekend?" Mia tossed a wadded napkin at her manager.

Natalie snatched it out of the air with impressive skill. "I'm doing a 5k with one of my sisters and then there's a family barbeque. Oh, you know what, in a couple of weeks we'll be doing Día de los Muertos. I mean, it's only a small thing, but you should come."

"Really? I've never been to one before." Mia perked up with excitement from not only being invited but she loved new experiences. A Day of the Dead celebration would be something different for her.

"So you've never done Día de los Muertos *and* you don't speak Spanish? Yeah, don't think I didn't notice how you passed that customer off on me who was just asking for some extra straws. Are you sure Laura's Mexican blood runs through those veins?"

Mia's ears grew hot and her smile melted away.

Natalie grew serious. "Oh, M, I'm just teasing. If it makes you feel any better, I never paid much attention to the tradition either. I'm not really a sentimental person. But a few years ago, my sisters and I went to the one on Olvera Street in LA and it really was amazing. They wanted to do it on a small scale here, so I help them out. It was at the community center, but, this year, we're doing it at St. Anthony's. We'll put together a community ofrenda, have some good food, and do face painting with the kids."

"I just feel awkward and maybe I don't belong. My dad has always had such a strong personality, like the Italian side just erased the Mexican side. I feel like I'm missing something."

Natalie straightened. "Of course, you belong. You can bring one of your mom's quilts, and put her picture on the table."

Mia's eyes burned and she covered them with a hand, attempting to keep the tears at bay. All she could do was nod her head in reply.

Natalie rubbed her arm. "It'll be okay. My sisters and I

will be there to help you. It's really a celebration, so maybe there will be tears, but we'll have fun, too. Plus, you can tell your mom you're working at her favorite coffee shop and we're friends. Think about how excited that will make her."

Mia released a blubbery laugh.

"I'm going to also talk to your mom and tell her all about your new boyfriend."

"You're such a brat." But Mia laughed and wiped the tears away.

"Anyway, back to the real dilemma about your lack of fun this weekend." Natalie's eyes drifted to the shop door which was covered in flyers. "Oh, I know just the thing. You should go to the silent auction."

"What? Why?"

"They hold it every year at the Masonic lodge down the street. It's to raise money for disaffected teens or something. We always throw in a nice gift basket with bags of roasted beans and a gift card."

Mia shook her head. "I suggest the fun patrol go back to the drawing board."

Natalie tossed the same wadded napkin back at her. Mia made an attempt to grab it but missed, and it bounced off the middle of her forehead instead.

The Pony Expresso manager laughed. "Serves you right. I'm just saying maybe you should look into it a little more. Not only because it's a good cause, but I'm also pretty sure the jewelry store participates. I might have seen him there once or twice. I'd go with you but, you know, family barbeque and all that."

"Hmm," Mia replied while taking a casual sip of her disgusting coffee.

"Think about it." A customer walked in, and Natalie stood, moving to the counter. "Oh, and M?"

"Yeah?"

"Your mom's regular spot was over there." Natalie pointed to the table on the opposite end.

Chapter Sixteen

THIS WAS THE fourth official year El Dorado Jewelry was a sponsor in the Assistance League of the Sierra Foothills Dinner, Dancing, and Silent Auction. The purpose of which was to raise money for the at-risk youth of El Dorado County. For the other three years, Luna had been the primary contact for the store, but this year it was Ross. He wasn't above commending himself for managing it all on his own. He submitted the financial donation on time and remembered to provide the donated jewelry for the auction.

In the past, he and Luna would make a brief appearance together. Correction. He would make a brief appearance to show his support and to grab a dinner of fancy appetizers. Luna was more of the wine-and-dine kind of person and made fast friends. She would stay longer to be the official ambassador of the store, letting Ross off the hook and giving him the ability to snack and run.

Appearing solo was uncomfortable for him, but it was for a good cause, so he dug deep and forced himself to circulate with the general population. If Ross was lucky, Aanya would make an appearance as well. She had been open to the idea when he was hanging the promotional flyer in the shop window.

People filled the old Masonic lodge, which was decorated with a half-hearted amount of blue paper streamers and balloon bouquets. A local country band played on stage, providing the proper mood for mingling. Not him though. Ross had never been a mingler.

One side was filled with finger foods and drinks. The other half of the room had tables set up with the many items available for auction. People loitered between the two sides, socializing as the atmosphere encouraged them to do. Ross's plan was to go straight for the food and breeze past the auction tables. He wanted to make a quick escape to spend more time with Hermes, who had gone through another round of treatment and was recovering at home.

"El Dorado Jewelry, right?"

Ross turned and was faced with a woman. He recognized her as one of the organizers of the event. Her gray hair was pulled in a tight bun, which seemed to pull her features along with it. The woman's name escaped him.

"Uh, yeah, that's right," Ross said.

"I'm Carol. You dropped off your item with me."

"Of course. Sorry, I'm Ross." He offered a hand, but she didn't release the handshake after what was the appropriate length of time. She held onto it as if settling in for a long conversation. It wasn't a good sign for his plan. This was what he didn't want to get roped into: a conversation.

"We're always so happy to have your jewelry store as a sponsor of this event. You know, it's such an important cause."

"Uh-huh." Ross tried to reclaim his hand without appearing as if he was competing in a game of tug-of-war.

"Well, I'm happy you decided to attend. But there was one thing I was hoping you wouldn't mind doing since you're here."

"Okay." The faster he agreed, the faster he would be free.

"We always like the businesses to fill out a thank you card to go with their item. You can just list the item that they won and then write a small word or two of thanks. I should have said something when you dropped the item off, but I forgot. Luckily for you, I brought a card, and you can just leave it next to your donation."

She released his hand. In its place was a small white thank you card and pen. The woman belonged on stage performing magic. Where had the card and pen come from? Carol came prepared and, at this moment, Ross was feeling the opposite. He remembered Luna filling out a similar card the previous year, but it hadn't crossed his mind at all until this moment.

Ross could do it. Of course, he could do it. But it didn't stop the anxiety from inching its way into his gut. With texting and typing, Ross managed fine. Handwriting a note…well, this wasn't as easy as Carol assumed. First of all, there was no auto-correct or spellcheck to depend on with handwritten words. He tended to give words their phonetic spelling, and, thanks to the complexities of the English language, he was wrong more than he was right. Even worse, Ross hated his handwriting, which rivaled grade school kids in its sloppiness. A simple thank you card was easily his worst nightmare.

As Carol turned away from him to speak to another attendee, his mind fell into its regular habit of searching for an exit, both figuratively and literally. How could he get out of this? Ross could call Aanya and see if she was planning on stopping by. He could conveniently forget to fill out the card. The person was getting jewelry. Did they care if they got a handwritten note on top of it? The whole thing was pointless, and he was annoyed to be bothered by the task when all he wanted to do was enjoy a selection of mini quiches and stuffed mushrooms.

"Hi, Rosso."

He turned.

Mia.

She stood there, wearing his earrings, and her presence was more welcomed than a table full of appetizers, like a golden light sweeping into the old lodge.

Her brow furrowed together with a slight tilt of her head. "Is everything okay?"

Hadn't he said hello to her? Had Ross only been blankly staring at her? He tried to pull himself together. "Mia. Hi. Did you just get here?"

"I've been here for about ten minutes. I was hoping my ring was going to be part of the silent auction. And it is, so I decided to put in a bid."

"Your ring?"

"Yeah, the pearl ring. It's my favorite. What's that? Is it secret bidding tips that's being hidden from me?" She indicated the card and pen in his hand.

Ross's eyes dropped as he ran his free hand through his hair. "They...uh..." He cleared his throat, trying again. "They want me to fill out a card with the details of the item and leave a quick note of thanks. It's silly. Whatever."

"You're kidding. They're already getting the most beautiful ring in the world for a good cause, and they need a thank you card on top of it? People can't just donate to charity, but they have to be patted on the back?"

"Yeah. It's ridiculous, right?" Ross replied.

"Well, if you're looking for someone with good penmanship, I'm your gal."

Without a word, he handed her the card and pen, a feeling of relief passing over him.

"Is there anything in particular you want me to write?"

"I don't know. Just say, *thanks for bidding on this ring.*"

"You're standing with the sweet-talking, people-pleaser here, remember? I'm sure we can do better than that." She lifted her lovely eyes to the ceiling in quiet contemplation for a few moments before bending over the table and writing words in elegant swoops across the card's blank surface. He couldn't take his eyes off her, possibly because his handwriting had never swooped in his life.

When finished, Mia read, "*Congratulations on winning this original gold and pearl twig ring. It was designed by local craftsman and talented artist, Ross Manasse of El Dorado Jewelry, who was inspired by the natural beauty of our city, the pearl of the Sierras. Your donation is helping at-risk youth and supporting local artistry. Thank you! El Dorado Jewelry.*" She glanced at him. "What do you think?"

Ross was amazed at Mia's ability to retrieve words with ease, as if they were books on a convenient shelf, waiting to be plucked at a moment's notice. Was her mind filled with beautiful phrases all the time? He could have spent a week and not come close to her level of finesse. "Yeah, it's fine.

Although, I don't think anyone has ever called Placerville the pearl of anything. And it's probably not necessary to pat them and myself on the back."

"You're lucky you have someone like me to do the dirty PR work for you." She set the card and pen beside the El Dorado Jewelry display before turning to him, her eyes glittering. "I also added, *P.S. Mia, the ring looks gorgeous on your finger. And you just scored a great deal on jewelry that's just as amazing as you are. With great respect and friendship, Ross.*"

"Uh-huh," Ross responded. He was sure she was egging him on, but this time he didn't mind. She remained rooted in place with a coy smile fixed upon her face. He drew nearer to inspect the auction clipboard on the table. "And what do you mean *great deal*? Just how much do you think an original ring from the talented Ross Manasse is worth bidding?"

Mia's eyes grew wide at her mistake. Using her body as a shield, she blocked his access to the clipboard. "Now, Rosso, you know I would bid a million dollars if I had it. That's really all you need to consider."

His arms snaked around her, trying to get a hold of the information he sought. "I think I would prefer the truth, rather than your fancy diplomacy talk. What are you hiding, Russo? Obviously, something shameful."

In response to his efforts, Mia leaned across the table with Ross looming over her. His fingers managed to claim the corner of the clipboard before she placed a flat hand on it, preventing him from gaining further territory. She wasn't going to make this easy for him, and, at this moment, he didn't want it to be.

A calm expression graced her face, not appearing at all on the losing end of this real-life Stratego, despite her disadvantaged position. "I'm a hardworking lady. What do I have to be ashamed of? You know what is shameful? Your relentless curiosity on something which is none of your business."

"It's my item. I think that makes it my business."

"I'm pretty sure this is against the rules. You're not supposed to be naming and shaming bidders. I don't think you're allowed to look."

He tried to claim the clipboard again, but she held him off, maintaining an expression of cheerful defiance. His own lips tugged in a smile. "It's called a silent auction, not a secret auction. It must be terrible for you to be so embarrassed."

"I'm not embarrassed."

"What is it? Twenty bucks?"

Mia stopped and gawked, her expression transforming into one of fake outrage. But she was unable to hide the sparkle from her eyes. "How dare you imply I would only bid twenty bucks? I am not that low. I find your arrogance and assumptions and…and…and your face offensive."

"What does my face have to do with this?"

"Isn't it obvious? That's where all the arrogance and assumptions are coming from."

Ross barked out a laugh, which led to Mia's dimple indenting deeper.

"Excuse me." Ross and Mia's heads swiveled, finding an old, impatient woman nearby. "Are you kids going to take much longer on this item? I wanted to take a look at it."

He realized how bad it appeared with Mia practically laid out on the table, and his limbs entwined around her. "I'm so sorry. Yes, she's done." Ross sprung upright, pulling Mia away from the table. He made sure to get a good look at the clipboard before moving away. "Thirty-five dollars, Mia? Really?" Ross followed behind her.

Despite her secret being revealed, Mia remained unperturbed. "Do you want to look inside my wallet? I, literally, had fifty-five dollars, and I used twenty dollars to get in here. And blocking the clipboard was my only strategy at keeping people from outbidding me. But now that old lady is making a bid. She's going to be *really* confused when she reads the personal postscript I put on the card." Mia lifted one of the other auction items, a wooden cutting board with cutlery as if considering making another bid.

"Thank you for writing the card, Mia."

She eyed him before returning to her inspection of the cutting board. Deciding against it, Mia replaced it in its original spot before moving to the next item. "And?"

"And what?"

"I was hoping you'd say, *Thanks for writing the card, Mia. How can I repay you for your amazing PR skills?*"

"I'm not giving you jewelry for writing a card."

"Of course not, that wouldn't be a fair exchange."

"Why are you suddenly so concerned about fair exchanges? I thought we were old friends."

"Hmm. I seem to remember a conversation where you informed me that we were never friends, and you only spoke to me because you didn't have a choice."

"I thought we agreed to forget about the afternoon where I was, quote, being an absolute asshole."

"And I thought we were only doing favor-for-a-favor

transactions." The light in her eyes became serious. "Even so, I'd always do a favor for you, Ross."

Ross didn't know how he could be annoyed with her one moment, and then whatever the opposite of annoyed was the following one. He was so mixed up his brain couldn't compute the antonym of *annoyed*. He sighed, his shoulders falling loose at the edges, "Thanks for being my PR card person. How can I return the favor?"

She smiled at this. "Keep me company during a light dinner." She indicated the food across the room. "And maybe you can treat me to a dance afterward." She nodded to the dance floor where a few couples were already occupying the area.

Ross swept a hand toward the food. "We'll start with the eating part. I'm not committing to dancing. I'm not much of a dancer."

"Neither am I, but I wouldn't mind having a little fun tonight."

They filled small plates with a variety of finger foods before grabbing a drink and finding an empty standing cocktail table. The Masonic lodge was mothball old with wood-paneled walls and flickering fluorescent lights, not exactly a romantic atmosphere. Not that this was a date or anything. Ross slid a glance at Mia. He wondered why she'd want to spend an evening with him, eating appetizers and listening to an average country band, but, deep down, he was thankful for the company. He was spending too much time alone, his days filled with working and taking care of his dog.

Ross watched her for a few moments as she took small bites from the items on her plate. "What made you show up tonight?"

"I told you I wanted the ring."

"The ring you thought you could get for thirty-five dollars."

"Actually, it would have been fifty-five dollars. I'm counting the twenty bucks I spent to get in here, which is no small fee. And, as I've noticed two people write on your clipboard since we've been over here, I think it's pretty safe to say I'm not walking out with a new Ross Manasse original. So, really, what am I getting for my twenty bucks but a few mini quiches, cheese squares, and some strawberries? I think the least I could get is a dance out of it?"

"It's funny how people can't just donate to charity, but they also have to expect dancing. You do remember this is for a good cause, right, Russo?" Ross popped a stuffed mushroom in his mouth.

She laughed in response, the tip of one hand patting her palm in muted applause. "Very good. I've been sufficiently put in my place. I'm also here because, you're right, it is a good cause, and it feels at least partly related to the family business. There should be one Russo representing here tonight."

"Oh? The Russo family believes in giving troubled kids second chances?" Despite the light atmosphere earlier, Ross retreated to a darker place at the turn in conversation. The napkin crunched within his hand.

"Of course. All kids deserve a second chance, troubled or not. It's what I was taught growing up, and I completely believe it."

Ross studied her for a few moments, his heart cooling

inside his chest. "And what would Little Miss Perfect, Most Likely to Succeed know about second chances?"

Mia's eyes snapped to his, appearing surprised at the brittle tone in his voice. Her expression shuttered to hurt before her eyes dropped to the table. She spent the following minutes picking at the leaves of a strawberry, letting the silence spread across their area like a heavy canvas.

Ross closed his eyes, a sigh drifting through him. He kept striking at her, hating every single time he did it. It wasn't fair to make Mia the lightning rod for all the frustration and anger stored up inside him over the years. He wanted to stop. The dance floor captured her attention, her face despondent.

"Mia."

Her eyes drifted to him, but there was no response.

"I owe you a dance."

"It's okay. You don't have to. I'm not much of a dancer anyway."

He abandoned his spot at the table and offered a hand to her. "Favor for a favor."

A light flickered behind her eyes, but there was no further movement. Ross remained standing with his hand outstretched, feeling foolish. "Please."

After several long moments, she relieved him of his awkward agony, placing a hand in his. He escorted her to the edge of the dance floor. Ross was far from confident this dance would be a treat for either one of them as his skills were lacking, but he'd do it for her.

The band began a new song, a slow, countrified cover of "Hotel California" by the Eagles. Ross took a deep breath, as if the air contained courage as well as oxygen, and drew her to him. One hand went to the small of her back, feeling the strength and warmth along her spine. His other hand wrapped around hers in a gentle grip. Mia's left arm touched his shoulder lightly as though he were a paper doll, and she didn't want to risk crushing him with too much pressure.

A faint but deep, rich scent of coffee beans expelled from her skin and clothes. The smell was as addictive as actual caffeine.

Her gaze slipped to his in a shy glance.

"You smell like coffee," he said.

She blushed, her eyes growing behind the lens of her glasses. "I'm so sorry. Is it bad?"

Considering all he wanted to do was place his face along the crook of her neck and take a long, greedy whiff, how bad could it be? He resisted the temptation, not wanting to come off as a creep. "It's fine," was all he replied.

"Did you ever go to any of the school dances?" Mia asked after a time.

"I wasn't really allowed to with my GPA, but I snuck into a few of them. I did go to the sophomore prom with Becca Brown. I asked her before I realized I wouldn't be permitted, nor did I have any money to buy tickets."

"So, how did you go?"

"I worked extra shifts at the store to borrow money from my grandpa, and then I begged one of the teachers to let me buy tickets, so I wouldn't be completely embarrassed."

"I don't think I remember Becca Brown."

"Another case of classmate amnesia?" He smiled. "Don't worry, you probably didn't know her. She wasn't in any of the AP classes."

They danced in silence for a while before Ross spoke again. "Did you go to the dances?"

"A few. I never went with anyone except friends. It wasn't really my scene. You know how it is." Mia grew more relaxed in his arms as she played with the seam at his shoulder. "Ross?"

"Yeah?"

"You know I don't think of myself as perfect, right?"

He pulled away to give himself a better view of her face. "Mia, I didn't mean to be so harsh. Just forget it."

Mia forged ahead as if she didn't hear his words. "I failed my driving test the first time I took it, not the written part, but the actual driving part. I lied to my friends, saying something came up, and I wasn't able to take it on my scheduled day. I was so embarrassed by my failure. Only my family knew, and they teased me about it for at least a week straight. And there was one time I went to a friend's pool party when I should have studied for a test. Luckily, the teacher let me make that one up. But the test with the B- was hung on the front of our fridge for a long time as a joke. Or the time—" She glanced at him, her cheeks coloring. "Anyway, I can't take the feeling of disappointing people. I'm afraid of failing, of not meeting the high expectations."

"I've only ever had the expectation of failure. Which one is worse?"

"Maybe it's the expectations themselves which are the issue, whether it's high or low. But you're not remotely a failure. You are a success. You have a business. You found your spot. I really admire what you do."

He wasn't sure if this was true, but he appreciated the sentiment regardless. Ross's heart warmed to her. "I know it doesn't matter, but, back then, I wanted to ask you to junior prom."

Her eyes, lit with surprise, searched his face. Seeing sincerity there, her expression softened. "I know it doesn't matter, but I would have said yes."

And it was true, none of it mattered. At the time, Ross had no money, a low GPA, and, by the time junior prom rolled around, he was a high school dropout. But before his life had fallen into complete shit, there was an earlier period when he had the smallest glimmer of hope, and life didn't seem too bad. There had been Mia, after all. She was kind to him. Plus, she had warm amber eyes and an adorable dimple. He was so hungry in those days, Ross craved whatever emotional nourishment he could find.

One time, at her home, they had been at the dining table when Mia giggled at something he said. Her dimple pierced her right cheek. Ross pressed his finger into it as if he would be able to feel her joy and not merely see it. Her smile had always been large as if it needed to convey the exact size of her heart. In the background, he caught her father's cool blue eyes drilling into him as the judge cleared his throat while taking a brisk path into the room.

"Hello, Mr. Russo," Ross blurted, retracting his finger from Mia's cheek.

The judge narrowed his eyes. "Doesn't sound like any work is being done."

"Judge, leave the kids alone," Mrs. Russo called from the kitchen.

He grumbled his displeasure before departing for another area of the house.

Even if Ross didn't have all the strikes against him and he had managed to ask Mia to prom, he was positive her father wouldn't have allowed it. But, tonight, she told him she would have said yes. He wanted to believe her, and this, at least, was something. A tiny crumb could satisfy the craving lurking beneath the deep, unexplored edges of his soul.

Ross spread his fingers across her back and adjusted his arms to hold her nearer, bringing their coupled hands to his chest. Mia settled into him, and the rich scent of coffee beans curled around them like a comforting blanket.

Chapter Seventeen

For the third time since they walked out of the Masonic lodge, Mia gave Ross a sideways glance. She wrapped her wool coat closer to her body. There was a chill in the air as winter inched closer every day. A chorus of chirping, invisible insects escorted them on their path across the parking lot.

She insisted Ross didn't need to walk her to her car, but she suspected he wanted to make his escape from the event as well. She wouldn't have minded dancing with him some more, enjoying being held close, but she also didn't push her luck. After all, she'd requested the one dance. *Dammit!* She should have asked for three and bargained down to two. She was losing her edge.

Even after she reminded herself about Placerville being a pit stop for the hundredth time, this did nothing to prevent the old wants from needling through her carefully constructed barrier. There were the classics: *See me. Like me.* To make it more interesting, a few new ones made their debut. *Kiss me. Want me.* At first, this shocked Mia. Ross wasn't going to kiss her. According to all the evidence, she was more than optimistic to even declare friendship with the man. And, yet, the record player needle was stuck at this exact point on the vinyl. *Kiss me. Kiss me. Kiss me.* She wanted to experience his lips against hers.

"And here's my car," Mia exclaimed too cheerfully when they arrived. "I don't think we'll have any dangerous black bear encounters tonight." She leaned against the driver's door, fixing her eyes on him.

"Don't get cocky. You never know when a bear will show up, especially when there's the smell of food in the air."

"If the bear pays twenty bucks, it should be able to eat as many mini quiches as it wants."

"Mini quiches go well with man-flesh."

She laughed. "Thanks for walking me to my car and keeping me safe once again." Feeling brave, Mia reached out and ran a light hand down his arm to his fingertips. Her gaze rose to his, and his eyes were dark with intensity. The snap of electricity had been sparking between them all evening.

Ross slipped his hands into the pockets of his jeans and squinted at the inky night sky scattered with stars glittering like gold flakes. The faint music from the country band drifted through the air. "You know, I've been formulating a hypothesis," he said after a moment.

"Really? Now you definitely have my interest. Please continue."

"I get the feeling you'd like me to kiss you." His obsidian eyes found hers again, a slight smile on his face, the expression as dangerous as it was exciting.

Well, Mia had never been good at being subtle. Still, she would prefer to keep him guessing a little. With all the calm she could muster, she adjusted the sleeve hemline of her wool coat and replied, "That's an intriguing hypothesis. But I need to ask if this is based on any sort of scientific study, or is it just wild speculation on your part? Maybe you're trying to boost your own ego."

"I don't know yet. That's why it's called a hypothesis."

"You could ask me if I want you to kiss me."

Ross drew nearer. "I could. But then I wouldn't be following the proper stages of the scientific method, and I imagine the experimental stage is the fun part. So maybe I'll run a test and end up with a theory. Am I doing this correctly? You are the know-it-all, nerd-girl, after all."

He was close with one minor correction. Mia was the know-it-all, nerd-girl, but she was transforming into a *very* turned-on woman. She swept a hand of permission toward him. "Please proceed. You seem to know exactly what you're doing, but, for posterity's sake, I'll be taking my own notes on your experiment. Sort of like a peer review, but no pressure."

With this, Ross took another step closer. Despite her projected calm demeanor, Mia was feeling anything but calm. She wouldn't have been surprised if the rapid, loud beating of her heart was interfering with the echolocation relied on by bats in the area. A gentle hand brushed across her chin, tipping it. His fingers slid along her jawline. She may have stopped breathing at this point. She worried she reeked of coffee and wanted to avoid overwhelming Ross with the scent. His face dropped nearer, but stopped inches away. If he didn't kiss her soon, she'd pass out from a lack of oxygen, which would be unfortunate because she didn't want to miss this.

"Is there something wrong?" she murmured after growing impatient.

"No, I was waiting to see if you were going to push me away or tell me to stop. I'm a very cautious scientist who's suddenly concerned about his own personal bias."

"For the love of all that is scientific and holy, I wish you'd proceed already."

And Ross did.

If she was baking soda and he was vinegar, childhood science experiments would dictate there would be a Mount Vesuvius eruption of bubbles. This was the best way to explain what happened when their lips met, but the explosion was contained inside the confines of Mia's body. Her soul burst like a firecracker. A fizzle of euphoria began at her lips and snaked its way to the edge of her toes. *More.* When she sensed Ross may be planning for an early departure, Mia took control of the situation. She rose on her toes, her hands traveling the length of his chest, staking a claim around his neck. His lips were hers, and vice versa. Mia pushed the kiss even further, opening up to him. Ross's hands latched on to her hips. He used his body to press her against the car, deepening the kiss even more as his tongue slid along her bottom lip before tangling with hers. A satisfied hum vibrated in her throat.

Mia could have kissed him forever.

But it didn't come close to forever. In an instant, he stepped back, cutting himself loose from their grasp. His eyes were dark and wide, appearing rattled. It was supposed to be a ridiculous experiment, except there was nothing at all ridiculous about the kiss. Even worse, it may have led to more in-depth experimentation. Mia knew it, and, clearly,

Ross knew it as well.

"Mia...I- I'm not looking to start anything. I have a lot going on with the shop...and with Hermes." The words tumbled from his mouth, his expression muted. "It's just that—"

"Ross, it's fine. I'm leaving eventually, so I'm not looking for anything either. Whatever. It's not a problem."

He released what seemed to be a sigh of relief, which did an excellent job of transforming her attraction into annoyance. She wasn't supposed to be *that* convincing.

But Mia slipped into a quick smile, wishing to convince him the truth of her words, regardless of how much she craved his closeness again. "Well, you know what they say, *words can be weapons of war or love*. Perhaps you should wield yours a little more carefully next time. You should know how all that nerd jargon can really set me off."

Mia fished her keys from her purse and unlocked her car.

He held the door, putting his other hand on the car's body, keeping her centered to him. "But I'll see you around?"

She studied him, wondering if Ross was more affected than he was letting on. There was immediate irritation with herself when Mia's eyes tracked to his lips again. "Sure. Maybe I'll stop by the store tomorrow or the next day with your images. Is that okay?"

"That's fine."

"Good night," she said, getting in the driver's seat.

"Good night."

He shut the door, and she drove off.

Her innocent wish of being the recipient of a kiss from

Ross was turning into earnest desire. Mia wanted more, but it wasn't in the plans. In fact, it was so far off, not only was it not on the page, it wasn't in the whole damn ream of paper. But, despite her effort at avoiding distractions, Mia wasn't sure anymore if she wanted to avoid this particular one. Perhaps it was time. What better distraction was there than Ross? And Mia realized her relationship with him could be heaven, or it could be hell.

Chapter Eighteen

"Hey." Ross was at the computer when Aanya walked into the office.

"Good morning," she greeted with her usual cheerfulness, coming into the room to remove her jacket and purse. She bent to pet a sleeping Hermes in his dog bed, who was doing a lot of sleeping these days. "Did you have a nice time at the auction?"

"Yeah, it was fine," he replied without removing his concentration from the computer screen. "You didn't miss much."

"I was there."

Ross glanced at her, surprised. "You were?"

"Yes, I came with my husband."

"Oh, well, I'm sorry that I missed you. I would have liked to have met him."

"There will be other opportunities. We saw you, but you were…occupied…with a friend."

With the twinkle in her eyes, she appeared to be finding their conversation this morning amusing. He was far from amused, being careful to keep his face void of all emotions. There weren't any emotions to be had. As far as Ross was concerned, it was a non-event. Why wouldn't his face reflect this? "We just happen to run into each other."

He was discouraged to see the twinkle did not dissipate. Instead, it spread to Aanya's mouth, which turned into a smile. "That's nice. I think she's a perfectly lovely and sweet young lady. You two look very good together."

"We're not together."

"Oh, well, that's…disappointing." She shook her head in disagreement, departing the office.

"No, it's not disappointing. We're strictly old friends," he called after her. Yes, old friends who kissed in the parking lot beside Mia's car. He dropped his head into the palm of one hand, rubbing his eyes.

He was the biggest bonehead for thinking kissing her was anything close to being a good idea. This ranked right up there with touching a hot stove, jamming a fork into an electrical socket, or putting his face next to a rattlesnake. Well, it was over and done with, and he wasn't going to waste any more brain cells thinking about it.

Goddamn Mia with her coffee smells and her dimple and her ability to mix him up so much, he didn't know which way was left and which was right. And this was before the kiss even took place.

Ross's first mistake was having a poorly thought-out plan. At the time, his reasoning was, *What the hell?* Let's give sixteen-year-old Ross a thrill, and the young, naïve kid would realize things built up inside the mind never met expectations. Twenty-five-year-old Ross wasn't worried because he could handle one tiny kiss with Mia Russo. Since high school, he'd had plenty of other kisses, and one more wouldn't make or break him. The moment would satisfy his curiosity but not be anything more than a one-and-done. There was a good chance this kiss would disappear from his mind before the end of the year, and then it would be his turn to pretend to forget. The idea was to deliver the kiss, offer Mia a thrill before wishing her a good night. Then he would whistle all the way to his truck without any further reflections on the matter.

He thought he was being clever, which was his second mistake. (When had he ever been clever at anything?) The idea train derailed from the shoddy tracks as soon as it departed the station.

His third mistake: the plan was concocted with only him in mind. After he gave the idea more in-depth analysis, he concluded this was probably the worst mistake in the bunch. With kissing, there's a partner, and he failed to account for her contribution in all of this. It didn't take Ross long to realize his glaring omission. In fact, the light bulb clicked on the exact moment the parking lot experiment started. It happened when Mia's eager mouth kissed him in return and her lips parted on a soft exhale. God, the kiss was heated and hungry and—

Exactly like putting his hand on a hot stove while using his other hand to jam a rattlesnake into an electrical socket. Or something like that.

Ross dragged a hand through his hair at the memory, exhilaration zipping through his veins.

Realizing a severe miscalculation had been made, his brain began registering a distress warning with a loud *Retreat!* Like the traitors they were, his hands defected to the other side, planting themselves on the supple curves of her body beneath her coat. Because his mouth was nearest in proximity to the brain, it was recruited next for the coward's cause of desertion. All he accomplished was adjusting the kiss's angle to a sweeter one, and the defenses fell at once. As a last-ditch effort, the brain sent a *Mayday! Mayday!* to the lower limbs, his legs to be specific. They were able to do the task the rest of his body was too weak to carry out, but not before the appendage between his legs perked up, finding interest in the whole situation. It was clear there would be no casual strolling and whistling to his truck after this man-made disaster.

Regardless, it didn't matter. It wouldn't happen again.

"Your old friend is here," Aanya said in a sing-song voice when he approached with a repaired ring in hand.

Ross raised his eyes in time to see Mia passing the large storefront window on her way to the door. *Shit.* His productivity today was at a historic low. Her visit would, no doubt, lead to even less work getting done—due to her talkative nature, *not* due to kissing. He made this quite clear to himself.

"She's here for business," he informed his employee, hoping to set her expectations at the exact point where they should be. Nowhere.

"Hi, Aanya," Mia greeted with a bright smile. Her eyes slid to his and, in a lowered tone, said, "Hey there. Are you available for some private time in your office?" For some reason, she thought it necessary to emphasize the words *private time*.

His mouth jarred open before he snapped himself back together. Ross strode to his office with a simmering agitation. As soon as she was safe inside, he allowed the door to slam shut. "What the hell, Mia?"

"What?"

"Private time? In my office?"

Her face settled in confusion. "Yeah, I wanted to talk to you about your photos, and I thought we'd do it in your office. Do you want Aanya to be part of this discussion? Should I get her?"

"No. Just…" He took a deep breath. "Can we just move on, please? You bug the hell out of me, do you know that?"

Mia provided a sweet smile in response. "Aw, Rosso, you bug me, too."

He didn't want to risk getting close enough to strangle her. Not when there was a chance he'd make out with her instead, and kissing was off the table—or at least it *should* be. It kept sneaking onto the table, like a persistent line of picnic ants. He cemented himself to his desk, crossing his arms and barked, "Moving on!"

Mia approached while holding up the jump drive she retrieved from her pocket. "Your photos."

"That's close enough," he replied, his palm out, cautioning Mia as he would a dangerous creature. He was Prometheus chained to the rock. She, the bespectacled eagle, was sent to consume his liver—or his heart. Not that he was using his heart, but it didn't matter. He didn't want to take any chances as far as she was concerned.

Her brow furrowed together. "Good lord, Ross. What's the matter with you? I'm not going to jump you if that's what you're afraid of."

"I'm not." He wasn't. Of course, she wouldn't. Ross was

being silly. What happened in the parking lot was a blip.

"Okay, good. Can I borrow your computer so I can upload your photos and show you what I did?"

Mia swooped in, taking ownership of his area behind the desk. Why did she swoop so much? Was it because she was part eagle? And why did it always mean invading his space? Ross shifted a stack of boxes to fit his body inside the same area as hers. Mia inserted the jump drive into the computer while raking her fingers through the locks of her hair, releasing the delicious scent of her shampoo. A flower mixed with another flower? What the hell did he know, except it didn't smell like coffee.

"So, I've created separate folders for each of your pieces. I gave each a name, but you can change the folder names to whatever you wish. For example, let's click on the pearl ring folder. Each folder has four or five of the best images. And I made them high res, so you can use them however you want or maybe pay for a professional print job and put up some damn photos in your store."

"What?"

"You need something on the walls, Ross. It'll look nicer. But you can do whatever you want with the images. So let's click on one."

The image opened on a closeup of the pearl ring. The setting and gold glistened in the light, providing a bright contrast to the muted, gray river rocks and white background. He could see why this ring was Mia's favorite. It was one of his favorites as well. But, in this case, it wasn't merely the ring but also the beautiful image. He couldn't deny Mia's photography skills; it was one more thing she excelled at.

"What do you think?" Mia lifted her eyes to him.

"Yeah, you did a good job."

She smiled, clearly pleased with his compliment. "Are you ready for a surprise?"

"There's a surprise?" Ross wasn't sure he liked surprises, especially from Mia. Whatever was going to happen, he'd prefer to see it coming from a mile away.

"Well, hopefully, a good surprise." Her fingers tapped the keyboard bringing up a webpage. "Welcome to El Dorado Jewelry on Etsy!"

He didn't say anything as his eyes took the page in. He should have been irritated with her overstepping her boundaries in his business, but, at the same time, it wasn't shocking considering teacher's pet always went above and beyond. The banner at the top of the page was a collage of the images she took inside his workshop. The avatar was pristine white with the store's name in swirling, gold font. All of it looked simple but elegant.

"You're not mad at me, are you? I know you don't need my help, it's just…I-I like doing this type of stuff. I might have gotten carried away, but I wanted you to see how it could all look together. Are you mad?" For once, Mia's tone lacked confidence, as if expecting his wrath was coming at any moment. "Please don't be mad at me. Okay, I'm sorry. I shouldn't have done—"

"I'm not mad," Ross murmured as he leaned forward, taking control of the mouse to scroll the page. The virtual store had several jewelry listings. He couldn't be mad when he was busy being blown away.

"Anyway, if you want anything changed, I can show you

how to do it. And you'll notice the prices are a little different. I calculated the costs of Etsy's fees, so you won't be losing any money on this. And to make it easy for relisting..." Mia reached for the mouse, her hand landing on his, causing his heart to skip a beat. "Oops, sorry. Can I have the mouse for a minute?" Mia re-clicked the tab bringing her images to the forefront. "You'll see I've created a document under each folder that's for Etsy posts. I listed all the fields you'll need to fill out when you post the item, like description, measurement, material, keywords, that sort of thing. But if you sell something, you can easily re-list it without starting from scratch. This way you're not wasting a lot of time doing something you don't like to do."

He cleared his throat, attempting to clear his head along with it. "How do I know if I made a sale?"

"It'll go straight to your main email. I got all this information from Aanya. You're basically set up and ready to go if you like it. Also, I listed key hashtags I think you should use for social media pages. Using the right hashtags will get eyes on your images, then you can add a link to your Etsy page, and it'll be easy for people to purchase from you. If your cousin doesn't have time to run the social media pages, I can fill in until she's ready. I really don't mind."

Ross couldn't wrap his head around the gift Mia gave him. It was clear she put a lot of thought and work into it. "Mia, I..." It was hopeless. He was lost. He couldn't find one adequate word to fill the void. "This wasn't part of our favor-for-a-favor deal. Now I feel like I owe you."

She ejected the jump drive before standing to face him, her body much too close to his. Her eyes took their sweet time scanning the features of his face. "Maybe it's time we stop keeping track of favors."

"I don't know if I can do that." The pulse rate of his heart increased as the distance between them began to shrink.

"I have an idea," Mia whispered.

"You do?"

"Mm-hmm." Her eyes dropped to his lips before lifting again. "Maybe you can be my friend."

"Why settle for so little? You could have asked for that matching necklace?" His gaze surveyed the edge of her jawline, debating where would be the best spot to press a kiss.

The corners of her mouth pulled into a smile. "I don't consider it to be little."

It would be so easy to—

His hand couldn't resist any longer, the pads of his fingers traced the edge of her jaw. Before he realized what was happening, his lips pressed to hers.

"I'm still not looking to start anything," he said before bestowing another kiss to her tender, responsive mouth.

"Neither am I," was Mia's light as air reply, returning his kiss with one of her own.

"So, it's settled then, this doesn't mean anything." He tasted her again.

"Nothing at all." Mia did her own tasting with a slow, torturous slide against his mouth, killing him in sweet, short increments.

"I'm serious, Mia."

"Me too," she exhaled between a delicate caress. "Do you

think I actually want to be kissing you right now?"

"Probably not as much as I don't want to be kissing you."

"This is the very worst kind of dilemma."

It needed to stop. It couldn't continue. Ross grabbed at the first wild idea his brain could envision. "How about the camera?"

Mia pulled away. "What?"

"Favor for a favor. The camera. It's yours." Serving as a perfect excuse, he made his escape, almost tripping over his feet as he went to the part of the office where the black camera bag was located.

"Does this mean you're rejecting my offer of friendship?" Her face held an expression he couldn't read. Disappointment? Sadness? It hit him straight in the gut.

"I've always been your friend," he heard himself say. "But the time and work you put into this seems like it should be worth more."

"You don't need to do that."

"Take it." He pushed the bag into her arms, shoving his hands into his pockets. "You'll get more use out of it than I will. I don't want to spend the time figuring out how to use it anyway."

"Really?" Mia's chest expanded from a deep breath as if a burst of happiness would soon rupture out of her. Amber eyes glowed. It was the most beautiful thing he'd ever witnessed. "It's funny. My boss was talking to her friend, who runs the boutique shop next to Pony Expresso, about the images I took. She might be interested in hiring me," she said.

"Great. Looks like I just helped by making a major contribution to your new business. Go do that."

Some of the glow shuttered from her eyes. "I haven't decided to do it yet. I really shouldn't."

"Why the hell not?"

"Well, because it's only a hobby. I have other things I need to focus on, and I can't keep getting distracted if I'm going to get out of here. And, obviously, I've been getting distracted a lot lately. I don't need to add another thing on top of it."

"What do you mean *get out of here*?"

"I'm applying to doctorate programs for political science. As soon as I get into a program, I'm leaving."

"Why?"

She looked at him in confusion. "Why what?"

"If you want to get into politics, why not just get into politics? You're obviously good at this stuff and have to be smarter than most of the people currently in it."

For the first time, her eyes flicked away, her fingers fiddling with the strap on the camera bag. "I… I might like research and teaching." It was a statement, but her usual enthusiasm was missing.

As he watched her mouth stretch into a flat line it hit him. "You didn't like working on the campaign."

"I didn't say that," was her quick response, before adding, "It was fine."

But Mia's discomfort with the whole conversation was evident as her vision locked on to the various objects in the office, and she continued to fidget with the camera bag.

"Mia," he said in an attempt to get her attention. Her

focus made a slow track to him. "You don't have the gleam for it, but you had it when you were doing photography and talking about setting up Etsy and Instagram pages."

Her face fell for a moment before she recovered and released a brief, humorless laugh. She moved further away from him. "Stop it. What exactly am I supposed to do? Photography? I can't do that."

"Why not? You obviously enjoy it."

"Because it's not a real job."

"I think there are professional photographers who would argue with you on that point."

Mia's eyes narrowed. "Okay, let me be more specific. It's not a real job *for me*."

He grew agitated at the new demeanor she adopted, running a hand through his hair as he leaned against his desk. "Says who? Mia, you're lucky enough you could probably do whatever you want. And if you can make something with only a camera, your intelligence, and your PR abilities, why wouldn't you want to try?"

"You don't understand," Mia said, crossing her arms tightly over the bag.

"You're right. I don't understand at all."

"I've already started the process."

"So?"

"Look, I'm just passing through here. I'm going to get my PhD. I'm going to get tenure. I'm going to write academic papers and books. I'm going to make something amazing out of my life and be someone important. I'm not going to be one of those people who peaked in high school, who are still living in a tiny, hick town, who haven't done or seen anything. I can't. Don't you understand. I *can't* fail." Her eyes were wide and shiny. Her chest rose and fell in short breaths.

Ross studied her in silence, understanding the straight honest truth behind her words. There was no people-pleaser, no brashness here. She was the person who pointed to the exact position where he stood in the grand scheme of apparent success. "You mean, someone like me—except I never even got to peak in high school."

Mia's complexion blanched, her gaze darted away while she chewed on her bottom lip, appearing on the verge of tears. "I-I would never think that about you," she replied in a small, strained voice. Hugging the camera bag close to her chest, she rushed to the exit. "I just can't afford to take risks like everyone else."

Chapter Nineteen

MIA MASSAGED THE skin along her temple, feeling wretched. Did it matter if she heaped an extra, cold serving of wretchedness onto her day? This was the reason she sat in her mother's craft chair, running fingers across an unfinished quilt block beside the sewing machine. All the necessary elements were there, and yet this was a quilt destined never to be finished. This knowledge depressed her even more.

What at first seemed impossible had become a reality. Mia found a weakened seam in Ross's leather armor and pushed until the edges pulled apart. This allowed a small part of her to slip through and touch him. But she had screwed up again and this time in the worst possible way. One moment they were kissing, the next, they were at odds. She had no hope this could be repaired, not again. She wanted to throw up.

In the chaotic, sloppy defense of her life decisions, she managed to slap down his entire existence, which was the furthest thing she'd ever meant to do. But he shouldn't have pushed. His insight into her life produced a bubble of panic within her gut. It was as if she was drowning on the inside from the overwhelming pressure. All she required from Ross was to acknowledge her situation with a nod of respect. Instead, those all-seeing, obsidian eyes took her in with x-ray accuracy. Her carefully controlled image was in danger of becoming wholly exposed, and she couldn't imagine anything worse.

Mia wished her mom was here. She was tired of the craft room door being closed all the time. While her father was Mia's northern star when she needed guidance in her professional life, when it came to matters of the heart, this was when she missed her mom the most. In the old days, the craft room door was always open.

"WHAT'S WRONG, MIA Sophia?" Her mother had asked when Mia wandered into the craft room one day while home on a rare winter break.

"Nothing," Mia replied as she took a seat near the ironing station.

Her mother continued sewing on a vintage Singer Featherweight machine, the constant whirring of a needle punching into fabric.

"How's the new quilt coming?" Mia was never interested in quilting. Still, she appreciated the hobby and the soft calming rhythms which came with it.

Her mother removed the square from the machine and pulled the new pieces apart to inspect the accuracy of her design. "Fine. I just have another few blocks left to do before I can start putting them together for my quilt top. Did you want to do something today? You're up early."

"No, I'm okay."

A steady hand slipped more fabric under the presser foot. "Are you excited about going back to school in a few days?"

Mia claimed a red tomato pincushion from the ironing board and pulled out random straight pins before jabbing them in again. "I guess."

The sewing machine activity stopped. "What's wrong?"

"Nothing," Mia insisted.

"You're getting fidgety, and you seem like you want to talk. Just tell me what's on your mind."

She sighed. "Mom…" But Mia couldn't bring herself to continue.

"Okay, now you're making me nervous. Are you about to drop some bad news?"

"No, no bad news. I just… Do you ever feel like you don't know what you're doing?" A more foolish question never came out of Mia's mouth, but what she was feeling didn't seem normal. This uncertainty couldn't be right. Maybe, with assurances, everything would line up in a perfect row again.

"Of course, Mia. Everyone feels like that. I felt like that for years after you were born."

"Yeah, I guess you're right. Everyone must feel it from time to time." She jabbed another straight pin into the tomato.

Her mother propped an arm on top of her sewing machine, resting her head against a hand. "Is this about school?"

"I don't know…maybe—it's just my interest in political science…what if it isn't what it used to be?"

"I'd say grad school is probably not going to be very fun

for you then."

Mia pressed her face onto the surface of the table in front of her and groaned.

"How long have you felt this way?" her mom asked.

"I don't know."

"Well, what would you like to do?"

Mia turned her head toward the wall, the pinprick of tears stunned her eyes. "I don't know," she stated with impatience, hoping to distract from the emotions which were threatening to surface. As a person who liked being anchored, the vast abyss of having nothing to grasp onto placed a heavy feeling of fear inside her.

"Have you talked to your father about this?"

"No," came Mia's soft answer.

"You know your dad isn't going to like this news."

"I know. It's just all the money—"

"I don't care about that. I want you to be happy. Going to school is not just about the education and career. You need to figure out what you want."

"Please don't say anything to him." She brushed the emerging tears away with her fingertips and cleared her throat. "I'm fine. I just—It's just a moment of nerves. Sometimes it can be overwhelming. I'm sure that's all it is."

Her mother frowned. "If you're really having second thoughts, talk to him. Do you want me to talk to him?"

"No. No, I… It's fine. I'm still thinking everything over. I need to come up with a plan."

"Neither Dad nor I can make your quilt for you, Mia. You need to do that yourself." Her mom gave her an encouraging smile.

The problem was Mia didn't know where she'd go if she did change direction or what her quilt should look like. All she wanted was to take a break from the constant pressure to succeed, to make sure her parents' investment paid off, to make them proud of her. A break would not have held up against the judge's scrutiny.

IN THE END, she never had a conversation with her father, and, with the sudden passing of her mother six months later, she lost her confidant. Instead, Mia forced herself to push ahead with the plan that had already been bought and paid for.

She did sometimes dream about what it would be like to start over somewhere new, where she had no history and no expectations. If Mia could have done anything she wanted, what would her life have been like? She envied someone like Ross, someone who seemed to be on such a clear path, doing what he was meant to do without question.

Mia wished she hadn't screwed it up with him, especially after he was nice enough to give her an expensive camera. And he had said, *I've always been your friend.* It wasn't until she heard the words that she realized how much she had yearned for them. Ross's sentence was a verbal hug, one which made her want to stop, close her eyes, and completely surrender to the warmth.

She never felt good about the way their friendship had ended in high school. Mia wanted something better this time around.

What would her mother have told her to do?

She wiped a solitary tear away while organizing the quilt squares into a neat pile. On the table was a small stationary pad with the motivating words, GET IT DONE! in a swirly black font and a sleepy, cartoon sloth along the bottom. Mia read the to-do list in her mother's familiar scroll.

PICK UP JACKET FROM DRY CLEANERS

GO TO FABRIC STORE

MAKE LASAGNA

It wasn't angelic advice from the great beyond, but it did give Mia an idea.

Chapter Twenty

"Wow, Ross, I'm actually really impressed. It looks great," Luna said on the phone. "Maybe the trick to getting past the Ross Manasse stubbornness was in front of me the whole time. All I needed to do was go ahead and do it. Is it better to ask for forgiveness rather than permission? Be truthful with me. How mad were you?"

Ross sat at the office computer, scrolling through the Etsy page on his screen. "For your information, I was perfectly calm. I was more in a state of shock than anything else. I was shocked right out of being mad. I couldn't believe it."

"This girl's really got you figured out."

And this was a big problem. He didn't want Mia to figure him out, to be vulnerable again, not with her. "Whatever. I'm not a complicated guy. Anyway, we've already made our first online sale. It's just a necklace—"

"Don't knock it. It's a good start. Once you upload some images for me on the cloud, I'll put in some time working on our Instagram page, but it sounds like all the hard work has been done."

"Yeah, sounds good."

Soon after ending the call, Ross found his thoughts drifting to Mia. It happened whenever he looked at her handiwork. With it being tied to his business at present, it wasn't easy to avoid. How many sales would have to come and pass for these thoughts to vanish? Or would it be a constant thing every time he re-posted a listing and stared at her images? After she left, it would be all he'd have of her.

His mind broke free at a soft knock at the door. "Come in."

The door cracked, and it was as if his thoughts conjured the physical when Mia popped her head in. "Hi, Ross. Can I talk to you for a minute?"

He groaned while returning his attention to the computer, clicking the Etsy page away.

She proceeded into the room, taking the free chair available. "How's everything going? How's Hermes doing?"

"Fine. What can I help you with?" Ross was determined to keep this visit short and herded toward the business end of things. There wouldn't be a handshake, let alone kissing, this time around. Now that he knew the reality of the situation, it was probably best if he didn't get himself in any deeper.

She pulled at nervous fingers. "What I said during our last conversation—I didn't mean to hurt you. I'm really sorry. Can I make it up to you?"

"How many times are we going to go through this? I don't want you to make it up to me. Let's just forget it. It doesn't matter anyway."

"But I don't want to forget it, not this time."

"Look, I can't exactly be angry about something you actually believe. At least you were being honest."

"Stop it. Here's what I believe. I think what you're doing

in this shop is great, and you're clearly doing something that utilizes your talents. Ross, you're lucky. And I-I feel like I'm still flailing around in life and it terrifies me. All I want is something certain I can hang on to, and I'm worried I may never find it. Or I'll find it, and it will be just one more disappointment. And then what? That's really all I was trying to express, and I, obviously, did it very poorly. It had nothing to do with you or what I think about you. And I respect you, so it's the worst feeling in the world for you to perceive my problems as a slight against you. I never meant to do that, and I want you to believe me."

If Mia had practiced this speech, she at least did a good job of sounding unrehearsed. He finally faced her, determined to keep this short and to the point. But when his gaze locked on her, it wasn't the confident, sunny Mia he was used to seeing. Instead, this was a woman who was worn around the edges with tired, glossy eyes and disheveled hair pulled in a loose ponytail. She kept her eye contact with him steady, her brow lifting in sincerity.

Ross didn't have enough energy these days to feel anything close to anger toward her, even during their awkward conversation a few days ago. The most he experienced was irritation, and he was more perplexed about this than anything else. Why did he care what she did? It was her life, her decision, and it didn't affect his situation whatsoever. Yet, it bothered him a great deal knowing Mia was on her way to being trapped and unhappy.

"You're making me nervous," she said. "Have you finally succeeded in your goal of hating me?"

He sighed, leaning back in his chair and rubbing a hand

along his jawline. "No. But maybe this is really for the best. I have a business to run. You're going to be leaving. So, what exactly are we doing here? Maybe you had it right from the start. Maybe the past really should be forgotten."

Her face fell further, her frown deepening. "If you don't want me to bother you anymore, I won't."

A charge of disappointment shot through him at these words, but he brushed it away and tried to dismiss it.

"But I would feel better if you gave me one last opportunity to make it up to you. Please," she added, her lips lifting in hope.

"You don't owe me anything, Mia. Trust me, you've done more than enough."

She held up a pointer finger. "One thing, Ross, for old time's sake."

"What exactly do you have in mind?" He couldn't help being curious. When was Mia not being intriguing?

"The Russo lasagna, my place."

"You can't be serious."

"I am. You always told us it was your favorite, and you certainly ate enough of it whenever we had it."

Mia remembered. Ross had stated several times that lasagna night at the Russo's had been one of his favorite things. He couldn't deny it now. Since those days, he tried many other lasagnas, but none of them came close to Mrs. Russo's. He should have declined the offer, but...

"How are we going to have this lasagna?"

"I'm going to make it." Her delicate jaw locked in determination.

"You cook?"

"I'm perfectly capable of following a recipe, Rosso. And I did help once or twice."

He tapped a finger on his desk. "No, I don't think this is a good idea—"

"It's just lasagna. Since when is eating a lot of lasagna a bad idea?"

"Right before going swimming or having sex," he shot back.

Mia released a hearty laugh, returning a lightness inside the room. "Okay, well, I don't have a swimming pool, and I won't try to seduce you. So, unless you make other plans after you leave the old Russo place, it shouldn't be a problem."

"What about your dad?"

"What about him?"

"He's probably not going to want me there."

Mia dropped her head back, her tongue making a *tsk* sound. "Good lord, Ross. He hasn't seen you in ten years. I doubt he'll remember you. Half the time, he can't remember if he ate breakfast or not. Besides, I'm inviting you for Thursday, and he won't even be there. He always goes to play poker at a buddy's house after work. What else do you have?"

"I don't think it's a good idea to spend close, personal time with you."

Her features scrunched in puzzlement. "Why?"

Because I can't risk making out with you again. Ross cleared his throat, leaning his elbows on his desk, and tried to find a less blunt way to get the message across. "Because recently…we've…you know…the kissing."

Mia rolled her eyes. "I will douse myself in coffee before you get there, and the smell will guarantee our separation for the evening. I already said I wouldn't seduce you. But I promise to keep my hands to myself and be on my best behavior."

The idea he would need to be protected from Mia was laughable. Except it wasn't. So what if she used coffee as a deterrent? Was she also going to put away the dimple, amber eyes, and cute glasses as well? But, at the same time, they weren't horny teenagers in high school anymore. They were two grownups. He could control himself, as could she.

His lips pulled into a slight smile. "Lasagna, huh?"

She grinned while doing an eyebrow wiggle, eyes glittering. "And the best part is, you don't have to do any homework beforehand."

Chapter Twenty-One

IT WAS FIVE forty-five P.M., and a frazzled Mia was wondering if her whole plan was about to explode in her face like an overripe tomato. Her kitchen showed signs of a possible catastrophe in the making. The countertops were topped with a cabinet's worth of dirty dishes and discarded ingredients. Plus, her apron was covered in red splotches due to a simmering meat sauce. She glanced at the kitchen clock again. If she didn't inspect herself in a mirror now, it wasn't going to happen.

At least the lasagna was in the oven. How it would taste remained a mystery. Judging by the mess surrounding Mia, the odds weren't very good. Why did she put herself in this impossible situation? As though she'd be able to replicate something as fondly remembered as the Russo lasagna. If it didn't taste close to the original, Ross would be disappointed, but Mia would be devastated.

Her mother had put together the recipe binder soon after marrying the judge, getting them from Grandma Russo. The famous lasagna dish was also one of her father's favorites, and her mother perfected it throughout the years so eventually she didn't need the binder. Italian, Mexican, or any type of food, Mia's mom was an amazing cook, but the Italian recipe binder was the only one she ever put together.

There had always been plenty of time to get other recipes. Until there wasn't.

All the favorite family meals her mom whipped up from experience and memory were gone. There wasn't a binder for Mexican cuisine, because her mother had never needed one and Mia had never cared to learn. Mia wasn't blessed with the same natural cooking talent, not that she tested herself much. Her last attempt at throwing things together based on gut instinct was a chicken enchilada verde six months prior. The meal was a flavorless mess, her tortillas broke apart, and it was nothing like her mom's. Mia had sat on her bed and wept a bucket's worth of tears while forcing herself to eat it.

But all wasn't lost. There was still the Italian recipe binder. She held onto this binder in the hopes it was still possible to taste some of the home-cooked meals she remembered fondly. If her ability to follow a recipe also failed her, Mia worried these food moments were lost forever.

Tonight the biggest question was this: Did her mother scribble the word *nutmeg* on the ingredient list? It did look like the words *dash of nutmeg*. Did nutmeg belong in lasagna, mixed in with ricotta cheese? Was this another Mexican Italian fusion only done by her mom? Maybe it was supposed to be something else and only looked like the word *nutmeg*. Perhaps Mia managed to ruin the whole lasagna with a sprinkle of holiday spice. She might as well toss in a pinch of cinnamon and ginger. This was definitely going to be a disas—

The doorbell rang.

She glanced over from her spot kneeling in front of the

oven. She focused on her disheveled reflection appearing in the black oven door, the closest she had to a mirror. Disaster, party of two, walk this way. Nothing she could do about it now. She raked her fingers through her hair in an attempt to be halfway presentable and less chaotic.

On the other side of her family's front door, Ross's appearance was the opposite of her own: calm, put together in a nice navy blue sweater and dark gray jacket, looking like a man who exuded good smells. *God, he looked amazing.* There was something about him, which made her want to snuggle up and press her face into the firm wall of his chest.

"Hi! Come in," she said, forcing a bright smile to her lips.

He hesitated, as though unsure if he should cross the threshold into the Russo home. But he managed to step forward through the time portal, and his eyes gave the living room a slow perusal. Mia could tell he was remembering, but his expression didn't reveal if they were good or bad memories.

"Is it weird being back?"

"Something like that." He gave her a quick scan. "Did you make a lasagna or fight one?"

Mia was still wearing the stained apron and yanked it over her head, snagging her hair in the process. "Ow," she said, as she brushed a hand through her locks to smooth them. "I have to be honest. It was a battle to the death and I think the lasagna won. This is the first time I've tried to make this meal on my own, so the kitchen doesn't look pretty."

A smile graced his lips at her confession. "It smells exactly how I remember it."

"Okay, well, that makes me feel a little bit better."

"You do have a green speck of something on your glasses, though."

He leaned closer, plucking it off the lens. Mia was sure she went cross-eyed as he held the green leaf between his fingers, because naturally she'd do the unsexiest thing when given the opportunity.

She took a guess. "Parsley, maybe?"

"Did anything make it into the lasagna? Because you seem to be wearing a lot of it."

"If you'd like an appetizer, you can taste me." *Oh god! Why did I say that?* Heat flashed across her skin as Ross stared at her. She'd never been so flustered in her life. "Never mind. Let's go into the kitchen."

He did a dead stop at the kitchen entrance, surveying the chaos. "Holy shit, Russo. How is it possible to make this much of a mess for one dinner?"

Mia dropped her face into a palm, her hair falling forward over her face. "I know. There's a lot that goes into a lasagna, plus I made the meat sauce from scratch."

"Mia, you didn't need to go to all this effort."

She slid her gaze to him. "I wanted to make sure it was *the* lasagna. That it tasted exactly the same, and if it doesn't…" She shrugged her shoulders in what she hoped was a carefree response because they were talking about lasagna, after all. She didn't want to appear too dramatic. "Well, as Grandma Russo would sometimes say, *Tutto finisce a tarallucci e vino.*" Mia did her best imitation of her tiny Italian grandmother with the tips of her fingers pressed together, striking through the air. "Which means it all ends with cookies and wine, and everything will be fine. But that assumes your version of fine is not eating the inevitable, disgusting lasagna I made and pigging out on cookies and wine instead."

"Did you finally learn to speak Italian?"

"Nope, but I still know those swear words. I've been using them all afternoon. I noticed you didn't ask about Spanish."

He gave her an amused look, clearly also remembering their old library conversation. "¿Tú hablas español?"

"I may have forgotten most of it since high school," Mia said.

"Aw, so both Spanish and I got the shaft on your memory real estate. Maybe I shouldn't feel so bad."

"Shut up, Rosso." She laughed, slapping him lightly with the apron in her hand.

He managed to snag it and used his grip on the apron to pull her closer. His dark eyes were warm burning embers again. "Well, what do you want to do while we wait?"

She considered lassoing Ross around the hips with her apron strings and—

Stop. She promised him she'd behave herself. "I don't know," she replied lightly.

"Your dad wouldn't approve of us doing nothing. I feel like I should have my backpack and be sitting at the dining room table with a school book."

"*The Odyssey*?"

"I actually finished it, on my own, a couple years ago."

"If you read every word twice, it means you've read it

one more time than I have."

"That's right," Ross said. "And I'm trying to learn Spanish."

Impressed, her eyebrows rose. "You've become quite a fascinating man, Ross Manasse."

"You're not the only one who likes a challenge."

They smiled at each other, the second hand on the kitchen clock ticking slower as the moment eased to a stop. The motivation to behave herself was beginning to crumble.

The timer went off.

A flutter of anxiety ran through Mia's veins at the arrival of Lasagna Judgment Day. "Okay, I guess it's time." She grabbed pot holders, cracking the oven door. She offered a silent plea to her Latina mother and all her Italian ancestors in the hopes nutmeg was the correct ingredient. She could use *all* the heavenly help available. She retrieved the glass casserole dish with the browned, bubbled cheese and curling steam wafting above it. As she set it on the stove, Ross drew nearer, hovering close enough for her to catch the wonderful spicy scent emitting from his form. Mia grabbed a handful of fresh-cut herbs, finishing the top with a generous sprinkle. "Buon appetito."

"That is probably the best-looking lasagna I've seen in a while."

Her chest inflated with a cotton candy swirl of happiness at his words. "Hopefully, it tastes as good as it looks." She scooped large portions onto white plates, and they ate standing beside each other at the granite-topped island in the center of the kitchen. They weren't digging into their dinner long before it was necessary to cool their mouths with a glass of cold water. The pasta was scalding. It was a good thing Mia wasn't planning on using her tongue for anything else. Anyway, she was too busy keeping her emotions in check, because the recipe had not failed Mia. Her mother was still here. And nobody cried over a plate of lasagna without looking ridiculous.

She stole a glance at Ross, who appeared to be in his own spiritual food moment, his lasagna portion half-eaten at this point. He stopped when he noticed her attention. "Never thought I'd be eating the Russo lasagna again. You did good, Mia."

She bumped his shoulder with her own, her optimism restoring itself, and with Ross here to share it with made it an extra bonus. "Maybe next time I can do it without bringing down the whole kitchen."

"Baby steps," he replied. "You don't want to push for the impossible. You're clearly not Little Miss Perfect, after all."

She smiled at the teasing, the feeling of absolute delight tested the boundaries of her heart. Was it possible Rosso and Russo had found their way to how it used to be?

He broke eye contact, returning his focus to the lasagna on his plate. "Can I ask you something?" he said after a few moments of silent eating.

"Sure. Are you going to ask what the secret ingredient is in the lasagna? I don't spill my secrets easily, Rosso."

"What happened during the political campaign?"

Mia's eyes dropped. She concentrated on slicing the corner of her lasagna with her fork. "There's not a lot to say. He lost."

"That's not what I'm asking. Why would I care about

some random politician?"

Her eyes slipped to his. Was he implying he cared about her? She'd hold onto this for now. "Do you think I have a killer instinct?"

"You're definitely ambitious. But if you're asking if I think you're cutthroat, I'm going to say no. At least, I've never seen that side of you."

Her fork swiped across her plate, spreading tomato sauce on the white surface. "You're not the only one to see this. People say they want someone brilliant or organized or simply 'the best' for their team, but sometimes what they really want is something I don't have. I'm branded as Little Miss Perfect or a 'nice girl.' Once I get this label, it's easy enough to dismiss my value as nothing more than a glorified office girl who's around to take coffee orders." Mia's lips pulled in a half-hearted attempt at a smile. "I guess it gave me some experience for working at Pony Expresso, where I'm still taking coffee orders." Her smile faltered when it wasn't returned. "Well, let's just say I wasn't really trusted enough to do the job I was hired to do. In fact, the male intern under me was allowed more responsibility than I was. The most excitement I had was writing tweets to clean up whatever mess the candidate got himself into with his mouth."

Mia didn't really want to have this conversation, not when it was better to keep things airy and light. This was especially true because her excuses sounded weak even to her own ears. Who did she think she was? Did she expect to burst through to the top of the talent pool? Maybe this was possible when the pool was smaller. But when it was an

Olympic-size pool, she was one tiny, insignificant cog in the system. And how could she burst through when her heart was never in it? Everything about it depressed her.

But Ross's expression was one of deep seriousness as he studied her. It was the familiar intensity he exuded when he was using his x-ray ability to pierce through to the marrow of truth.

She sighed, her shoulders slumping. "Also, the more I learned about the candidate behind the scenes, the more I came to dislike him. I just grabbed the job because it felt like what I was supposed to do. It was clear he had no moral compass and winning was more a matter of pride than civic duty. Here I was trying to paint a good picture of the guy for the public, but I knew it was a lie. So either I was lying, begging people for campaign funds, or getting coffee orders. That was my whole experience. Anyway, the work I was doing didn't make me feel very good, like I was in the process of selling my soul." She sneaked a peek. "Does that make you think less of me?"

"Why would I think less of you?"

"I don't know. If I help someone with no moral scruples, maybe it means I don't have any either. Anyway, I'm glad he didn't win, so I guess it's a good thing I'm not applying to work for other campaigns right now."

"So why stick with it?" he asked.

"There are other options for politics, like going into academics. I have a plan. Plus, when you make an investment like my parents did...well, the investment better pay off. Otherwise, it's just a waste."

"You haven't lost your soul. You're still you, Mia. And

anyone who doesn't see your true value deserves to lose."

When his dark eyes caught hold of hers, she became captivated. His words meant everything, and Mia's heart overflowed with the sentiment behind them.

"Nutmeg!"

"What?"

"That might be the secret ingredient in the lasagna," she said.

The corners of his mouth kicked up in a grin. "You can trust me with your family secrets, Russo."

Something inside told Mia she could not only trust him in this but in all things. Ross would always be someone she'd be safe with. If she'd learned one thing from her independent venture into the real world, it was how rare this feeling was.

But Ross might not be able to trust her. She had made him a promise, a promise involving keeping her hands to herself. All Mia's hands wanted was permission to roam his body, and her lips were requesting the same for his face. She knew why she shouldn't do this, and it was for all the reasons Ross provided earlier. But she was tired of playing everything in her life with a calm rationale. He made her want to dive headfirst into the lake without checking the depth beforehand.

"Ross," she said, turning toward him. Mia suspected he was reading her thoughts or contemplating similar ones, because he was nearer, his eyes softening as they took her in. The electric spark of a kiss floated on the horizon, and neither one was going to fight it. She sucked in a breath, her eyelids fluttering shut, as their faces drew closer.

"Ahem!" The gruff throat-clearing shattered the moment

from the kitchen entrance.

They sprung apart as the judge strolled in.

"Dad, what are you doing here?" She took a sudden interest in her dinner, swiping a strand of hair behind a reddening ear.

"Why wouldn't I be here? This is my house. And what the hell happened to my kitchen?"

"Nothing. I just made lasagna. I'll clean it up. Did you want a piece? It should still be warm."

Her father studied Ross with a growing intensity. The subject of the judge's scrutiny kept his own eyes downcast. "Well, I don't want to interrupt anything, but it does smell good."

"Yeah, okay." Mia retrieved a plate for her father, loading it with a large slice. "By the way, this is Ross. We...uh, went to school together. He owns El Dorado Jewelry downtown." If her father had disliked him before, as Ross believed, she didn't want to jog her father's memory too much. Perhaps this time, the judge would form a more fair opinion.

Her father appeared set on eating dinner at the kitchen island, instead of his usual habit of eating in the living room or in his office.

"So, you own a jewelry store?" her father asked Ross.

Ross gave her father a brief glance. "It's a family business. My cousin owns it. I'm just the bench jeweler. I'm keeping an eye on the place while she's away."

"Ross makes all the beautiful pieces they sell. Mom would have loved it," Mia provided with an upbeat tone.

Her father ignored this, keeping his attention on Ross. "Your family is really putting a lot of trust in you then."

The first hint of an awkward tension was developing in the air. Mia jumped in. "Dad, what happened to your poker game? I thought you always played with your buddies on Thursday."

"Phil's kid was sick, and it was canceled. So, you guys went to school together?"

"Mm-hmm," Mia provided.

"Did you go to college?" her father asked.

"No," Ross replied.

The judge pointed his fork in her direction. "Mia here studied at UC Berkeley, went to grad school and everything. Top of her class. Did she tell you that?"

"No." Ross pushed the remaining sauce around on his plate.

"Well, she did. And now she's planning on getting her doctorate. But I always knew Mia would go far."

An internal cringe went through her at the turn in conversation. "Alright, we don't really need to talk about this, Dad."

"What were you talking about before I interrupted?"

"Just old school stuff."

"Oh yeah? Did you tell him how you used to tutor some real duds in high school?"

Mia's eyes snapped to her father's face. The full shock at his statement was incapable of penetrating her mind. Her father's metamorphosis was instantaneous as he shifted from a beloved guardian to an omniscient judge.

Her father continued. "You always have to wonder about kids like that. What kind of life can they truly have? Especially the ones who lack brains and have a penchant for trouble. Ah, well. Not that you were one of those. Right, Mr. Manasse?"

"Thanks for dinner, Mia. I think I'm going to take off." Ross didn't wait for a response before walking from the kitchen and out the front door.

Her father turned an innocent gaze toward her and shrugged. "What did I say?"

Mia glared at her father before going after Ross.

She caught him outside on the driveway before he got to his car, her hand latching onto his arm. "Ross, please—"

"I don't want to talk about it. I'm going home. This was a mistake."

"I'm sorry, but my dad... This doesn't make any sense." Her brain struggled to understand. What was she missing?

He let out a bitter laugh to the night sky before facing her. "Really, Mia? Don't be so naïve."

"Even if he doesn't like you, I don't think—"

"No, this goes way beyond the judge having a simple dislike. He punished me before, and, in his effort to protect you and your future, he's going to keep punishing me."

Mia stilled, her hand clutching the sleeve of his jacket, refusing to let go of him or the issue. "What do you mean he punished you before?"

"You know exactly what I'm talking about."

"No, I don't."

Ross's dark eyes swept to the house. "Your dad is watching us from the window."

"I don't care. I want to know what you mean."

"You're trying to tell me you don't know what happened to me in high school?"

"Is it the cheating thing? I don't care anymore."

He stopped, his expression a mixture between anger and confusion. "What the hell are you talking about?

"Did—didn't you get kicked out of school for cheating?"

"No. I... Where did you hear that from?"

Her grip tightened on his cuff. The answer stuck in her throat, but it didn't matter because it was obvious.

"Mia."

She raised her gaze to him.

"I never cheated. I really tried to do well in school."

"Then what happened?"

His shoulders fell as he closed his eyes and rubbed a hand across his forehead. "I ended up in your father's courtroom."

"What? What for?" Mia's hand fell away as she took a step back. After believing the cheating story for so long, this new twist took her by complete surprise.

"Shoplifting. My friend and I were hanging out, basically avoiding school, and we were bored. We went into a store, and I saw a copy of *Butch Cassidy and the Sundance Kid*. It was Grandpa's favorite movie, and his birthday was coming up. I never had any money, but I really wanted to give it to him. Obviously, I got caught."

She let out a breath. "Okay, well, it's ironic you would steal that particular movie given the subject matter."

Ross's lips stretched into a frown. "This isn't funny, Mia. You have no idea what it's like to go through the system."

"You're right. I'm sorry. But as far as kids getting into trouble, it's not that bad. I'm sure my dad sits on these cases all the time."

"That's what the public defender said. He told us I'd

probably get a warning, community service, or restitution." He took a breath. "The judge sentenced me to sixty days in juvenile detention."

Her world froze. "What?"

"Your dad made sure I got the worst punishment he could give me. It wasn't simply petty theft, but also burglary with intent. I took a twenty-dollar blu-ray. We didn't even have a blu-ray player, so that shows you how much thought I put into it. Your father even threw in truancy for skipping school."

"Had you done this before?"

"No. First and only offense."

"Ross, I... It doesn't make any sense. What else aren't you telling me?" Mia was desperate to find an explanation, one which fit neatly inside her existing reality.

His expression remained flat. "That's the whole story. There is nothing else."

"No. That can't be it. Just tell me. I don't care what it is. I just want to know the truth."

"There's nothing else, Mia."

"I can't believe that."

"So, you think I'm lying?" His question was edged in anger. Every muscle in his body locked together. His calmness seemed to be held together with nothing but a thread.

"Or maybe you don't remember everything that happened. My dad is strict, but he's not like that, Ross. He wouldn't do that. It doesn't matter if he dislikes you, he's always been fair. He's always believed in second chances."

The thread snapped. Ross's hands gripped into tight fists. "I'm not the one here who forgets things. And how would you know, Mia? Are you there in the courtroom with him? What do you know about any of this? All I can tell you is I was a poor kid with failing grades who made a mistake and ended up behind bars to be forgotten by everyone but my family. By the time I got out, continuing with school seemed like a huge waste of time since I wasn't going to graduate anyway. That's why I dropped out. So, yeah, I was foolish, and I paid the price. Your dad made sure of that. If there's anything more to the story, you'll have to ask him."

Mia's insides were hollow. "I don't believe you."

His jaw tightened. "Well, you already believed I was a cheater, so now you can add thief and liar to the mix. I don't care." Ross yanked open the door to his truck, slammed it shut, and peeled out of the driveway. She remained rooted in place as a mist of rain began falling from the sky. With a heavy heart, she returned to the house.

Mia put away the extra lasagna and started the slow process of getting the kitchen in order. She was standing at the sink when she heard footsteps behind her. She glanced at the blackened window and saw her father's reflection watching her.

She continued washing dishes. "Do you only hate him because of me?"

"I don't appreciate the accusation, young lady."

She faced him, wiping her palms on a nearby dishtowel. "Well, he told me the most fascinating story."

"I don't know what you're talking about."

"You told me that he was kicked out for cheating!"

"No. I told you he got in trouble."

She tossed the towel on the counter, her hands snapping

to her hips. "You said—"

"You need to calm down. You're obviously not remembering things correctly. That kid—"

"Stop it. I'm not a kid. Ross is not a kid."

"That's even worse. He is, and will always be, a distraction and not worth your time."

"Uh-huh. So is that why you did it?"

"I didn't do anything but follow the law. That's my job as a judge. And protecting you is my job as a father."

Oh god. Mia gripped the countertop to keep herself from crumpling to the ground. Everything Ross said was true. Their friendship altered his life in a way she hadn't known. No wonder he was angry.

She narrowed her eyes. "You always told me the law was only one part of your job. The rest had to be made of common sense and heart. What happened to that, Judge?"

Her father's expression tensed, his face coloring. "He broke the law, Mia! Was I just supposed to ignore that because you liked him or because your mom thought he was a good kid? When you break the law, there are consequences in this society. Do you expect me to give your friends special treatment? I thought I raised you with better ethics than that."

"No, not special. Fair treatment. And I would like to believe you can put your personal disdain for a person aside instead of purposely using your power to crush someone."

"You think you can be a better judge than me? I've been doing this for over twenty years. I think I can see people, read them, and know them better than you can. You can give people second chances, even third chances, and they still end right back in the same spot. Not everyone gets out, Mia. You don't know. You've been protected, and maybe that's my fault, but in the real world—"

"No, don't you turn this around and try to make this be about my issues. This really had nothing to do with me, until you made it that way."

"The problem is you're too emotional. Like your mother. You can't see this from a logical point of view."

Mia scowled, her own frustration coming to the surface. "Oh, so the only one who gets to be emotional when they make decisions is you? Because what you did to Ross was nothing but emotional."

Her father's face burned red with anger. If she were to come closer, her skin was sure to blister. "You don't get to talk to me like this." The words were hard and unyielding.

She glared at him as her own temper flared around her like flames. "This is not a courtroom. You are not a judge here. If you don't like that I'm not blindly accepting your explanations, maybe they're not as logical as you think. Is that the real reason you didn't tell me ten years ago?"

"The kid was a troublemaker!"

"He took a *fucking* DVD for his grandpa's birthday!"

"You don't understand. That kid—"

"Did he skip school? Was he poor and didn't get good grades? Spare me. What am I missing?"

"Isn't that enough?" her father shouted. "You don't understand. As a judge—"

"I'm sure you've seen hundreds of kids exactly like him. And if you're trying to tell me that they all got the same treatment as Ross, then I find your type of judgment disturbing. The only thing I don't understand is why."

The judge didn't respond, and he didn't need to. The answer was already clear enough to Mia. He had treated Ross that way because he could.

Chapter Twenty-Two

Ross retrieved a bottle of beer from his fridge. It was one of those nights which required a stronger drink, but there wasn't one. The beer would have to do. He twisted off the cap, taking a long sip in his darkened kitchen while staring out the window.

This was precisely what Ross was trying to avoid. Why exhume all these unhappy events when he put so much effort into trying to forget them? Mia, the bespectacled eagle, swooped into his life, her wings sweeping away his carefully established walls. All he requested was a quiet life with Hermes and to make jewelry in his workshop. Sure, Mia's presence delivered light and warmth. But at the same time, her massive wings also gathered the clouds overhead, bringing the memories roaring back like the current storm happening outside his home.

He remembered the scared sixteen-year-old Ross. The kid who was snatched by store security, handcuffed by local police, and a disappointment to his grandfather once again. Sitting on the hard wooden chair in the courtroom, he'd fixated on the plaque reading Honorable Vincent D. Russo. He had a flicker of hope in the man who was to be his judge. The person with the title of *Honorable* knew Ross and knew he wasn't a bad kid. In the end, it had been silly of Ross to hope for anything different. No one ever saw him as anything but someone lacking in potential.

Ross was jerked from the memories with the appearance of headlights pulling in front of his home.

What. The. Shit.

He plunked the bottle on the countertop and strode to the door, jerking it on its hinges. He hadn't made it past the porch before a jacket-less Mia jumped from her vehicle, the rain coming down heavy around her.

"I'm done discussing this with you! Go home, Mia!" He jabbed a finger in the general direction of it.

She remained locked in place. "I know you're angry. I don't blame you."

"I don't even care anymore. You can believe whatever you want. Just leave me alone."

The porch light basked Mia's skin in a golden hue. Drops collected on the lenses of her glasses, obstructing her eyes. She removed them and lifted her face to the sky, her features scrunching as if in pain. He did his best to harden himself to it. What did she know about misery? Her whole life was one of charm and success.

"I care, and I *do* believe you." Her tearful words reached him across the driveway.

It was too late. Ross's anger wasn't going anywhere, not this time. Tears would not soften him. He zeroed a cold gaze in her direction and steeled his voice. "As horrible as being put behind bars was, what you did to me afterward hurt even more."

Mia ignored his previous command, trudging forward to

where he stood beneath the covered patio. He couldn't tell which drops on her face were tears and which were due to rain. Her arms were folded tight across her chest as she shivered, bowing her head. His ears caught the slight hitches in her breathing. "You're right. I've been the worst kind of friend." A hand pressed across her eyes as her mouth stretched in despair.

"I came back, Mia. After the two months, I came back. They told me you didn't want to tutor me anymore." When she had given up on him, it felt like everyone had.

"I'm so sorry, Ross. I was so focused on the possibility that you cheated, and how it may have reflected on me, it was all I considered. I allowed myself to be persuaded into thinking that talking to you was suddenly wrong, and that I didn't know you at all. You weren't the only foolish sixteen-year-old back then." Her eyes remained fixed on the cement stoop beneath her feet. She tightened her arms more, her body trembling.

"You're going to get hypothermia."

"I don't care. I'm not leaving like this. Not this time."

The stiff line of his shoulders softened. He sighed. "Let's go inside."

She followed him into his home, and he left her in the entryway before returning with a clean towel. Draping it across her shoulders, he rubbed along her upper arms in an attempt to dry and warm her shaking limbs. Mia remained silent, allowing him to work the towel over her body and watching him with those big, warm eyes. When he finished, her hands clutched the plush fabric to her shoulders. "Thank you."

"I thought you didn't believe me," Ross said.

"It's not that I didn't believe you, it's that I don't want to believe these things about my father. He's always been someone who I've admired and used as my standard of morality. It's why I thought I couldn't work with politicians anymore, because they weren't meeting these standards. It's hard to get your brain to switch over and accept something so different than what you've always known. To find yourself disenchanted once again."

"I think I went through a similar thing with you."

She burst into a fresh crop of tears.

"Mia—"

"No, you're right. The school failed you. The system failed you. And I failed you. I don't blame you for hating me."

Whatever anger remained in his heart seeped away, leaving nothing but weariness behind. He was so used to the anger, so used to pushing. For once he didn't want to push. Rather he wanted to pull something toward him. And the person he pulled was Mia, right into his chest, wrapping his arms around her damp frame. Her body softened against him, allowing herself to be enveloped.

"I don't hate you. I've never hated you."

"You should," she murmured against his chest. "This whole thing was a mess, and it was pretty much all my fault."

Ross dropped his mouth to her ear. "I think you're giving yourself way too much credit. Everyone knows you're brilliant and capable, but you're not that capable. You're not the reason I got into trouble when I was a kid. You didn't cause me to take the movie. You don't have any control over your dad. I can take responsibility for my actions. You don't need to saddle yourself with a bunch of stuff you didn't have any control over."

She gave a short sniff. "I'm sorry I disappointed you."

"It happens. Trust me, I've been a disappointment many times in my life." He pulled away, taking her face between his hands. Her eyes were wide and shiny. Her dark lashes were clinging together in spikes across pink cheeks. Her glasses were still in her hand, and he wasn't used to seeing her without them. It didn't matter, glasses or no glasses, she was beautiful either way. And she was here, listening to him, choosing him.

He traced his thumb along her brow, outlining the edge of her temple before sliding its way across her cheekbone. She closed her eyes at this, light breaths exhaling from her lungs. He was tempted to capture each breath, to allow himself to bask in her warmth.

Just once.

"You should go home," he said.

Her eyes held his. "I don't want to."

Don't push. Pull. These were the last things that went through his mind.

Ross covered her mouth with his own, drawing a luscious kiss from her. Mia's arms slid around his neck, locking them together. Lips pressed. Tongues met. The air between them became charged with desperate desire. These were not the soft, tame kisses of springtime but rather the hungry wants and needs after a long, barren winter. Measure for measure, she returned his kisses as volcanic as Ross gave them. His mind teetered on the edge of a cliff, and he was powerless to do anything about it.

Requiring extra support, he pressed her against the wall. His lips claimed her mouth again and again until the surrounding atmosphere was filled with nothing but hot, panting breaths. Nothing about this felt enough. His body wanted more skin, more heat, more of her. As Mia's hands drifted down his chest, electricity crackled and spread inside him. There was a tug on his waistband as Mia worked to undo the button of his pants.

Ross managed to tear himself from her lips. "Mia," he said, using his hands to pacify her busy ones.

"Ross, please," was her breathless response. "I'm on birth control if that's what you're worried about."

He'd been impulsive before and look where that got him. Ross didn't want to be impulsive with Mia. She had come to mean a lot to him. With an impressive amount of restraint, he took a step back. "We're not going to do this tonight. I think we can both agree it's been a strange evening with a lot of emotions. It's probably not a good idea to add something else to the mix."

She actually released a small whine, and he smiled while tucking a strand of hair behind her ear. "Are you working in the morning?"

"Yeah," she responded.

"Maybe we can have dinner tomorrow—"

"Okay."

"Let me finish. Go home. I'll stop by the coffee shop, and you can tell me yes or no to having dinner here, a designated dad-free zone. Whatever you decide is fine, but I want you to really think this over. I don't want this to be something impulsive you do because you're mad at your father."

Mia studied him. "How do I know you also aren't motivated by anger toward him?"

Ross brushed his lips across her temple. "Trust me. If I'm doing anything to you, the last person I want to be thinking about is the judge."

"How about we make a deal and just keep him out of this altogether."

"Deal. But I still want you to take time to think about it."

Mia groaned. "Fine."

Ross was tired of fighting this attraction. He could finally admit to himself he wanted her. But, above all, he wanted *her* to be sure.

Chapter Twenty-Three

IF THERE WAS one thing Mia was good at it was being an overthinker. It may have started when her sixth-grade teacher, Ms. Reid, commented on one of her essays with *Push yourself harder, Mia*. At the time, Mia thought she had been pushing herself. But perhaps she hadn't. How was she supposed to know which effort was simply *hard* or she reached past it and achieved the level of *harder*? It made her look at everything with extra scrutiny because maybe her original perception was wrong.

When she departed Ross's place, her mind was set. She wanted to be with him the following evening. During the whole drive home, one word played in her head: *Yes*. And why not? They were aware of each other's situation, and as long as they stayed upfront about everything, it wasn't a big deal. But, as Ross seemed to predict, time had a funny way of making one less sure, and the overthinker took over.

On the one hand, it was just dinner. It's not like Ross was asking her to move in. Dinner could mean a lot of things. Or it could mean nothing. Besides, dinner tended to be an all-consuming endeavor. Not many people were capable enough to shovel food into their mouths, and participate in an additional activity at the same time. Eating a meal was a completely normal everyday event, and she just happened to be doing it at Ross's home. Thinking it meant something more might be considered presumptuous.

On the other hand, this dinner would be shared with Ross. This was a beautiful man with desirable and kissable lips, not to mention some sexy forearms. A guy who worried about her getting hypothermia, and accepted her for who she was, nerd-girl and all. So, yes, it was dinner but, at some point, there would be the time *after* dinner. A time when there wouldn't be the single focus of bringing a fork to her mouth. And maybe she'd become preoccupied with other things that could be brought to her mouth. *Mia, you in danger, girl,* said her internal voice. Yes, yes, she was. Because Ross drove her wild with distractions, and she didn't even care anymore.

Mia had already submitted her applications, turning her life into a long waiting game. She could have her distractions if she wanted, and she didn't want to waste time thinking about where she might have to go next. New York, Washington, DC, Texas, Virginia. It didn't matter. Until she got accepted somewhere, Mia had to squeeze in whatever she could.

The next morning, she was still going back and forth in her mind, attempting to dissect all the possible outcomes like it was a Choose-Your-Own-Adventure book: romance edition. As though she'd be able to look ahead in the pages and see what fate she could expect before committing to a decision.

"You're getting that far-away look in your eyes again, M," Natalie said.

"Hmm? Oh, yeah. Fine."

Natalie gave her a funny look before laughing. "Okay, well, now I know there's something going on."

Mia blushed. But she craved someone to confide in and Natalie was the closest thing she had to a girlfriend these days. She leaned near her manager. "Ross asked me to dinner."

"Who?"

"The jewelry guy."

"Ooh. Tell me and tell me now." Natalie bit her bottom lip while wiggling her eyebrows. "I think it's time for you to get yourself some dinner *and* some dessert."

"Natalie!" Mia offered an apologetic glance to the customer as she handed over the drink she had made. "I- I haven't answered yet."

"And *why* the hell not? You guys clearly like each other."

"Well, I'm leaving eventually. I'm not sure there's a point."

"So he doesn't know you're leaving?"

"No, he knows."

Natalie shrugged. "Then the point is sometimes you both need dessert. If you don't live when you're young, when are you going to live?"

It was at this moment, Ross pushed through the door with his kissable lips, flushed cheeks, and wind-tousled hair courtesy of the crisp blustery weather outside the shop. When his intense, black eyes made contact with her, Mia dropped the creamer container on the counter. It splashed in her face, leaving white dots of residue on the lenses of her glasses. *Ugh*. Real smooth.

It was a good thing an extra-friendly Natalie took Ross's order because Mia had enough trouble acting like a person with functioning hands. Could Mia be satisfied if it was a single night? She slid a glance at him as she prepared his Americano. There was no doubt in her mind that dessert with him would satisfy all her sweet-tooth cravings.

Mia popped the lid on his cup, turned, and she found him standing at the counter. This had the immediate effect of throwing everything off-balance. His gaze remained steady, waiting, and she swallowed hard, her movements stiff and awkward as she placed his coffee on the counter.

"Yes," she managed to squeak out. Ross took the cup without a word and walked away.

Natalie gave Mia's arm a light pinch. "Hey, M. Make sure you don't fill up on dinner. Dessert is the most important meal of the night."

Chapter Twenty-Four

ROSS WAS SURPRISED. And it wasn't because Mia said yes. She could have done so for any number of reasons. Maybe it was a late bloomer's rebellion against dad. Or she was bored. Perhaps she genuinely liked him. There was a part of him that didn't care what the reasoning was. When there was a strong possibility Mia would reject him, he found himself hoping she wouldn't. The surprising part was how much his heart buoyed due to her single-word response.

But now he had to scramble to plan an actual dinner. Feeling frustrated at his brain's lack of help and creativity, he settled on Victor's favorite dish: paella. It had been a long time since Ross made it, but the more he thought about it, the more excited he grew. He told Aanya he was leaving the shop, and he'd like her to close.

"Is everything okay?" Aanya asked, clearly thrown off by his announcement. Her reaction wasn't surprising since Ross was always there until closing and sometimes even after.

"Yeah. I need to go to the vet to refill Hermes's prescription, and then I just have some plans later."

She gave him a sly smile. "Oh, good. I hope it's something fun, like plans with…a friend?"

"Something like that," Ross said as he scooped the dog

from his bed.

With a twinkle in her eye, Aanya returned to cleaning the glass display cases and humming a light, pleasant tune. He didn't find her humming annoying this time, possibly because he wasn't hanging around.

Leaving the store during work hours gave him the most unnatural feeling in the world. It was as though he was a vampire discovering he could walk around in the daylight without being singed by the sun's rays. He brushed the feeling aside and proceeded with his errands.

As he chopped his ingredients, the small, familiar voice in his head whispered its doubts. Perhaps Ross was reading the whole situation wrong. Or maybe starting something with Mia was a mistake. What exactly did he think was going to happen here? It was clear whatever this was had no future.

But when did he become the type of guy who worried about things like futures? He had come to accept that his day-to-day existence would continue the same as it always did with little change. To consider a future meant to have hope, and Ross wasn't gullible enough to get sucked into that type of optimism again. Instead, he'd stick with his one-day-at-a-time approach. He used his knife to slide his chopped vegetables into his skillet and pushed his doubts away.

He had nearly finished cooking when she arrived.

"It smells delicious," Mia said as she entered his kitchen. "Wait a minute. Did you really make something, or are you heating takeout? This kitchen is way too clean."

"I clean as I go. You should try it."

"Smartass." She leaned to peek into the cast iron skillet.

"What is it?"

"Paella. Have you had it before? I grew up eating it with chicken and sausage but decided to spring for some prawns tonight."

"Oh, come on, Rosso. I already like you too much. I have to leave someday, and I don't want to be crying. You don't even have a recipe card out."

"Reading just slows me down. I cook by taste, and this was Grandpa's favorite, so I've made it a lot. Just enjoy dinner and accept that you're going to be crying." He couldn't stop the grin from taking over his face, his doubts becoming quieter at Mia's admission that she liked him.

She ambled to the refrigerator. "Is this him?" She studied the photos posted on the refrigerator door. It was covered with images, but she focused on one in particular. It featured his grandfather, Ross, and Luna sitting on a hay bale at Placerville's harvest festival. Victor's arms were around each grandchild, and all three shared matching happy smiles.

"Yes," Ross said as he focused on stirring their dinner. "With Lulu and me. I think I was about ten there."

"And you with Hermes, back when he spent more time awake than asleep." Mia pointed to another picture and froze. "And—" she took a closer look. "You play the guitar? Dammit, Ross. Do me a favor and hold something back. I don't want it to look like I get swept off my feet so easily."

"Then you'll be happy to know I only play a little and I can't read music. Grandpa was definitely better at it than me."

"I'm sorry I never got to meet your grandpa. He sounded amazing. Was there anything he could do that *wasn't* better than you?"

He eyed her with amusement. "I'm sure there's something."

She arched an eyebrow. "I guess I have to stick around until I discover what that is."

With dinner done, he scooped large portions into bowls, and they took it to the small, wooden dining room table with mismatched chairs. Mia blew on a forkful of rice before slipping it into her mouth. He tried not to watch her, concentrating on eating his own dinner. His eyes may have slid to her once or twice in anticipation of her reaction.

"Ross?"

He met her gaze. It seemed as though Mia was attempting to appear serious but failing. The corners of her lips ticked upward.

"I know you don't trust compliments, and you think I'm just a people-pleaser, so I'll try and say this in a way that might make it easier for you to accept." She paused as if organizing her thoughts. "I hate…that you're a good cook."

He returned his eyes to the food, careful to temper his own expression but feeling pleased. "You like it then?"

"Good lord. If someone cooked this for me for the rest of my life, I would die happy." Her smile stretched across her face as she said it. She leaned on the tabletop. "I'm definitely falling in love—with the dish, not with you. You're just okay, and I bet your grandpa made it better than you. See? I'm not getting swept off my feet."

He chuckled at her comment. Talking with Mia, whether about good things or bad, was never dull, and he was coming to enjoy their conversations more and more. Ross wanted to be guarded, but he already knew it was too late. He missed having someone to talk to, and Mia kept surprising him.

She leaned her head against her palm as she continued eating her dinner. "What happened after?"

"After what?"

"After you left high school."

He pushed his fork around the edge of his bowl. "Well, I went through a period of not wanting to do anything and getting into small-time trouble with friends. Grandpa finally got to the end of his rope and threatened to kick me out, which was terrifying. His health had started to go downhill, and this was even more terrifying. When he had his first stroke it was sort of a wake-up call. Someone needed to help him and make sure Lulu was taken care of. He had already started to teach me the jewelry business, but it was then that I took it seriously. And I learned that I was good at it and I liked it."

Ross rubbed a palm across his jaw, feeling the tiny prickles of facial hair against his hand. "I knew if something happened to him and I wasn't prepared, the business would be gone, and we would have nothing. I decided to go back to school. Lulu pushed me to go to an adult literacy program, and it was there that the mystery into my reading issues was solved. After that, I went through the process of getting my GED."

"And the reason you insist your cousin owns the business is?"

"Because she does. We thought if we ever had to go to the bank for help, it would be better if it was a person who didn't have a record for stealing."

"Did your grandpa see you get your GED?"

"Yeah. He was really sick by then. I wasn't a great grandson, but at least I was able to do that."

She watched him with a clear, steady gaze. "I'm sure he was very proud of you. You've done well for yourself."

"I've done okay. It's no PhD."

Her mouth pulled into a straight line. "You need to stop comparing yourself to other people, thinking you'll never do things as good as your grandfather, or what you do is worthless because it's not a PhD."

"I feel like similar advice could be given to you."

She laughed. "Why do you always have to throw my words back at me? Let's start with you. You are Ross Manasse, and that means you're a talented jeweler, in your own right, who can play the guitar, make an amazing paella, slow dance well. You're clearly a very accomplished young man."

"Mia," he said skeptically.

She smiled at him, patting his arm. "No, I mean it. You're like a Renaissance man, but without the huge ego."

Ross appreciated the way she explained things. Mia had a way of talking as if she had the ability to inflate a cloud under a person. Perhaps she was a people-pleaser, but he believed her, and he liked it. He couldn't help liking her.

Mia's hand continued to rest on his forearm, the tips of her fingers grazing the skin there. He pulled it back until his hand slid beneath hers, and he could hold it within his grasp. Ross's thumb brushed across each joint and knuckle as he studied the details of her hand—the curved lines, the callus on a finger, the small freckle marking her skin. Her eyes were also stuck on their hands as if fascinated with the way their fingers intertwined together.

"Do you want more?" he asked.

"Yes," she blurted.

"Well, there's plenty of food."

"What? No—Sorry. No, I'm done. I-I'm full." Mia brushed a hand across her face, her cheeks blushing. She was never more adorable than when she was flustered. He wanted to keep flustering her.

They stood, each picking up their own bowl. Mia followed him into the kitchen. She rinsed their dishes, putting the items in the dishwasher as he packed the leftovers, placing them in the refrigerator. Nothing was said, but it was a comfortable moment of domesticity as if they'd done the exact thing many times before.

The question was, with dinner finished, what was supposed to happen next? Ross knew what he wanted to do: take her into his arms, press his lips to hers, and get so hot and bothered the heat alone would devour them, leaving behind a pile of ash. Without any witnesses, it would be attributed to another mysterious case of spontaneous human combustion.

When he faced her, those amber eyes were like lava, hitting him with force, and he was helpless to do anything but swallow. Now he was the flustered one.

A warm smile fixed upon her face. "Thanks for dinner, Rosso. I don't know how regular food can ever compete after that."

"Are you leaving?"

"Do you want me to stay?"

"We can watch a movie or something."

"Okay."

Even with their plan decided, neither one of them moved. All he wanted was to run his hands across every inch of her skin, to see her hair splayed across his pillow, to hear words of pleasure fall from her lips. Ross couldn't take it a moment longer. Closing the distance between them, one hand went to her waist, the other grazed her cheekbone. His mind was split between overwhelming desire and sheer terror. He didn't know what was inside this Pandora's box, but he was sure it wouldn't be all rainbows and sunshine. How could it be when it was clear both of them were on different paths? Despite this, he was tempted to rip the lid off. But he couldn't open it, no matter how much he wanted to. It would have to be Mia, and he'd provide her with any reason he could to discourage her unless she was a hundred percent positive.

Her arms slid around his back, bringing them closer, lifting her face in expectation of the kiss she was sure to receive.

"What if someday you decide you want to get back into politics? Maybe run for something yourself," he said while stroking the soft skin on her cheek.

Her expression shifted to confusion. "What?"

"It's not a far-fetched possibility, right?"

"I don't know. I mean, I doubt it, but I guess."

"But you don't know."

She blew out an impatient breath. "What exactly is happening right now?"

He hated himself for doing this, but he felt forced to at least see the conversation through to its logical conclusion.

As much as his hormones were screaming to be unleashed, this felt too important. Ross ran a hand down her spine before pushing a strand of hair behind her ear.

"If there's even a chance of you pursuing politics, it's probably not smart to get involved with someone like me. Sure, it's a juvenile record, but I'm sure people will dig up anything and try to use it against you. I don't want my mistake to ruin your chances. I don't want to be your skeleton."

"Ross—"

"This isn't just fun and games. You need to be serious."

Her fingers stilled and her eyes darkened. She pulled away from him completely, leaning against the countertop opposite of him. "You want to be serious? Fine."

Ross wasn't sure what he expected from her, perhaps for her to wake up and realize good times with him might not be worth the hassle. Or maybe he just wanted to save himself from eventual heartache. For the first time in his life, he didn't feel strong enough to handle it, like whatever part of his heart remained, it was stretched so thin these days, it wouldn't take much to cause an irreparable hole.

Mia cleared her throat, running a frustrated hand through her locks. "I don't know what I'm doing," she said. The confession made her face appear pained and he almost drew her into his arms again. "I don't know what I'm doing and I don't know what's going to happen. I already told you this scares me. And I know nothing can be planned because life is always going to throw a couple of curveballs. As far as politics are concerned, I honestly don't see anything more than research and teaching—"

"But you don't know."

"Okay, let's say maybe I decide to do something more. It doesn't matter. Whether I get into politics or not, you will never be some dark secret in my closet. You shouldn't be a dark secret in anyone's closet. Do you hear me, Ross Manasse? You are more than just one mistake. I like the whole man, and that includes the bones and muscle, heart and soul. And most of all your mind. God, when I look at you, seeing something shameful is not even worth entertaining because you'll never be that to me."

He stood there, unable to move, let alone respond. He tried to get his legs to move forward so he could wrap her in an embrace, press a grateful face into her neck and breathe her in, one floral note at a time.

She must have assumed his brain stopped working because her fingers went to the buttons of her shirt and she began to achingly undo one after another. She stepped close to him again, pressing kisses along his jawline.

He closed his eyes, releasing a jagged breath as shaky hands slid into the opening of her shirt, skimming silky skin. She already felt so good: warm, soft, pliable, everything he needed.

"You're sure you want this?" His voice sounded gruff to his own ears.

"Good lord, Ross. All this skeleton talk and, yet, you still can't pick up on how much I want you to bone me. How much clearer can I make this?"

A laugh rumbled through his chest. "*Bone* me? Nerd-girl, your vocabulary is already becoming so pedestrian."

"Maybe it's time for you to tutor me in a thing or two?"

He reached lower, grabbing her thighs, and lifting her up. With a gasp, her limbs wrapped around his torso. Ross gave her mouth a biting kiss. "It might be time for a little extracurricular activity."

She laughed as she continued to press kisses to his face, and he carried her to his bedroom, fire burning through his veins.

When Ross laid her on his bed, her grasp on him loosened. He carefully removed her glasses, placing them on the nightstand. Then he took hold of the T-shirt on his back and pulled the garment off while Mia discarded her own shirt. Her finger traced a line along the ridges of his chest, her eyes dark and hazy. He couldn't wait to do his own touching, and she seemed to be reading his mind when she rose to unhook her bra before unceremoniously dropping it on the floor. Mia reclined as if presenting herself like a platter ready to be sampled. Every part of her was breathtakingly beautiful.

"Taking your bra off was supposed to be my job," he said, unable to resist kissing a path from her collarbone to each breast, and she moaned in pleasure.

"After all this back and forth between us, I might be feeling a little impatient."

Just as she had the ability to inflate a cloud under him, he'd do anything to do the same for her. He started undoing the zipper of her pants with clumsy fingers. "All right, Miss Most-likely-to-be-taking-notes-while-being-seduced. Just so you know, if anyone is going to be taking notes tonight, it's going to be me."

"Is that right?" She lifted her hips so he could peel off her remaining clothes.

He nodded. "I'm studying what it takes to shut off that overworked brain of yours. I've never considered myself a people-pleaser, but right now I'm going to try my hand at being a Mia-pleaser."

That shut her up. Her mouth parted on a soft intake and her skin developed an attractive flush.

Ross was becoming equal parts agony and hope. Agony because his body had convinced itself that if he didn't have her soon he would possibly die. And hope because, even if this was contained to a single night, it was one moment where she would be absolutely his.

He traveled down the length of her body, nipping and kissing a path along her skin. Her breathing was increasing but he wouldn't be satisfied with just that. His shoulder wedged her legs apart as he fit himself between them.

"Ross—"

He pressed his mouth there, ignoring her and began to kiss and lick. When Mia started to squirm, he latched an arm across her hips as he continued tasting her, running his tongue through her.

"God. Ross," she gasped, her hands going into his hair and pulling strands. He did his own grunting at the pain and pleasure of it all. He didn't let up until her breathing reached a pinnacle of hyperventilation and she suddenly arched, moaning something intelligible. Pleasure and satisfaction swirled within him at the knowledge he could steal all her words with nothing but his touch.

"What did you say?" he asked, lifting his head and letting his gaze peruse her spent body.

"I said, you really are a Renaissance man."

Ross smiled against her stomach. "I'm not done yet."

"I should hope not," she said between heavy breaths while reaching for the fly of his pants, and undoing them.

Ross pulled away so he could quickly rifle through the contents of his bedside stand, his panic growing until he was able to locate a single condom.

He finished undressing, rolling on the condom, and re-settling on top of her. He paused. His agony and hope had morphed into desperate want, but he was afraid of losing all sense and reason. "Mia—"

"I swear to god, if you keep teasing me…"

He pushed into her and she groaned his name into his ear. There wasn't any way he was going to maintain any sort of control here. Ross was reduced to pure energy and need. He gave in to the rhythm of her. Either he was hers or she was his. It didn't matter.

The world had already shifted beneath him and he was in trouble.

Pandora's box had been opened.

Chapter Twenty-Five

MIA KICKED UP crisp fall leaves while walking through the parking lot of St. Anthony's Catholic church, leaving a trail of golden-hued confetti.

"Mia." Natalie waved from where she stood at a long table in the church's rec room. Mia approached while undoing her scarf.

"Hi." She gave her a quick hug as she tried to settle the nerves in her stomach, feeling both excited and anxious that today might be something important but also emotional. "What are you doing? Do you need help with anything?"

Natalie appeared to be in the middle of decorating the table, which was already covered with colorful fabric, various framed photographs, small baskets of fruit, and a smattering of candles. Above the table was a string of papel picado, bright squares of tissue paper with cutout designs. For a spot dedicated to the dead, it was all quite cheerful and bright. Mia set her bag beside the table.

Natalie scanned the room which was already filling up with other people setting up tables and food. "Not sure where my sisters went. You can help me with these tissue paper pom-poms." She set two small potted marigolds on the table. "One of my younger cousins is learning to drive and he accidentally ran over my grandma's front yard flower bed. She was so mad, and it's really hard to find summer flowers this time of the year. My sisters came up with the idea of supplementing our lack of marigolds with tissue paper ones."

From her bag, Natalie pulled out what appeared to be folded bundles of yellow and orange tissue paper. Mia chose one and followed Natalie's instructions for pulling out alternate sides until the bundle transformed into a delicate, marigold-like pom-pom.

"These are cute," Mia said as they taped the pom-poms to the wall around the table.

"It does look pretty nice," Natalie agreed.

"What's the significance of marigolds?" she asked, becoming more intrigued.

"El oro de Maria," said an elderly voice behind her. Turning, Mia found a small, frail older woman beside her.

"The Virgin Mary's gold," Natalie translated. "But I'm pretty sure the flowers have been used going all the way back to the Aztec period. It's the flower of the dead."

The older woman said something else in Spanish to which Natalie rolled her eyes. "This is my abuelita. She's complaining that the tissue paper versions don't have the smell. Apparently, it's the scent that brings the spirits. They follow it or something." Natalie responded back to her grandmother. "This is Mia. She doesn't speak Spanish."

"No Spanish?" the older woman repeated.

"No. Sorry," Mia responded. Her cheeks flushed and she was beginning to feel awkward again.

But the older woman smiled. "It's okay. You did very good on the flowers."

Natalie laughed. "Yeah, of course, Mia did good."

Abuelita reached toward Natalie's shoulder and gave her a small pinch. "Okay, okay, you did good too, querida. Where are your sisters?"

It was at that moment Natalie's two younger sisters breezed in, chatting a mile a minute. Natalie did all the introductions even though Mia had met one of the sisters once before when she came into the coffee shop. They were both younger than Natalie but Carla was the youngest one. She wore her curly hair in two equally sized buns on top of her head and wore jogger pants and a crop sweatshirt. She looked like an adorable Latina anime character. The other sister was Mariana who had a sharp, sleek bob and wore a weathered leather jacket. She'd be at home as a kickass secret agent in an action movie.

"Mia?" said Mariana. "Are you the one dating the jewelry guy with the dog? Carla is a little jealous of you."

Finding herself in a group of way-cooler-than-her Gonzalez-Torres women, Mia couldn't help feeling a little smug.

"No, I'm not!" Carla said, her cheeks turning pink. "I just said he was hot. I say that about a lot of people."

"No, you said, *why can't I hit that?*"

"Again, I say that about a lot of people. But at least I do occasionally hit it, while Natalie's dating life is like the desert. No life."

Natalie shook her head. "What are you talking about? There's lots of life in the desert. There's cactus, snakes, scorpions..." Her sentence petered out as her sisters gave her raised eyebrows.

"This is what you're going with," Mariana said.

"No," Carla inserted. "I think she's right. The desert is a fitting metaphor for her love life"

"Ugh, stop. I don't plan on getting married so it doesn't matter now does it," Natalie replied.

"Ay, dios mío." Her abuelita did the sign of the cross as though Natalie's pronouncement was blasphemy to her ancestors.

"Who said anything about marriage? I said *hit it*. Anyway, don't care because I'm more interested in what's going on with the jewelry guy." And Carla's big brown eyes turned toward Mia.

Mia was having a good time with the teasing up until this point. "Oh, uh, we're just friends. Not exactly dating."

The women all spoke at once with Spanish mixed in and pointed to a lit religious candle that featured the Virgin Mary. It was clear she was being warned against lying in front of dead souls and paper marigold pom-poms. "Okay, okay. I hit that," Mia confessed.

"Finally," Natalie said. "Although you might have to repeat the whole story since your mom hasn't arrived yet."

"Oh, should I...?" After this, Mia wasn't sure she was ready to bring down her mood quite yet...or ever.

"Yeah, it's fine. This is a community table."

Mia took a steady breath and reached into her bag. She carefully pulled out a framed photo of her mom sitting in front of a fountain. She set it on the table before reaching for the small quilt she brought. "My mom also loved flowers. She appliqued her favorites on this one." She pushed down a lump in her throat as she set the item beside the photo.

The girls gathered her in a side hug, and Abuelita handed

Mia a stick lighter. "For the candle."

"Oh. Okay." Mia set the wick of a votive candle aflame. She stared into it while taking a few moments to think about her mother.

"Your mamá must be very proud of you," Natalie's grandma said.

"I hope so," Mia replied. "I'm sure there are some things she would be disappointed about. I didn't come home during my breaks as much as I should have. I didn't take enough photos when I had the chance. I was always so busy trying to do another program or just do more with my schooling. I'm afraid it won't be worth the sacrifice."

The older woman studied her. "You have that time now. This is Día de los Muertos. We celebrate what we had and continue to have because they stay with us."

Mia wiped a hand across her nose.

"Es la verdad. The truth. You find the truth in yourself. That's what makes mamás proud."

After spending the day with Natalie's family, walking around the other tables to see activities for kids, and witnessing a procession in the parking lot while drinking Mexican hot chocolate and eating pan dulce, she felt loved and connected. The whole thing was bittersweet but lovely.

But the last thing she wanted to do was go home afterward. Things were still rough with her dad, and she was actively avoiding him rather than engaging. She couldn't pretend she wasn't still angry over the whole situation.

Her mind instead turned to Ross. Their dinner had been a week ago. She hadn't reached out to him again, nor had he reached out to her. It seemed like they had both agreed the whole thing was going to be a one time thing. Something to get out of their system. As much as she told herself she was fine and it didn't matter, she had a sneaking suspicion getting him out of her system would never be so easy.

She parked her car along the sidewalk in front of his house. She didn't even know if he was home or—

Ross stepped out the door, wiping his hands with a dishtowel. "Hi."

"Hey." She wasn't sure what to say to him. Telling him she simply wanted to be near him, see him, might come off as creepy. So she didn't say anything, choosing to remain fixed to her car.

"I take it you're here for me," he said.

Mia smiled, glancing down at her shoes before meeting his eyes again. "Well, I'm not here to reminisce with the dog."

"I'm glad you stopped by."

"You are?"

"Mm-hmm. We never got to watch that movie."

She laughed. "Darn. You're right. Total fail. Well, you know what they say, if at first you don't succeed…"

"Try, try again," he finished for her. Ross's hand beckoned her toward him. She came because she couldn't help it. He was her opposite magnet and the rules of science dictated this pull each of them had on the other. She walked straight to him and didn't stop until her body was pressed to his and her arms wrapped around his waist. She lifted her face, her chin poking into his firm chest.

"Hey, Russo."

"Hey, Rosso. I like the way you kiss."

His eyes grew soft, his gaze traveling to her mouth. When his lips kissed hers, it was sweet and tender, giving her that warm feeling of connection again. They stayed like that for a moment before Ross lifted her by the waist, dragging her into his house and to his bedroom.

Chapter Twenty-Six

ONE MORNING IN March, Mia was pulled from her heavy slumber by a warm, gentle squeeze across her midsection and his voice low in her ear. "Time to get up, Russo. You've had enough sleep. Come on, I made breakfast."

She pressed her face into the pillow and moaned her complaint like a fussy toddler. Although she had to admit, it wasn't the worst way to wake. It beat the ear shock of an alarm and a bruised banana for a quick breakfast, as she raced out the door.

As soon as Ross vacated the room, she cracked an eyelid. Reaching for the nightstand, she fumbled until she located her phone and glasses. She sat, yawned, and did a quick finger comb through her hair as she slipped on her glasses and checked the time. Sunbathed in the morning light, Mia bent her knees, drawing them to her chest, propping her head on a palm as she stared across the bedroom. Hermes sat in the doorway threshold, watching her, his long pink tongue rolling out in a happy pant.

Welp. She woke up in Ross's bed. Again.

During these last few months, Mia spent more time in Ross's home than she did at her father's when she wasn't working or taking photos. The Lanza-Manasse house was a place where she could actually breathe, one that was lived-in and comfortable, plus Ross was here. His home didn't have sad memories of her mom or the new eggshells she had to walk on because of her dad. One day, Mia even snuck a printed selfie she took with Hermes and placed it onto the crowded surface of Ross's refrigerator. When he discovered the new addition, he smiled while shaking his head, but the photo remained in place. Mia could admit it was silly, but this was her way of leaving one tiny mark on a place that felt like home, even if it was a temporary one.

Hermes gave a small bark from the threshold. Seems like he was having a good day. Mia called him to her and pulled the small animal onto the bed, cuddling him. While he wasn't out of the woods yet, the veterinarian told Ross she was feeling optimistic about the dog's prognosis and he responded well to the treatment. Just in case, Mia gave Hermes lots of kisses and told him what a good dog he was until he squirmed away and darted out of the room.

That was her cue to get out of bed. Mia crawled out from the covers, and dressed. Ross stood at the stove wearing a dark gray T-shirt, and sweatpants. His raven-colored hair was disheveled from sleep and those sexy forearms were making her breakfast. She couldn't imagine a more appealing scene.

The delicious scent of smoky peppers and caramelized onions filled the air. Mia's stomach responded with an embarrassing grumble. His eyes turned to where she stood in the bedroom threshold ogling him like a creeper.

"It's about time," Ross said.

She approached him. "What are you making? It smells good."

With a wooden spoon, Ross did a quick stir of the ingredients in his frying pan. His other arm drew her to him, and he tucked his face into her neck, pressing his lips there. She tried to dismiss the warm feeling of comfort and safety this simple gesture produced inside her chest. She could pretend there were no calendars, warning her of a Ross-less future, nor any maps, threatening to distance her away from this kitchen. She wanted to soak in the moment, revel in her contentment, live in the now.

"It's just a simple chorizo hash and eggs. No big deal," Ross said.

Her arms threaded around his waist as she snuggled into him, kissing his scratchy jawline. "I think we have different ideas of no big deal," she murmured before kissing him again, "Considering what I normally scarf down for breakfast, this is a feast."

Ross smiled as he basked in her affection. "Says the overachiever who's always looking to score extra credit on everything."

"Oh, I'm not complaining, Ross Manasse. I like being spoiled, but I'm not sure that's a good idea on your part."

"Next time, I'll kick you out with nothing but a stale granola bar. But you better grab us a couple of plates since I've already gone through the trouble of making it."

With their plates filled, they sat at the dining room table. She took the olive green chair with the chipped paint. Mia sat in this particular spot enough times to claim ownership of it in her mind. She was tempted to use a steak knife to carve her initials into the wood. This act might declare her intention to sit in this chair for the rest of her life. It was a ridiculous dream, but it didn't stop her from eyeing the steak knife on the table.

"I take it you're not working today," Ross said.

"Not today," she replied while staring out the window. She was thankful to have a day off. She didn't mind working at the coffee shop, but she was starting to feel restless about her situation. Although she enjoyed working with Natalie and her coworkers, coffee didn't seem to be her life passion either.

"Do you have any plans?"

"Nope." She studied the food on her fork before putting it in her mouth.

"I was going to drive to the city to see my buyer."

"Your buyer?"

"To get supplies for the shop," he said.

"Do you mean like gemstones and stuff?"

"Yeah. Because of the online shop someone set up, I have to get supplies more often now."

"Sounds like a good problem to have and that brilliant person should get a special thank you later. You have to go to Sacramento every time?" she asked.

"No, I usually do it online, and he just ships it to me, but I thought it might be nice to go to the city today."

Mia suppressed a grin as she studied her plate. "Yeah, you should go to the city then. It looks like it's going to be a nice day for it."

"Mia," he replied, a visible expression of frustration sweeping across his features.

Her own brow raised in innocence. "What?"

"It's just…I… Dammit, Mia."

Mild laughter escaped her lips. "You're not much of an angsty bad boy when you're afraid to ask the woman you're sleeping with a simple question."

He pushed his chair close to hers, wrapping his arm around her shoulder and pulling her close. "Come to the city with me today?" It wasn't so much of a question as much as it was a request fringed in hope.

Mia swept her fingers through his hair so it no longer stood on end. "See, that wasn't so hard. It kinda feels like a date."

Ross returned to his breakfast plate. "It's not a date." He mumbled the phrase which had become common between them, ever since they agreed at the beginning that what they were doing wasn't dating. They needed the constant verbal reminder, especially when they did things which suspiciously looked like dating, such as a non-date at the local movie theater where they shared non-date popcorn.

Ross shrugged. "It's just a work thing and I thought you might like to take a trip to the city."

"Will you take me to lunch?"

"Yes, I will take you to not-a-date lunch." He shook his head. "Although, I don't know how you're so concerned about lunch when you're eating breakfast."

"It's the key to my success, Rosso. I like to think ahead and plan," Mia responded, scooping more delicious hash onto her fork.

He studied her for a few moments. "And what you and I are doing, you've thought that through?"

Mia dropped her eyes. It wasn't as if she didn't have a reply, but she didn't have one she wanted to give. The answer was simple. No maps. No calendar. Complete denial. Not everything in her life could be packed into a neat, organized box, her relationship with him in particular. She lifted her eyes to him once again and smiled, thinking of something better. "Oh, can we go to Sacramento Shutterstop? It's supposed to be a really great camera shop and I've never been."

"Yeah, whatever you want. Are you looking for anything in particular?"

"Remember, I told you about the boutique that wanted me to take some photos for them. The woman came into Pony Expresso last week and we got to talking. I decided I want to do it. Maybe I'll pick up a real reflector at the camera store, be a real professional about it." As much as Mia wished to downplay her excitement, she did feel a thrill when talking about it. She was so used to hiding that side of her.

Ross, though, felt safe and she wasn't disappointed when he lifted her hand, pressing a kiss to her palm. "You be my navigator, and I'll take you to any camera store you want. You're a great photographer and she'll love your work."

Mia left the table with her heart full of happiness, but the feeling dissipated when she drove to her dad's house after breakfast. Despite being on edge, she planned to take a quick shower, put on fresh clothes, and then wait for Ross to pick her up so they could drive to the city together.

She was blotting her wet hair with a towel when her father appeared in the doorway.

"So, you do still live here after all. I feel like I hardly ever see you anymore. What have you been up to these days?"

This wasn't entirely correct. They'd seen each other in passing but, since their fight, there hadn't been much communication between them except for the bare minimum. Their relationship had never been awkward on the surface before. It was as though neither wanted to risk reigniting the flames. The judge, standing in her doorway and questioning her, made Mia wary.

She glanced at him as if he was a solar eclipse, and she couldn't risk staring at him for too long. "Nothing much. I've just been working and hanging out with friends."

"Hanging out? With friends?" Her father repeated the phrase as if the words themselves were unfamiliar and foreign. Perhaps, in regards to her, it did sound strange and unnatural. Even in high school, Mia didn't spend much quality time with friends outside of school.

She sighed. "I've been mostly hanging out with Ross."

As an intelligent man, her father would have no problems connecting the dots. In this case, there weren't many of them, and they were placed in a convenient straight line. But her confirmation must have proved his worst fears as his eyes grew dark and severe. "Mia—"

"I don't want to talk about it, Dad. We're going to the city. I have to finish drying my hair before he gets here."

Her father remained rooted in the doorway. It crossed her mind he might consider becoming a permanent fixture in order to prevent her from leaving. "You've changed, Mia," was all he said.

Her tongue tsked as she rolled her eyes and turned from

him. Mia grabbed her hairbrush and jammed it through her locks, glad to have a task to focus on.

"No, I mean it. You've changed," he stated again.

One part of her, the people-pleaser side, wanted to burst into tears at the disappointment in his voice. The other part, the angry Mia, pushed the people-pleaser down the stairs to barricade the door. She couldn't get past that everything her father stood for had been a lie. She was ashamed at how much she had unquestionably accepted over the years, how much she let him influence who she was. Not anymore. "I hope so. I'm almost twenty-six. You always wanted me to be an independent adult, to think critically for myself. Well, guess what? That's what I'm doing."

"I don't care how old you are. You don't just stop being my daughter."

"I know," Mia replied with resignation.

"I love you, and I only want what's best for you."

Her heart peeked out from behind the wall. "I know that, too. And I love you, Dad. But you also have to trust me to make decisions for myself, regardless if you agree or not. I know it's hard. You're used to being the sole, important voice of reason most of the time, but I don't need to be taken care of."

If she was hoping for her father's face to soften, then his unshaven jawline locking together was disappointing. "You say that, and, yet, what am I doing but taking care of you. You have a place to live. I've put money into your schooling. And for what? So you can get all indignant like you're an actual adult here. If that was your goal, young lady, you failed. You're a coffee barista."

Her reaction to these words couldn't be stopped. Tears sprung to Mia's eyes. She willed her own jaw to remain firm, for her voice not to break. "I'm working. I've done my submissions. What exactly have I done wrong here? Am I not supposed to have fun during my free time? I have spent years killing myself doing everything I was supposed to do. When do I get that small pocket of time to not worry about school or what my future is supposed to look like or do something just because I want to?" A fissure popped in her voice, and a murky, thick layer of turmoil was threatening to squeeze through the cracks.

"I've only pushed you because it's important, Mia. You've always been someone who's going places, and I don't want you to lose your focus. Getting stuck like this has never been who you are. I don't understand why you're letting this guy distract you. What happened to that drive? You've changed. And I'm only telling you this because I love you and I'm looking out for you."

She gave him one last look, one made of steel, one like her mother reserved for special occasions of justified indignation. "Well, thanks for your concern, but I'm going to the city."

Mia wasn't sure if it was her words, her expression, or a combination of both, but an invisible force swept through the room. Her father's form wavered like a malfunctioning hologram, and her eyes were granted a new view of him. It wasn't her perfect Atticus Finch, judge of a father who stood there. Instead, what she saw was a man whose shoulders were hunched from age, hair gone gray and wispy, and his features sagging from a life spent on a bench in front of troubled kids. With one last look in her direction, he turned and left behind a void of uncertainty as empty as her doorway. It was clear their relationship was on a precipice of being transformed forever and was never returning to the way it was before. Her father was right. Things had changed and it wasn't only her.

Chapter Twenty-Seven

WHEN HIS TRUCK pulled into Mia's driveway, Ross spotted her sitting on the porch. A happy feeling passed through him at the thought of Mia being eager for his arrival. But when a smile didn't light her face as she got into the passenger side, he realized his first instinct was wrong. Since climbing into his truck, she hadn't said much of anything.

"Is everything okay?" he asked.

There were a lot of adjectives he could use to describe Mia: sunny, optimistic, smart, empathetic. One word he'd never use on her was quiet.

He slid a sideways look at her profile. "Mia?"

"I'm okay. Just lost in thought," she responded.

"Is there anything you want to talk about?"

"No. I'm okay. Really." She returned to staring out the window. "It's just…things have been strained between Dad and I since lasagna night. My relationship with him has never been like this."

Ross recognized the guilt developing inside him, the knowledge his big mistake was still rippling across the surface with unintended consequences. "I'm sorry," he said. "Would you rather not have known what happened?"

She gave a slight shrug. "Would I rather look away from reality just for the sake of comfort? No. I want to know the truth, but I also don't like how this feels either. Does that make me horrible?"

Ross shifted in his seat, adjusting the seatbelt strap across his chest. "What you feel is what you feel. No one likes their world turned upside down."

"I found out my dad is not quite the moral saint I always believed him to be. I helped him put up his election signs. I was so proud thinking I was doing something great and important. I look at him now, and all I can see are his flaws. I feel silly for being naïve enough to put anyone on a pedestal. And, at the same time, I'm sad he'll probably never be there again, and I'll just continue to live with an empty pedestal. But I got exactly what I asked for. I know the truth, and I should have wanted the truth a long time ago. But compared to other people's upside-down world turning, it's very inconsequential. The size of my world is small and insignificant."

Ross regretted this conversation was occurring at a moment when he couldn't draw her to him. They were locked on their own sides of the truck. "The size of the world doesn't matter. It's your world regardless. And he's still your dad. Maybe things have changed, but you're strong enough to handle it."

Shiny eyes turned to him. "How are you not angry and bitter about all of this? I want to be angry and bitter for you. Do you want to climb up on my pedestal? I just had a spot open up."

Ross gave a short laugh. "I *have* been angry and bitter,

but ten years is a long time to hold on to all of that. And I don't want to be on any pedestal, even yours. I've screwed up way too much to know I don't deserve to be anywhere near one. Maybe you should figure out what you can do to be on your own pedestal."

The truck filled with silence again.

"What happened to your parents?" A flash of horror swept across her features. "Sorry. I didn't—I've always been curious, but you don't have to answer."

"It's okay. They were killed in an accident. It was my mom's birthday, and they wanted to go to the state line to gamble and celebrate. My grandpa was my babysitter." Mia's hand slipped into his which had been resting on his right thigh. He squeezed her hand in return. "They didn't even get there. Got a flat tire around Kyburz, pulled off to change it. But, you know, it gets so dark and curvy there. Anyway, some other car hit them."

"Oh god. That's horrible."

He nodded.

"And Luna lived with you guys, too?"

"Yeah. Apparently, my aunt was a little wild and Luna was the result of one of those times. Lulu's father was never in the picture. They both lived with us for a time but then Aunt Amy decided she needed a hundred percent fresh start and for some reason that meant moving to the other side of the country with a new husband and leaving Luna behind."

"What? I can't even understand that. Did she even stay in contact?"

"She did at first, but it got to be less and less frequent. Lulu used to get so upset, and she broke one of the windows in her bedroom. She didn't deserve to be treated like that. We would just hold her and let her cry. Anyway, that was our world."

Mia turned to the passenger window again. "I know it hasn't always been easy, but I'm glad our worlds connected. You're a good person, Ross."

He swallowed, and silence lingered in the atmosphere. No matter how casually Ross could discuss his past and his flaws, there was no denying that they continued to trail him whether he wanted it or not. After he'd taken his jewelry store responsibilities seriously, Ross preferred a life spent in the solitude of his workshop. He could put his head down and focus on work alone. Cutting himself off from most of the outside world was both intended and desired. Ross could tell himself he didn't care about society as much as it didn't care about him. The separation had been mutual.

Except this wasn't true anymore. Mia had invaded his life like a swarm of dazzling golden butterflies, and Ross realized how much he was missing. Now that he had it, he didn't want to lose it or for his world to return to one without butterflies. But, in its uncertainty, what she gave him no longer felt substantial enough.

It kinda feels like a date, she had said earlier at breakfast.

Ross didn't want it to *feel* like anything. He wanted it to *be*. But, same as knowing she would have accepted his invitation to the prom, it didn't matter in the grand scheme of their temporary companionship. And he didn't want to reveal his own hunger and vulnerability.

He would keep these locked away. Instead, he'd revel in the tiny moments. Like when her body curled into him, she'd always release a soft, satisfied sigh. His heart was filled to the brim with these little sighs.

Or when she'd pop into the store during the day bringing tea for Aanya, Americano for him, and a day-old muffin for Hermes. The smell of coffee regularly invaded his workshop like a ray of sunshine, and Mia would hug him from behind as he sat on the stool. *Hello, Rosso*, she'd say before pressing a kiss to his neck.

Her conversation used to be filled with things about scholarly papers and submissions, but lately this had been replaced with things that ignited a gleam in her eyes which had nothing to do with school. Perhaps this gave Ross the greatest hope of all.

He glanced at her at the other side of the truck cab and reached across the expanse, his fingers slipping her hair behind an ear. "Are you excited about going to your camera store?"

For the first time since she got into the truck, a spark lit her eyes. "Yes. I feel like I'm eight, and my parents just promised me a trip to the toy store."

Seeing her happy became the most important thing for him at this moment, and she had given him an easy mission to fulfill. "We'll go after I finish with the buyer."

With this, the old Mia Russo returned. Throughout lunch, she was all grins, sparkling eyes, and dimple as she teased him and made him laugh. His mind was ruthless and unforgiving in its ability to remind him this wasn't a real date. Mia wasn't a real girlfriend. What he had wasn't a real future. Still, he had become greedy and wanted it. All of it. The hand-holding, the commitment, and being able to count on a partner to share life's minutes, months, and years with. He wanted the full calendar. Going back to what Ross had before was like telling a person to be satisfied with stale bread after spoiling them with a feast. Now he could see how starved he'd allowed himself to become before Mia.

As they were leaving the sandwich shop, a voice called to her. "Mia! Mia Russo!"

They turned, and a woman with burgundy curly hair and an unflappable force, smiled a wide, toothy grin at Mia.

"Lizzy!" Mia exclaimed, and the two women launched into a full-body hug as if celebrating one of them no longer being lost. "Oh my god, I can't believe this. How are you?"

"Girly, you are in big trouble, do you know that? You're lucky I'm still talking to you. You never replied to my text."

Mia snapped a hand across her mouth. "Oh my—You're right. I did see it and then I got busy with something else and forgot. I'm so sorry."

Lizzy's deep brown eyes gave Ross's body a slow, careful perusal. "Yes, I can see you've been busy."

"Oops, sorry," Mia said. "This is my...friend, Ross. Ross, this is my cousin, Liz."

He shook her hand and said a quick hello before the two women were buzzing in conversation again as if trying to pack in as much information as possible in a minute.

"You should have told me you were coming to the city. We could have met for coffee or something. We need to catch up. I have so much to tell you about the family and, of course, they'll want to know all about what's going on in your life."

"It was a last-minute idea," Mia replied, "I'm dying to

hear how you've been."

"Well, what are you doing right now? I just got out of a meeting with a client from hell and was going to take a caffeine escape."

"Oh, well, I can't right now. We have—"

"Mia, why don't you go for coffee," Ross said.

The women stopped, both pairs of eyes turning to him.

"It's fine," he replied. "You can catch up with your cousin. I'll take care of business and then meet you at the coffee shop when I'm done. It shouldn't take me very long, and what I'm doing is not very interesting anyway."

Mia studied his face.

"Come on, cuz. I'm dying to catch up. Let's do it," Lizzy said.

She appeared to be giving it more consideration as her eyes locked with his. "Are you sure?"

He rubbed a hand across the length of her arm. "Yeah, I'm sure. It'll probably take me an hour, tops, then I'll come get you, and we can go to your store."

"Okay," Mia agreed after a moment. "We'll be in the coffee shop across the street, but I did want to see what treasure chests full of jewels look like. It does sound interesting."

"You can come with me next time," Ross assured her.

He wasn't happy about the situation, but when Mia smiled and gave him a hug, it removed some of the sting. "Thank you," she whispered in his ear.

"Okay," he said. "Go on. The faster I walk over there, the faster I'll be done."

He spent a moment watching Mia and Lizzy lost in conversation with each other, making sure they crossed the street without incident. He wasn't sure either one was paying attention to their immediate surroundings.

Ross sighed before continuing on his path alone. God, he wanted more from her. He wanted everything.

Chapter Twenty-Eight

"SO, ARE WE going to talk about the tall, dark, and handsome elephant in the room?" Lizzy asked.

Mia shook her head before taking a sip from her caramel mocha. "I was wondering how long you were going to hold out for." She eyed the clock on the wall. "It only took ten minutes. I applaud you for your restraint."

"Thank you. That's practically forever in my world." Lizzy grinned.

"Like I said earlier, he's my friend, Ross."

Her cousin snorted. "Yeah, okay. We may not be roomies anymore, but I can still detect your bullshit and right now you reek of it."

"It's complicated."

"That I believe, because Mia Russo always has to make everything complicated, even when it doesn't need to be."

"I'm beginning to remember why I hated living with you."

Lizzy laughed. "Because I'm always right?"

Her older, street-smart cousin lived for being right and she usually was. Mia also used to believe the same thing about herself, but lately history revealed that Mia didn't know as much as she thought she did.

Lizzy clapped her palms together to wake Mia from her daydream. "Quit stalling. As soon as my mom hears about this she's going to be mad I didn't drag you over for dinner with the fam. At least give me something I can offer her to soothe her disappointment."

Lizzy was right. Her Aunt Sylvia would be disappointed she was in town and didn't plan a visit. Her mother's side of the family was scattered around Sacramento and was a large, close-knit group. Growing up in Placerville, and always involved with school and extracurricular activities, meant that, as a kid, Mia always felt a little bit of an outsider with the Diego family. Visits were rare. Now that she thought about it, she wondered if the judge had something to do with this as well. Her father was also on the outside when it came to Diego family gatherings, not one to encourage a trip to Sacramento as he'd rather stay home. At the time, Mia felt protective of him. With present-day insight, it added one more additional strike against the judge. Neither she nor her mother deserved missing out. He should have tried harder to consider them.

Despite this, the family had always been welcoming whenever they did visit. When Mia decided to take the job in Sacramento, the family embraced her, including Lizzy offering her a place to stay. They became two young professionals sharing an apartment, Mia in politics and Lizzy in graphic design. During that year, she got to know her mom's side of the family. Unfortunately, she hadn't been great at staying in touch since she left the city.

"I don't want to disappoint Aunt Sylvia, but I doubt Ross wants to be dragged to an impromptu family reunion only to be peppered with questions like I'm currently getting from my very annoying cousin."

"We were always nice to Tom and we didn't pepper him with questions...much. Although, I don't think any of us wanted to know him any further than we had to. Did he finally land that corporate lawyer job?"

"I have no idea. I don't make it a habit of keeping up with ex-boyfriends." She was glad they were no longer together. Probably the only person who wasn't pleased with the breakup was her dad, who really liked Thomas. She could now see how her ex had always dictated the terms of her relationship, and, like a good people-pleaser, Mia went along with it. Perhaps there was a good reason Lizzy always mispronounced his name as Thom-ass in the privacy of their apartment.

"You don't make it a habit of keeping up with your family and friends either." Lizzy propped her chin on a palm. "But what about new boyfriends?"

"I told you, it's complicated."

Lizzy dismissed her words with a swift wave of her hand. "Well, you definitely have something. Let me offer this observation. If someone were to take a photo of you now and compare it to one taken during the campaign, night and day. However you're living life now, it obviously agrees with you. Whatever it is, let's package it. I'll design the marketing around it, and we'll sell it and rake in millions. You and me, fifty/fifty partners. In fact, I'll be an owner and a customer. After this last client meeting, I'm close to hitchhiking all the way to Ol' Hangtown myself and starting over."

"I can't imagine you doing small-town living."

"We haven't confirmed if it's small-town living or small-town loving yet." Lizzy's eyebrows wiggled with humor.

Mia leaned against her hand, letting the reality of the situation somber her. "It doesn't matter. It's temporary small-town whatever because I've applied for my doctorate and I'm not staying."

"And I've never seen someone look so miserable about it."

"I'm living with my dad and working in a coffee shop, I should be ecstatic. I don't know what's wrong with me."

"I noticed you're not grouping your *it's complicated* friend, Ross, in there." Lizzy did lazy bunny ear quotations with one hand around the phrase *it's complicated.*

"Ross is…" Mia tried to think of what she wanted to say, but nothing seemed adequate. "I don't know," she confessed, dropping her forehead on the table.

"That doesn't sound like the Mia Russo I know. Do you like him?"

"Yes," Mia murmured into the hard surface. "He's talented and smart and puts up with me and kisses like a dream." She popped her head up, supporting it on her palm. "But at the same time, it's like what am I even doing, Liz? I'm leaving. Thomas broke up with me because of the whole long-distance thing, and it does make things complicated. But every time I get an email, I'm worried it'll be the one that'll take me away. I'm not being fair to him or to me, and we should stop, but I can't help myself. I get around him, and instead of seeing bright red lights, the lights are all yellow, and I'm jamming my foot on the gas, trying to get through the intersection before it turns red." Mia dropped her head on the table again with a thump. "I hate me."

"I mean, have you considered…" Lizzy's sentence died almost as soon as it began.

Mia returned to her cousin's brown eyes. "What?"

Lizzy tried again. "Have you considered maybe not jumping back into school and just seeing where things take you? Maybe being back in your hometown has been a good thing, and your future is something else. You can take a breath and reassess what you really want. I can tell you right now, it wasn't campaigning. Watching you do that job was like being between two parents who stayed together even though you could tell both of them despised each other. Staying for the kids is never a good thing."

"Do you think I'm stuck?"

Lizzy's expression became serious. "No. I refuse to believe that. You are good at working with people and selling your ideas. Like me, you just have to find your people, those that have your same ideals. They're out there."

Mia gave Lizzy a flat look. "Ugh, when did you become more optimistic than me?"

Lizzy laughed at this. "It's not optimism, it's the truth and you know I'm a blatant truth-teller. People always think the truth is what they want it to be, not what it is. Anyway, you deserve to enjoy living your life, Mia, instead of constantly pushing yourself toward something."

"Or you could be wrong."

"Possibly, but you act like dream kissers are waiting around every corner. I can tell you, they're not."

"Okay, but you're painting a future with nothing but kisses—"

"What's wrong with that?"

"It's a fantasy. And I don't know what that future actually looks like. I don't like a mysterious future, it terrifies me."

"Every future is a fantasy until you make it happen."

Mia released an exasperated sigh. "Okay, thanks, Mom. God, you're really making me regret running into you. Do you know what you're making me give up right now?"

"Making out with Ross in a back alley somewhere?" Lizzy guessed with a smile.

"How about we talk about you and your life? Give me a chance to offer you some advice. Are you still doing graphic design work?"

Lizzy's gaze drifted away. "Yeah, I'm mostly freelancing. It can be a real drag some days. I'm currently doing some design work for a new tech startup called Garbandzo, it helps small bands set up local gigs. Oh, I've also been working with a nonprofit group." Her eyes brightened. "You should look into them. They advocate for justice reform measures. They're a really great group although a bit disorganized. I'm pretty sure they could use someone with your skillset. I mean, there isn't any money or national prestige but, you never know, they might be your people."

Mia paused. Maybe Lizzy was right. Maybe she had been looking for her people but had been looking for them in all the wrong places.

"Your man friend has returned." Lizzy nodded her chin to the door.

Mia glanced behind her in time to observe Ross's handsome form strolling through the threshold.

"That was fast," she said.

He took a seat beside her. "Was it? It took me at least an hour. You two must have had a lot to talk about."

Mia peered at her half-empty drink. It wasn't her favorite and she no longer had the desire to finish it.

"I was just telling Mia that I think small-town life suits her glowing complexion, and she should consider sticking around. Why mess with a good complexion?" Lizzy said without an ounce of subtlety.

Ross's eyes met Mia's, and they warmed to burning embers as he slipped an arm along the back of her chair. Mia resisted leaning into him, knowing if she gave in to the warmth, she might never crawl out again. It would be like trying to leave the coziest of beds on the coldest of mornings.

"Hopefully, she listens to you more than she listens to me," he said.

"Did you get your business taken care of? Did you buy all the jewels?" Mia asked, eager to change the subject.

"Jewels?" Lizzy's eyebrows jumped on her forehead. "What do you do?"

"I'm a jeweler," Ross said with minimum fanfare.

"To be more specific, Ross designs and makes jewelry. He made these earrings." Mia swept her hair away to flash the sparkling pendants dangling from her ears.

"Ah, I love them. Do you have a business card or a website? My mom's birthday is coming up and she loves unique jewelry," Lizzy said.

Ross reached into his pocket and removed his wallet.

"I thought you didn't have business cards," Mia accused.

"I never said that. I said *you* couldn't have one." Ross dropped a small white card on the table.

Mia snatched it up. "How old are these? You really should get new ones with the Etsy shop address." She pulled a pen from her purse and wrote the web address on the backside. "You should check out his online shop, Lizzy. I'm not the designer here, but you'll at least love the jewelry." Mia handed the card to her cousin when she finished writing on it.

Lizzy's brown eyes studied it. "Have you ever considered re-branding?" she asked Ross.

Oh, god. She knew the exact point of destination Lizzy was heading. Is this what Ross had to deal with when Mia came bounding in with her ideas? Was she still doing it? A tinge of shame seeped into Mia's bones.

"Uh, no," he responded. "It was started by my grandfather, so it's been the same for a long time."

"I see," Lizzy replied. "Well, I don't mean you should get rid of the family legacy or anything but maybe consider adding the legacy to your brand. What's your grandfather's name?"

"Victor Lanza."

"I'm sure El Dorado Jewelry has been a part of your family for a long time, but the name is pretty generic. Something like Lanza Fine Jewelry identifies your shop as something unique and special while honoring your family. People like that. It's putting a family history behind the place, which is great for an old town like Placerville. I'm willing to put in a little work into helping you out if you'd like to redesign your brand." She tapped the edge of the card against her chin. "I do like those earrings and I'm a person who likes things nice and *uncomplicated*, especially when it comes to friends and family." She winked at Mia. "Also, I'm sure you're not like the nightmare customer I currently have. Speaking of which, I really should get back to work."

Mia stood as Lizzy did. "I'm glad we were able to catch up, Lizzy. Don't let Aunt Sylvia get too angry with me. I promise to plan a special trip and see everyone before I leave for school."

Lizzy pulled her into a hug. "You better. And don't ignore my texts. I'm one of your people so you're not allowed."

After waving to Ross, Lizzy was gone. Mia returned to her chair.

"Are you ready for your camera shop?" Ross asked.

She took a deep breath. "Ross, my cousin has a tendency to run away with an idea once it gets in her brain. You shouldn't feel pressured to change anything if what you're doing is working for you."

He gave her an amused look. "I would say that's ironic coming from you."

"The fact that you're not wrong doesn't make me feel particularly good about myself. It is your business, and you need to be happy with it. I know I should keep my nose out of it. I'm sorry if you ever felt I was acting like a pushy, boss lady. I'll try to be less so."

He drew her to his chest, and this time she let him. It was like slipping on her favorite sweater. "You may be a bit of a know-it-all boss lady, but it doesn't mean your ideas aren't good and that I don't need a little push in the right direction every once in a while. And maybe your cousin has the right idea, too. I kind of like the idea of having Lanza in the name. It's something I can talk to Lulu about."

She closed her eyes as she accepted the transfer of comfort from his body into hers. "Okay, whatever you guys decide. I'll do what I can to help out. Not because you need it, but because I like being a part of your jewelry world."

Ross didn't say anything for a few moments, his arm tightened around her, and he rested his cheek on her head. "Alright, should we go?"

"You seem to be just as excited as I am about this camera store."

"Maybe I'm excited to see an eight-year-old Mia go on a toy store shopping spree."

She laughed as they stood before giving his face careful examination, her mind returning to the conversation she had with Lizzy. She tried to picture what a different future could be. As hard as she attempted to imagine, the vision was too limited, like wearing a pair of sunglasses at night. But Mia couldn't deny the balloon of happiness inflating within her chest, testing the capacity of her ribcage.

As they departed the coffee shop, she slipped her hand into his.

Chapter Twenty-Nine

Ross was in the workshop but could hear Aanya speaking to someone inside the store. He found it easy to block distracting noises and returned to his work until he heard a laugh. *Her* laugh. Ross would recognize Mia's laughter anywhere, and it stopped his activity in an instant.

He lifted his magnifier glasses to the top of his head and glanced at the vintage analog clock with the yellowing face. It was almost closing time. They didn't have any formal plans to get together, although they rarely made them. Everything between them happened in a casual, spontaneous way. Ross and Mia were drawn to each other. Time between meetings was never very long, and either she sought him out or the other way around.

He was tinkering with an old camera he wanted to give to Mia for her birthday but hid it away, deciding to investigate the activity in the shop. As soon as Ross pushed through the workshop door, their gazes collided. Mia gave him a smile, complete with a dimple, as bright as the sun as she crouched down to place a simple wildflower wreath on Hermes's head. He was still surprised to learn there was an actual beating organ inside his body. He could hear the blood pulsating inside his head.

"Well, well, well. If it isn't my favorite bench jeweler."

"Hey, Mia. I should be finished up soon."

"Someone's getting a bit egotistical. How do you know I'm here to chat with you?"

"I knew from the first day you walked into my store."

"Considering that you were the only one working that day, you were pretty much my only option."

Oh, he was for sure going to make her pay for that one. But he realized their eyes had locked onto each other as if they were the only two people in the store. He blushed when Aanya, who stood between them, cleared her throat.

"Well, I'm off. I'll leave you two kids to enjoy your evening," Aanya said, moving toward the office to gather her personal items.

"Aw, Aanya, I was hoping you could help me convince Ross to put some images on the shop wall." Mia kept her eyes, lighted with humor, still focused on him.

He shook his head in response. Mia would never give up until she'd whittled his resolve from redwood log to toothpick.

Aanya strolled out with her purse under her arm and tugged her jacket into place over her stout shoulders. "I don't think it's a good idea for me to get in the middle. I'm sure you two can handle it quite well. Do you want me to open up the store tomorrow, Ross?"

"Why would you need to open it up? I can do it."

"Just offering. Well, I'll see you tomorrow then."

After Aanya walked out, he locked the door and flipped the open sign around.

"Now that Aanya is gone, looks like I'm your only option again," Ross said as he flicked off some of the main shop lights, bringing the level of dimness to a fraction above dangerous.

"Huh. Funny how that worked out. Maybe your ego is on to something after all." Her voice revealed nothing but a general pleasantness even as her eyes sparkled.

"What were you ladies talking about?" He made his way to the workshop with Mia trailing behind him.

"Just what I said. I was trying to recruit her into talking to you about putting images on your walls. Your walls are tired of being naked."

He removed his leather apron, hanging it on the door hook before giving her face a slow perusal. She really was quite lovely. Every time he found himself facing her, he had nothing but a desire to sink his face into the different parts of her. "You've never had a problem with naked before. And what happened to your promise of not being a pushy boss lady regarding my business?"

Mia's mouth opened to speak before it shut again, and she pressed a hand across her face.

Pleased with her lack of snappy comeback, he smiled, pulling her to his chest. He placed his lips to her ear. "I finally won one. I think I'll savor this moment forever."

She lifted her face, revealing a pout. "Okay, you got me. But I didn't know that meant I was expected to quit cold turkey. This suddenly seems very unfair."

He laughed before pressing a kiss to her forehead and releasing her. Ross returned to his work stool and organized his space. "You said it. I'm just here to remind you."

"Hmm," Mia replied. "It's very considerate of you but

also very aggravating."

"How about this? You and Aanya can look over your images, and pick the ones you like best. With the online store doing well, I can probably figure something out with our budget."

"Okay, now it's *extremely* aggravating. Where did this easygoing Ross come from? I came all the way over here—"

"Yes, so far." He rolled his eyes.

"*All the way* over here to seduce you into making some improvements to your shop and, just like that, you foil everything. I hope you're happy because I'm certainly not. Making convincing, seductive arguments is the only fun I have these days."

He took his time to study her body with the appreciation it deserved while he bit into his own lower lip. "Don't mind me. I'm certainly not looking to ruin your fun."

Mia pushed her way between Ross's stool and his workbench. "I should hope not."

He locked his arms on either side of her, boxing her in. "If you ask for something else, I promise to be more difficult." The workshop was not the place for any kind of romantic rendezvous with its poor lighting, surfaces covered in plaster dust, and old machinery. Besides, he could have her home in ten minutes and do things properly. Mia enjoyed teasing him and talking big, but that's all it usually was. This didn't stop his brain from taking an unexpected detour, his mind wandering across the activities he'd like to do at this moment. There were parts of him that didn't care about things like impracticalities and plaster dust.

She grinned even wider. "You being difficult does make

things more fun."

"When trying to get what you want, you don't consider torture, do you? I'm embarrassed to say I'm not as tough as I look. I break easily."

"Do you consider this torturous?" She planted a slow kiss upon his lips. It grew and flourished at a leisurely pace, spreading pleasure throughout his body. It was warm and smooth like syrup, and he had already developed a vicious sweet tooth for the stuff.

"Actually, yes," he said when she pulled away. Everything Mia did made him want to lose his damn mind. Maintaining his ability to think straight could be construed as torture of the worst kind, especially when it came to his body's internal thudding.

She laughed at him, running fingers through his hair. Her expression was carefree and filled with light. "You poor, tortured man. How you suffer. Did you have a good work day?"

"Pretty normal. You didn't work today?"

Mia smelled of sunshine rather than coffee. "Nope, I walked around town with my camera. Natalie said we could host a special local artist thing at the end of the summer and I'm thinking about submitting something. I got my inspiration from my Día de los Muertos experience when I went with her. I thought about taking images of colorful items around town in order to create a photo collage. The images on their own won't look like much but as a whole it's going to look like a graphic version of a marigold, the same flower used in Día de los Muertos altars. It's just something I want to do in memory of my mom."

While there was a touch of bittersweet sadness to Mia, he could also detect some of the inspired gleam as well. Ross rubbed his hands along the length of her arms. "I really like that idea. It's like you're creating a quilt from photos. I think it's the perfect way of honoring her."

"A photo quilt. Yes, I love that. Anyway, Natalie has been texting me all day about things I can take pictures of that are on the gold color spectrum. It's actually been fun just walking around town and looking at the old buildings in a different way."

"Good. I'm glad you're doing it. Have you heard anything lately from any of the programs you applied to?"

Her face lost some of its sunniness, her focus drew to the security window between his workshop and the storefront. Ross kicked himself. He shouldn't have said anything, but it had been awhile since she mentioned it. If he was going to face something unpleasant, he liked to have a chance to prepare his heart. It wasn't fair to leave him unprotected.

"Mia?"

"Is that window really one-way?" They could see out into the empty shop, but it was a mirror on the opposite side.

"You've been on the other side of it, so you should know," he replied.

Mia gave it one final examination before saddling onto his lap and weaving an arm around his neck. She kissed him with an aggressive appetite as if her sole desire was to melt him down one kiss at a time, leaving a puddle of molten metal on the floor.

With both of them sharing one seat, their physical situation was risky, but Ross no longer cared. He had his own hunger to satisfy. His hands followed their own travel itinerary unimpeded as he sought a deeper connection with Mia, slipping a hand under her sweater and palming a breast. Touching her, hearing her breath hitch, became all consuming.

Mia had her own agenda as the hand on his chest made its way to the top of his pants, undoing the button. He didn't mind fooling around, but this wasn't the best place for anything more, especially for someone like Mia. She deserved something better than an old, grungy workshop.

"Mia," he said while breaking away, "I don't think—"

"Ross, when I think of you during the day, I think of you here, making your pretty jewelry, and I like it."

He pushed a strand of hair behind her ear and imparted a gentle kiss on her lips. "When I think of you during the day, I imagine you with a soft, daydream look on your face because your brain is busy thinking up beautiful thoughts. The sparking between neurons must make the inside of your head look like it's filled with glitter."

Mia's full lips parted before providing a smile so sweet he couldn't help kissing her again. That's twice in one night he'd won their verbal sparring and it provided a wonderful boost to his ego. But it was his turn to be speechless when she removed herself from his embrace and stood. With a confident look, she undid her pants, the clothes on the lower half of her body slid to the ground in a graceful striptease. Ross's mouth must have jarred open at the sight.

He hated himself for putting an end to anything so beautiful. "I don't have a condom."

"I told you, I'm on birth control. No STDs. Are you

good?"

He nodded.

She returned to straddling him on the stool, and he swallowed hard as she finished undoing his pants, pulling out the full length of him and stroking it.

"I want you." Her words were needy and breathless.

"You can have whatever you want."

"Good." She captured his lips before lifting her hips and taking him inside her.

God. She reduced him to a quivering pile of groans. He clung to her as a firestorm blazed through his veins. A dewy sheen developed across her neck, and Ross couldn't resist placing his lips there, wishing to lick the sweet drops from her skin. Possessive fingers gripped her thighs tighter as he made her work him over harder, faster. What would she ask from him? Jewels? Hers. His business? Hers. Hell, he might even give her Hermes if she asked him at this moment. Would she ask for his heart? The others were less risky to give in comparison. But when he came into her with an uncontrolled shudder and moan, he knew his heart was already on a platter, befitting an offering. How could it be anything different? His DNA had been completely dismantled and rewritten with her name grafted onto every sequence.

"I think you made a tactical error," he said, panting hard. "You went straight to torture and never asked for anything."

She pressed a kiss to him. "I think I got exactly what I wanted."

To be fair, he didn't ask for anything either, and he wouldn't.

Chapter Thirty

"LANZA JEWELRY?" Ross's cousin tested the phrase on the other end of the phone. "First photography on the walls and now this. Although, it all makes sense to me. Grandpa would have liked it. Maybe we can do some special relaunch for the shop's thirty-fifth anniversary next year or something."

"Yeah, that's a good idea," Ross agreed.

"I'm really proud of you."

He stared at the scenery outside his kitchen window as he drank a beer, not allowing Luna's words to penetrate too deep. "What? Why? I didn't come up with the idea."

"Because," Luna replied, "instead of being the bitter, old-at-heart guy hiding in the back of the shop all the time, you're opening yourself up to new ideas and considering them. That's a big deal."

"I'm not *that* stubborn," Ross protested.

"I tell you all the time. You're a smart guy. You just have to trust yourself more."

It didn't matter how many times someone told him this. The compliment made him uncomfortable. "Yeah, well, I'm just doing the best I can in trying to manage this without you."

"You're doing fine. Besides, it doesn't sound like you're completely alone."

"Aanya does well. I think she charms more sales than you ever did."

Luna didn't miss a beat. "And Mia?"

He lifted his bottle to the light to see how much beer remained, trying to decide if he should grab another one. Hermes settled at his feet with a deep sigh. "I would tell you that she doesn't work for the store, but I have to give her credit since the online shop she created is pulling in regular business. Our mail lady has gotten into the habit of asking for pickup packages whenever she stops in."

"Nice sidestep. I only care about it on a personal level, and I would say she's been good for you. I'm glad you found someone nice, Ross. I can't wait to meet her when I'm back for the summer."

"Maybe."

"What do you mean maybe? Do you not want me to meet her?"

"No, I do. It's just—I don't know, Lu."

There was a moment of silence before Luna pushed ahead. "You guys are together, right?"

Frustration simmered inside of him. Any other relationship, any other woman, the answer would have been clear. If it had been a multiple choice question, all three options would have the same word: *Yes.* Mia liked him. He was wild about her. She was in his bed so frequently, it felt like something was missing if he didn't fall asleep with his arms wrapped around her. He was even planning something special for her birthday in a few weeks. This temporary relationship had already lasted longer than any of Ross's previous ones, and it seemed more real. Every single ingredient that made up a steady, growing relationship was there except for the most important ingredient of all—verbalized commitment.

He massaged the space between his eyebrows. A headache was on the horizon. "I don't want to talk about this with you."

"Who else are you going to talk to? Hermes? Seriously, Ross, you can talk to me if you want. I'll even do minimum Judgy McJudgerson."

"Yeah, right. Besides, what do you know about these things?"

"I've had a relationship or two."

"Does dating someone for a month count as a relationship these days? We've had Brita filters longer than some of your relationships."

"I can't help it if I'm particular. And I don't think you're one to talk."

Ross scoffed and almost choked on his drink. "*Particular* is a funny way to say Judgy McJudgerson, Lulu."

"Whatever. I'm not completely naïve on the topic of love," Luna said, her voice fringed with hurt.

He was about to snap back at this statement because what Ross had wasn't love. But the words became stuck in his throat. At the same time, he didn't trust himself to recognize it. This was something that happened to other people.

Ross and his bottle of beer settled on the couch in the living room. He leaned his head against the top of the sofa.

"To be honest, I don't even know how to define whatever it is that we have. Fling, I guess. All I know is that whenever Mia talks about the future, I'm nowhere close to being in it."

"You've had flings before, and they never seemed to bother you."

"I guess because I was the flinger and this time, I'm being flung."

Luna laughed. "I believe we have a name for this, and it rhymes with *schmarma*."

"I thought you said you were going to hold off on judging."

"I said minimum judging, which means there will still be *some* judging. Let's put it this way, instead of getting a gut buster, half-pound burger, you're getting a gourmet slider made from the most tender of judgment."

When he didn't respond, she continued. "So, I take it you don't want this to be a fling."

"It doesn't matter what I want," he muttered in grumpy resignation.

"Of course it matters."

"No, it really doesn't. She's already applied to all these programs. It's only a matter of time before she's gone. What exactly am I supposed to say? *Don't go*? I can't do that. This is something I can't compete against, so I'm not even going to try. And even if I was able to say something, what exactly would I be offering her to make the sacrifice worth it? I don't have much. We've scraped by our whole lives and no matter how many sales we make, I can't imagine anything differently. I'll probably end up in a secondhand coffin. Plus, her father hates me, and Mia deserves someone better." He didn't mean to express so much, but it all came rushing forth like an avalanche of frustration.

"You're offering her *you*—"

"That's not enough."

He must have shocked her because there was silence on the other end of the phone.

"Have you told her this?"

He set his bottle on an end table before running a hand through his hair. "No, of course not."

"I think—"

"I'm not telling her," Ross interrupted.

"I don't think you necessarily need to tell her all that. But, since it sounds like you've never even had a conversation on the topic, maybe give her something, so she knows she has a different option if she wants it."

"What? Of course, she has an option. Mia always has the option to stay here in town if she chooses. She doesn't need me to tell her that."

"A lot of mistakes can happen because of assumptions. Maybe she feels like she has to go. Maybe she doesn't think you're open to committing. Maybe she's never considered it. You're not going to know if you don't have a conversation about it."

Ross considered his cousin's words. In the early days, Mia discussed her future freely, but she appeared resigned more than anything else. It was as though her fate was decided, and Mia accepted it with a shrug of her shoulders. These days though, she never wanted to discuss it, preferring to talk about setting up the local artist showcase at Pony Expresso instead. Perhaps she had changed her mind.

It had all become complicated and he hated complication. "And if she stays and it doesn't work out between us, then I just ruined her life for nothing. I've been disappointing people my whole life, and you know it. I don't want to do it anymore." Ross was afraid his Atlas lacked the upper body strength to hold the globe of Mia's hopes for the future. He'd rather not hold it at all.

"Good grief, Ross. I'm not telling you to kidnap the woman and force her to be with you. I'm only saying you offer her an alternative and let her make the choice. Yes, she can make a decision to just stay in Placerville if she wants, but that's jumping into a completely unknown situation. I don't know anything about Mia, but I would be scared. Besides, even if she does decide to go, it doesn't have to be the end of it. People have made long-distance relationships work before, and she won't be in the program forever."

"She could be gone for years and out of state. I'm trying to run a business. She'll be knee-deep in her education, and even after she finishes, she'll have to go to where the jobs are. Placerville probably doesn't have a lot of opportunities for someone with a doctorate in political science. And I'll still be here, fiddling in the workshop, the same old Ross."

"What exactly do you want? No excuses. Just straight want."

Ross didn't have Mia's vault of fancy words ready to be used at a moment's notice. All he had were the raw words of longing for something out of his reach. "I want Mia. I want all of her and everything that comes with it."

"Alright, then. Talk to her. If you feel you're going to lose her anyway, what do you lose by telling the truth about how you feel? And if you let her walk away without saying anything, then you don't deserve her."

Chapter Thirty-One

"HE ASKED ME to go camping with him for my birthday," Mia moaned to Natalie after explaining why she had to trade her weekend schedule with one of her coworkers. She draped her upper body across the counter. Her despair over the situation warranted it.

"You don't like camping? My family loves to go camping near Tahoe," Natalie said.

"I don't know. I've never been."

"Wait. Like *never*-never? M, look at me and tell me you're joking. What about when you were a kid?" Natalie shared a look with the customer who stood at the register. "You hear this, Fran? Mia, here, has never gone camping and now she's freaking out."

Mia snapped up and began putting Fran's regular drink order together. "I slept in a tent at a friend's sleepover one time, but it was in the backyard. And I'm not freaking out...not much anyway."

"That doesn't count." Natalie replied while finishing the transaction.

"Doesn't count," Fran agreed.

"My mom wasn't one for roughing it, so we never went. I've always wanted to try it, though."

Natalie turned to face her. "Then why are you upset about your jewelry man taking you camping? And he's doing it for your birthday? That sounds really sweet."

"I'm not upset about the camping. I'm just..." Mia couldn't think of the words to express her frustration and instead flung her hands in the air with a groan.

"Is it not going well between you two?"

"Is the magic gone in bed?" Fran guessed.

Mia and Natalie both swung their gazes to the octogenarian who seemed more at home tending geraniums rather than engaging in sex talk.

"Good lord, Fran. Here's your drink." Mia waited until the customer got bored and scuffled her way outside.

"Okay so what is it?" Natalie asked when it was quiet again.

"It's not him." Her palms pressed into her eyes to keep from crying. "He's great as usual. He's planning the whole trip and won't let me do more than bring s'more supplies." Her voice broke. "I love s'mores."

"Then what's the—"

"I've been accepted into a program. And it's in Texas." The time for ignoring maps and calendars had reached its conclusion. She'd become a doctoral candidate.

Natalie's mouth formed into an *O* shape before her own face fell into a frown. "Does this mean you're leaving? Are you giving me your two weeks' notice?"

"Yes. No. I mean, I don't have to be there right away. The program doesn't start until the end of August but I'll probably leave sometime this summer, so I can find a place to live and get settled in. But I really haven't decided on a firm date yet."

"Does the jewelry man know yet?"

"No," she whined. Not even her dad knew. Mia had kept her video interviews with faculty committees quiet. To be honest, she was surprised to be accepted when all her answers were practiced and her smiles forced. She accepted the first offer just to get the whole thing over with. "It doesn't make any sense. I was so eager to leave when I first got here, and now I just want to cry. I know not telling Ross is selfish, but I just want us to be in our bubble a little longer before reality bashes its way through."

Natalie sniffed. "Who cares about jewelry men and camping and true love? What about me?"

Mia stifled a laugh between tears. "Right? I'm going to miss working with you so much. You've really been the best. We'll still be friends, right? I've never been great at keeping in touch with people, but I want to be better. And I'm sure I'll be back for visits."

Natalie pulled her into a big hug. "Oh my god, you better, M. You're like my best adult friend that I'm not related to. Can I say congratulations at least, even if you know I completely resent it?"

Mia nodded again, but the congratulations felt empty in her heart. She didn't feel like celebrating.

WITH THE TRUCK unloaded and the tent set up at Camino Cove campsite, Mia moved toward the shore's edge. This part of El Dorado National Forest was more woodsy and peaceful than Placerville. The air was crisp and sharp while light breezes teased her hair during the warm May day. The waters of Camino Cove were a flat mirror of moss-colored glass. She took a deep breath, her nostrils filled with the spicy scent of pine needles and nature.

She rotated her view to the campsite. Ross, with Hermes at his side, was busy setting up the propane stove. Here was a man who wasn't able to let tasks go undone. As long as there was something to be taken care of, he was doing it.

Mia lifted her camera, and took pictures of the surrounding wilderness. A few colorful tents dotted the landscape. Even with neighbors, they were as secluded as they could be. She returned to the campsite, the dry sand and pebbles crunching beneath her shoes.

"It finally happened. Now I'm worried about bears and wishing I brought some bear spray. If one comes by, he's probably going to come straight for the person who brought the s'more supplies." Mia pointed to herself to make the statement more obvious.

His gaze shifted to her. "So getting through to you isn't a lost cause? Good to know."

She narrowed her eyes, peering into the dark forest thicket for any large, suspicious bear-like shadows. "For someone who worries about bears, you don't seem particularly nervous."

"We've got Hermes. He'll protect us."

She eyed the dog, all three legs of him. "If you tell me he lost his leg saving you from a bear attack on a past camping trip, I'll probably believe you. All I care about is being assured I'm not going to end up as bear shit this weekend."

Ross concentrated on re-doing the circle of rocks around a makeshift campfire pit and filling it with fresh logs. "I don't know how fast a bear's digestive system is, but I don't think it's that fast. I would probably guess maybe mid-week would be more realistic. He'd probably still be hungry from hibernation."

"Smartass."

Ross's eyes remained averted from hers, but a smile slid across his face at her response. He did have a beautiful one. She decided it was worth the risk of bears to see it, and she was *really* going to miss it. Mia wondered if an uglier smile would make things easier. Probably not. He could have only a single tooth in his whole mouth, and she'd miss ol' toothy and his one-eyed dog.

There was a long log nearby with Ross's backpack leaning against one end. It was the perfect place for her to relax while watching him, and Mia took a seat at the opposite end of the blue backpack. When her weight settled on it, there was a brief moment of confusion as her view of the world became skewed. Her final resting spot was sprawled in the dirt. The logs of the world seemed to be in a conspiracy to make Mia appear as klutzy as possible.

"Ugh, I'm beginning to think my mom had the right idea," she complained as she righted herself and patted the dirt from her clothes.

"Oh, yeah. I was going to warn you that the log wasn't completely level."

"Thanks, I think I figured that out." Her palms pressed on the log to make it steadier before trying it again. It wobbled but being more prepared, she didn't fall.

Ross approached the log with Hermes at his heels and sat at the other end near his backpack. This made her sitting position more precarious as her end tilted beneath his weight. "Ross!" Mia yelled, clamping on to the sides as if it were about to transform from tree into bucking bronco.

"You know who Archimedes is?" he asked.

"I'm going to guess some ancient Greek so-and-so. Philosopher?"

"If this was a class, you just earned a red checkmark." He scooted six inches closer toward her end of the log. "He was an ancient mathematician and inventor."

"Did he also take a girl camping and find it amusing when she fell off a log into the dirt? Maybe there was a lesson for you to learn, but you completely missed it."

"I don't know. But he was the one who said, *Eureka.*"

Mia knew the answer to this one. "I've found it."

He inched closer on the log, dragging his backpack with him. "That's right."

"So it doesn't have anything to do with an old prospector striking gold?"

"Maybe some discoveries can feel like the same thing."

"If you're attempting to seduce me, I have to tell you it's working."

He scooted closer, his position approaching the center of the log. Mia decided to remain fixed at her end. She didn't want to make it too easy for him when he was already playing with all the cheat codes.

"He was also the first to understand the concept of a lever. If your seesaw is uneven, the person who weighs more can move toward the center and, before you know it, the lever will be even. It's all about balancing each other out."

Mia blinked, her eyes dropping to the log. She shifted her weight, and it didn't budge. It was as steady as the ground underneath. "Okay. Well done. But this means you're stuck in that spot forever."

When her eyes lifted again, Ross held a small vintage camera in his hand. "Eureka," he said.

If the log wasn't as solid as it was, Mia would have fallen off it once again. Confusion descended on her brain. "What?"

"I...uh...finally checked out that junk shop across the street and Gary gave me a good deal on this, because I told him it was for your birthday. I've cleaned it up and put some film in it. I didn't know if you prefer black-and-white or color, but I took a chance and got color film."

"You got me a vintage camera?" Mia wasn't sure if she wanted to cry or laugh or maybe a combination of both.

"Yeah. Are you going to take it, or am I just going to hold onto it all day?"

She scrambled toward him, uneven levers be damned. She took it in her hand, letting the expensive Samsung hang on its strap, forgotten. "It's a Hawkeye."

"I know. Trust me, I've been over every part of that camera. I think some kind of tiny spider used to live inside of it. I thought maybe you might want to take some images for your marigold collage."

"You got me a Hawkeye."

Ross's face scrunched in confusion. "Do you like it or not? I'm having trouble figuring it out."

Mia nodded as she turned the black Bakelite body over

in her hands, chewing on her bottom lip. Her eyes must have decided crying would be the best reaction. "I don't think I've ever gotten a more thoughtful gift before."

"What about that expensive camera around your neck? This one only cost me five bucks. The shipping of the film cost me more."

"The Samsung was payment for services rendered, not a gift. There's really film in here, Ross? I can take pictures with it?"

"Yeah. Do you want me to show you how to use it?"

"You know how?"

"I watched a YouTube video on it."

Mia considered Ross sweet, but he was growing sweeter with each passing moment. She suspected there was honey running through his veins instead of blood. This might be the real secret behind why she found his kisses to be perfect. They were laced with a genetically modified sugar, created to be more addictive. The idea she would have to go through withdrawal sounded like an absolute nightmare.

"Show me, please," Mia replied, scooting close enough to lean against his chest as his arms encompassed her frame.

He demonstrated how to wind the film, open the shutter to take an image, and how to create a long exposure.

"With only twelve shots, it feels like a lot of pressure. What if I screw up?" Mia asked.

"Then we buy more film. It's not a big deal."

"What should I take a picture of?"

"Whatever you want. It's your camera."

Mia's gaze searched the surrounding area as she considered this. When it landed on Hermes, the dog gave her a slight wag of his tail and a single bark. These days the pooch was more active, becoming spritely once again.

"Hey, Hermes, do you want to be a beautiful model for me? You just can't wiggle around too much, or you may end up out of focus, and we won't know until we get the film developed." The dog responded with another bark and wiggled around even more. "I don't know if handsome here is going to cooperate. Can you hold him?"

"You want to take a picture of the dog and me?" Ross asked.

"Sure." Mia stood to face him on the log. "I should have at least one photo of the pair of you for my scrapbook, then I have something to look back fondly on."

She may have caught a dark flash in Ross's eyes, and she internally cursed herself for being careless with her words. But when she glanced at him again, there was nothing there.

"Come here, boy," Ross called, patting his lap to catch the dog's attention.

Hermes responded as if he lived and breathed to be noticed by Ross. He scrambled on the log, snuggling into the man's chest and lavished his owner's neck with sloppy dog kisses. Mia wished she and the dog could change positions, with Hermes taking the picture instead. There was a good chance the dog wouldn't mind. He didn't have one jealous bone in his whole body. Mia should be more like Hermes.

Her eyes dropped to the viewfinder located at the top of the camera, centering her favorite subjects, and swiping her hair behind an ear. "How did you get Hermes? Was he from the animal shelter?" She pushed the shutter button, and it made a satisfying click in response. Mia would gladly fill the whole film roll with images of Ross and Hermes. Wherever she ended up living, she could have her own refrigerator covered in their pictures.

"Are you implying Hermes doesn't look like a pedigree from a top breeder? This is the best dog in the world." Ross released the squirming, excited animal, who returned to the task of sniffing for small animal clues in the dirt. "He showed up at the shop one day, looking pitiful, and wouldn't leave me alone until I finally gave in and let him stay."

Mia returned to her seat on the log as she twisted the knob on the Hawkeye, preparing for the next shot. She chuckled at Ross's response. "It seems like Hermes and I share the same friend-seeking technique. I don't know how I feel about this. Either he's a genius, or I'm not as smart as I thought. Let's go with the first option."

"I thought it seemed familiar. I'm obviously the world's biggest sucker."

"Well, Hermes's method paid off, and now you're a proud dog owner. I think it suits you."

"It wasn't on purpose. I didn't want a dog." Ross slipped his arm around her waist, bringing his lips to her neck. "I didn't want a girlfriend either," he murmured.

Mia's heart stuttered in her chest as if traveling across road bumps. Did his lips detect the aftershocks in the pulse running along her neck? She resisted the urge to pull away from him, not wanting him to sense her internal panic at his words. "Oh god," she said with a nonchalant air as she studied the details of her new camera with extra scrutiny. "What's the girlfriend equivalent of Hermes?"

"One dimple would probably qualify. It makes you lopsided."

She turned to him in faux outrage, eyebrows raised and lips set in a firm smirk. "Did you just imply there's something wrong with my dimple?"

"Having only one might be considered a defect to some," he stated matter-of-fact.

She pushed her finger into his chest and provided a wide smile so he'd get her solitary dimple in full effect. "I'll have you know, I'm using my one dimple as criteria for finding my future soulmate. Someday I'm going to meet someone with a single dimple, but on the other side of their face, and it'll be like salt and pepper shakers coming together." She pointed from the dimple to the dimple-less side of her face to illustrate her argument further.

Ross's brow pinched in the center, and his mouth stretched into a straight line. Was he angry? Did Mia take it too far? Her sole purpose was to keep things light.

"Okay, that's it." And in a sudden blur of motion, he grabbed her around the waist, throwing her over his shoulder as he stood.

A gasp followed by laughter bubbled out of her. "I beg your pardon. And just what do you think you're doing? I almost dropped my treasured camera."

Ross marched them to their tent. "You can only push a person so far, Mia. I planned a nice camping trip for your birthday, and I didn't do it to hear about some bastard salt-and-pepper-shaker, dimpled soulmate. It's too much."

Hermes bounced around them, barking wildly and wagging his tail. "Bite him, Hermes." She laughed again.

Ross had to set her down to undo the tent zipper, but

she didn't move, looking forward to tackling him herself. "Get in," he growled, "and prepare to accept your punishment."

He followed her inside, leaving Hermes outside to continue sniffing the grounds, while he zipped them within the tent. Soon her cameras were carefully stowed away with her glasses and he began peeling her clothes in between light nips against her skin. He carefully tucked her into the sleeping bag and after removing his own clothes, joined her.

"Maybe I can hang around until you find this other mystery man." Ross's lips pressed kisses along her collarbone.

"What man? I don't even know what you're talking about anymore," she said in return, her fingers curling in the hair at the nape of his neck.

His mouth stretched into a beautiful grin. "Did I just discover a natural memory eraser or is this typical Mia Russo forgetfulness?"

"I don't believe it's an actual discovery until you exclaim *Eureka* like your friend, Archimedes." Her mouth slid against his in a deep kiss, their tongues mingling together.

"Eureka," Ross whispered when they broke apart. "I've found it." His eyes were like ink, taking a determined glint, looking as if he actually had found something. She should have panicked, but she was trapped within that gaze.

Ross propped himself on an elbow, a hand stroking through her hair. The way he looked at her during these moments was always unsettling as if he discovered some part of her even she wasn't aware of or didn't want to be aware of. It was too deep, too vulnerable. In keeping with her standard practice, Mia pushed for action, reaching for him, encouraging him to do more. She didn't care what happened as long as he stopped staring at her.

This time, he resisted. Pulling her hands off him, Ross gave her a lazy smile. "Slow down there, Eager Beaver," he replied.

"Ross—"

"We're camping. It's your birthday. Relax. There's time."

But was there? Guilt invaded her conscience.

"Happy Birthday, Russo," he said. A single finger did a slow slide down her face, stopping at the epicenter of her cheek. *X* marked the exact spot her dimple would emerge from. She'd allow Ross to unlock the treasure anytime he wanted with nothing more than the different parts of him: body and mind. The buzz of unspent energy was already snapping along her spine.

His finger remained fixed on her cheek. "This. I like."

Mia smiled, releasing the indentation beneath his finger. "Oh? You don't see it as a defect anymore?"

He shook his head, his eyes never leaving her cheek as if hypnotized. Ross bent his head, leaving a measured kiss there, and Mia closed her eyes. His lips worked a path along her neck, dragging slow, gentle kisses across bare skin. She may have heard the soft uttering of her name, but it was so faint her ears weren't sure they perceived an actual word or a sigh. It didn't matter because her mind was doing its best to capture the experience by touch and scent and sight. She wanted it broken down like a strip of film, frame-by-frame, to be referenced later whenever she needed it.

An internal heat swept through her, the surface of her skin sensitive to his touch. Ross was no longer paying attention to her eager-beaver hands as she scraped her nails along his back. *God.* Whenever they were together, she was always on the verge of falling. Falling apart. Falling into. Falling…At this moment, Mia wasn't sure what other type of *falling* people did, but whatever it was she must have done it.

He focused on her lips, drawing forth heavy, lush kisses from her mouth as he guided himself into her. Something about this time made it unique. Was it the fresh pine air? The freedom from everyday life and work? The seclusion they had inside their tent as though they were the only two people in existence? Was it Mia's knowledge that this was one of those moments she'd remember forever regardless of how old she got? She couldn't put her finger on it, but something had shifted. Ross's movements, as he rocked against her, were slow and deliberate.

"Look at me," he said, his voice low and gravelly.

Maybe she could this time. Maybe she had to. Just this once, she'd let him unlock her.

The thing with dark intense eyes, the type that seemed to peel armor away from a person, leaving nothing but the bare essence, was that they weren't a security window. She could see into him as well. Past his fevered gaze, she saw Ross. Compassionate. Supportive. Kind. He was a man who had a lot to give and was just looking for someone to take it.

Too bad it couldn't be her.

She wanted to cry. Instead, she wrapped herself around him, pressing her face into one strong shoulder, inhaling him, kissing him. She was a rubber band, and with each stroke made between them, Ross was stretching the band to its limits. Until it snapped. She broke apart in a mixture of sparks and tears, his name tumbling from her mouth. His own groan reverberated at her temple. What Mia felt for him seemed too big to be contained within her chest. She tucked her face into his neck, waiting for control and for her breathing to return to normal.

Ross gathered her to him as if she was a precious bouquet of Shasta daisies, his arms encircling her with tenderness. Though bedtime was hours away, Mia's own eyelids were drooping, ready to drift off into a peaceful nap of a spoiled cat. It didn't help that Ross was brushing his lips across her forehead with a light touch.

"Mia?" she heard him say somewhere from the other side of hazy consciousness.

"Hmm?" Mia didn't have enough energy to give him anything more than a murmur.

This was met with continued silence on his part. She was about to follow up with more encouragement. But the low whine of an impatient Hermes outside the tent's wall interrupted the tranquil atmosphere.

"I better put out a food bowl for him and start cooking something for dinner," Ross said, pulling himself from their embrace. Mia turned to watch him as he retrieved his clothes.

"What can I do to help?" she asked.

He gave her a quick glance. She imagined her hair took on the appearance of a fluffy love nest, and she finger-combed it to tame it.

He gave her a warm smile. "I got it. Relax. Just come out when you're ready."

"Are you sure?"

"Yeah. Don't worry about it." Dressed, he gave her a final kiss on the head, then let himself out of the tent to take care of camp business, zipping the entrance behind him.

Mia rolled to her back, basking in contentment as she closed heavy eyes, ready to surrender to a few minutes of light napping. This could be the most luxurious activity she ever allowed herself. His warm, loving kiss was still imprinted on her skin and—

Mia's eyes snapped open.

Ross loved her.

Her demure side wanted to ration away her quick jump in judgment. Mia told herself it was nothing but pure ego making this ridiculous assumption about his heart. Sure, he never said the phrase aloud or uttered the word *love* in her presence. Not even when talking about innocuous things such as a love for peanut butter, sunny days, or camping trips to Camino Cove.

Regardless, Mia knew. She had seen it in his eyes, a burning ember so bright it glowed like gold and could have been seen from a mountain top. It was in his gaze, his touch, in every single kiss he laid upon her. And she accepted each individual element as if there was no responsibility or additional meaning behind the action. The revelation was heart-stopping. Their situation was more precarious than she originally predicted.

Ross's love was a beautiful, iridescent bubble, and she stepped so close, it formed around her. Like a real bubble, the walls were flexible but fragile. There was no way for her to step out of the bubble, no matter how gentle she did it, not without popping it. It was either stay in the bubble or pop it. There were no other options.

The problem was, Mia didn't have a choice. This perfect life on the campground was not hers, no matter how much she wanted it. Her life had a plan, and what she was doing at Camino Cove was one last elaborate act of pretending, as if she could live a simple life and be the person who had it. The reality was, the fates were dealing one more bad hand of cards as far as Mia and Ross's relationship was concerned. She had to play it, even if it meant everyone lost, including her. She was destined to disappoint Ross once again. One final time.

The bubble was going to pop.

Chapter Thirty-Two

SOMETHING WASN'T RIGHT. Sure, on the surface, Mia was her usual cheerful self. But at some point, during the weekend, a switch had been flipped. He wasn't sure how it was possible for her to spend whole days in his presence and still appear as though she was avoiding him. It could have been the lack of eye contact or how she flitted from one inconsequential topic of conversation to another. It was also due to the fact she had long conversations with Hermes. His own dog was getting more attention than he was.

It wasn't as though he didn't try to move the conversation into a serious realm a few times, but Mia was a skilled boxer with shuffling, lightning feet, and dodged all of his attempts. By the time they were driving home, he had an entire weekend of frustration building inside him, ready to burst. Bursting could be messy. He didn't want messy, especially in regards to something he considered to be important.

They arrived at his home after a long drive. Mia's car was parked in his driveway, exactly where she'd left it before their trip, covered in a layer of soft, forest dust. He pulled alongside her car, putting his vehicle into park. They met at the truck bed as Hermes trotted across the yard to sniff shrubbery. Mia's backpack was slung over her shoulder.

"I'll help you unload," she offered with a smile.

"It's okay. I can take care of it."

"I know you can. You've been taking care of it all weekend. You should go inside, relax, and I'll take care of it for a change."

"Thanks for the offer, but I think I'll pass." There was a brief moment of silent awkwardness between them. Ross was stacking the final blocks of his courage together.

Her mouth opened, shut, and then she chewed on her lower lip for a moment before blowing out a breath. "Okay, well, I better be heading home. Thanks for my first real camping trip. I had a great time."

It wasn't as though he wasn't going to see her again, but this window he gave himself, one of the reasons he wanted to take this trip, was closing with each step she took toward her car.

She was almost there when he called her name.

Her pupils might as well have been two big question marks as they watched him approach. Ross's brain raced through every thought he had during the car ride home, leaving him with a few precious moments to pull it all together in a smooth, convincing argument. He decided to go with, "Move in with me."

Was it too late to start over? It was clear he settled on the worst possible option as he watched her sunny disposition melt into slacked bewilderment.

"What?" Her voice was nothing more than a crack in the silence.

It wasn't the reaction Ross was counting on, and a bubble of turmoil was forming in his gut at her response. Mia already spent half her nights at his place. Maybe asking her for the full week wasn't a big deal, but it was a big deal *to him*. He'd never asked someone to move in before. He'd never had a desire to ask before now. But he had allowed himself to feel a glimmer of hopefulness in this particular woman.

There was no chance for a do-over. He had no choice but to plow straight ahead. "I asked if you'd move in with me." *Great.* There was nothing like repeating the same exact thing which had been declared a mistake the first time around. This wasn't going well at all.

He took a deep inhale and tried again. "Look, I... Let me just say a few things before you jump in. I know you have your plans, and if you have your heart set on that, then it's going to happen, and there's really nothing I can say. But I just want you to know you have another option." Ross paused, drawing closer. "Me."

He swallowed hard, doing his best to smother the poor self-esteem threatening to break the surface. "I know it doesn't sound like much of an offer compared to the dream of going off and doing big things, but...I want to be with you, Mia. You can have whatever you want, go wherever you want. I want to stay in your world. Is there an option here where I don't have to lose you?"

She slumped against her car for support, her hands spreading across the surface of her face. "Ross, if I stayed I wouldn't have any real job prospects here. Believe me, I wish it was so easy for me to stay."

Ross leaned against his truck, jamming his hands into his

pockets. "It doesn't have to be difficult. You could make that decision."

She sighed, her face still partially hidden behind her hands. "I've been accepted into a program. It's in Texas. I'm sorry."

"Oh." The word was insufficient to describe the air being punched from his body. She'd known the whole time. No wonder she was avoiding him. Ross felt foolish for even hoping.

She removed her hands from her face but avoided eye contact with him. "And I always thought leaving would be easy. But now there are things I don't want to give up, like you and Hermes and your beautiful refrigerator covered in photos. But if I don't, it's like I'm admitting I gave up, that I'll never succeed, and maybe I'll just work in a coffee shop forever. And you're amazing and wonderful, but I have no idea what my future looks like if I stay."

"Come on, Mia. Do you think any of us knows what's going to happen in the future? Do you think I saw you walking into my shop and back in my life?"

"You know what I mean. You're asking me to walk willingly into a completely dark room. I don't think I'm strong enough to do that. I'm sorry to disappoint you again."

Ross stepped nearer, brushing the length of her arm and taking her hand in his. "I don't believe that. I've never seen you back away from a challenge, and you may be walking into a dark room, but you won't be walking through it alone. I'll be there with you. I'll hold your hand."

Mia's eyes sprung with tears, and she pushed her face into his chest. "I wish you hated me again. Life was so much easier back when you hated me." She cried hot tears into his shirt.

He held her, soothing her weeping form with his hands. "I told you, I never hated you. And I'm never going to, because…I love you." Ross originally considered that his declaration of love would have been the most difficult thing to tell her, but with it being out, he discovered it was the easiest three words he'd ever said. Whatever effect he thought this would have on her was wrong. If anything, she blubbered harder. All he wanted was to fix the situation, but he didn't have the first clue how to accomplish this.

He dropped his head and spoke into her ear. "I will always do whatever I can to help you because all I want is for you to be happy. And I don't care if it's becoming a photographer or a social media person or working in politics. The important thing is you know what you want. I'm offering you the time to figure it out, without pressure or expectations. I will take one of those rooms in my house and build you a darkroom if that's what you want."

"And if I still fail?"

"Then, you fail. You'll survive. Trust me, I've done it a hundred times in my life. I love you because of your strength and tenacity. If you fail, you'll pick yourself up and move on to the next thing after spending a few moments with me, your safety net, and expert failure."

"I should already have this figured out," she explained between tears.

"First of all, that's not remotely true. Anyone who believes all twenty-six-year-olds should have everything in life figured out is a clown."

"You just called me a clown," she hiccupped between a sob before swiping her hand across a runny nose.

"Secondly. Who cares? Who exactly is keeping tabs on everyone? There's not a secret accomplishment board at our old high school. What is life, but a series of constant adjustments? Our high school selves are not allowed to dictate what the rest of our life should look like."

"You don't understand. All the time, energy, and money that's been invested, all those times I didn't go home to see my mom. It would all be a waste. I'd have done it all for nothing."

"I don't see it that way. Everything you've done has led you here. That doesn't have to be a bad thing, and it's definitely not a waste."

She released a humorless laugh. "But I was already here. I went backward. I'm most likely to succeed at being a huge joke."

"I don't mean *here* in the literal sense. I mean, who you are as a person. And you're intelligent and funny and insightful—"

"And, according to you, also a clown."

He gave a slight chuckle as his hands continued running soothing lines along her spine. "It would make me feel better to know, even you, can have your moments. But, regardless, I love who you are right now, and your experiences shaped you into this person. How could that be a waste?"

As she continued to cry and recline against him, she didn't say anything for a few moments. Perhaps his words were having an effect for once. His hand took hold of her jawline, damp from tears, and tilted her face to his. Behind her glasses, her eyes closed. Saturated, dark lashes came to rest on her cheeks. "I'm not a pretty crier," she said.

"What the hell is a pretty crier?"

"You know, someone who can look pretty while crying. I always look like a wet, snotty mess."

"I don't care," Ross replied. "I'll take you, snotty mess and all." He captured her mouth with his, pouring all his love, hope, and dreams into this single kiss, his last good argument remaining. Mia leaned into him, returning his kiss with a desperate press of her own as if this romantic act could tether them together forever.

But she broke it off, taking in a ragged breath. "Ross, I can't. I can't do it."

A surge of frustration flooded through his veins. He rubbed a hand across his face. "Mia—"

"You don't understand—"

"You're right, I don't. I've never understood. And I don't care what you say. You're never going to convince me that continuing down this same path, the same one you're already miserable in, is going to make you look successful. Who the hell are you trying to impress? People at our ten-year reunion? No one gives a shit!"

"No, that's not it at all. It's for me. I have to do something meaningful, something that matters in my life."

His jaw shifted into a locked position. "I'm getting a little tired of the implication that being with me somehow means you're giving up a life of purpose, and nothing matters."

Her expression dropped. "Don't."

"Don't what, Mia? What exactly am I supposed to be

hearing? Because it sure sounds like the life I'm living is okay for someone like me, but heaven forbid if you should ever have to lower yourself. Getting down in the mud is fun for a fling. But as for something more serious? Let's get real. It wasn't even an option, was it?"

"You're acting like I planned this. Like I wanted it."

"You didn't want it?"

"No, I-I did want it, but I never thought of you as beneath me. Maybe not thinking everything through was the problem. I didn't think about anything and just did it." Mia sighed, her vision drifting to the sky. "You're angry with me. I get it. But what you're saying right now is not only a slam on yourself but hurtful to me, too."

"I don't really know what you expect from me. How did you imagine this whole thing would end? Was I supposed to kiss you on your cheek and then watch you drive off into the sunset with nothing but warm, fuzzy memories? Is it wrong for me to actually want something from this?"

Mia blew out an aggravated breath. "And what do you think I'm hearing, but more expectations? My whole life has been filled with expectations and me trying to fit into whatever box people want to put me in. Now I'm getting them from you."

A frustrated hand rubbed the nape of his neck. "It's not expectations, as much as it's me caring about you and wanting you to be happy."

She narrowed her eyes, her cheeks were dry from tears but stained with streaks of pink. "And why would that matter?"

"Are you saying it doesn't matter?"

"Do you think expectations came from people who didn't care about me? My parents cared about me and loved me, and they had the highest expectations."

"Is that what this is really about? Does this have something to do with your father?" Ross couldn't hide the harshness from his questions as a darkness crept its way into his soul.

"What?"

"You don't want to disappoint your father, and he would definitely be disappointed if you stayed with me. Are you sure you just turned twenty-six? Because waiting for your father's approval over your life sounds like the persuadable sixteen-year-old Mia again." A bitter venom was already invading his bloodstream and he couldn't do anything to stop it.

Mia's mouth opened to respond but only jagged breaths came out. She sucked in her bottom lip, her eyes closing as if searching for inner strength. When she opened them again, they locked on to him. "You don't know how exhausting it is to feel stuck, to feel trapped in between. I honestly don't know what the answer is. Do I trust that my father knows best? Do I throw it all to the wind and take a risk? I don't know. I really don't. And I don't want to disappoint him or you, but at the end of the day, someone is going to be severely disappointed in me, and it's eating me up inside."

Mia swallowed, tears pooling at the edge of her eyes again. "The last thing I want to do is hurt you because I know you care about me. I know this. And I care about you. I've always cared about you, and I've always seen you as someone of value. Not in the mud. Not lesser than. You're a beautiful man who makes beautiful jewelry and cares for a sweet dog and supports his cousin, and then on top of that, you want to take me on as well. You give so much of yourself, and I wish I could return it all. You deserve to be happy, too. But...all this was decided a while ago, and I'm stuck."

"Fine. Go home, Mia."

"Ross—"

"Looks like the choice wasn't so difficult after all. I just wish you would have told me as soon as you made it. It's not fair you get to pull yourself away, while leaving me completely in the dark."

"I'm sor—"

"I don't want to hear anymore apologies. You have to do what you have to do. I should have known better. You gave up on me once before. It was really only a matter of time before it happened again, wasn't it?"

Mia's face fell, a frown deepening into her features. "Ross..."

"Go home."

Chapter Thirty-Three

THE DRIVE WAS such an uneventful blur, Mia didn't remember one moment of it. Her path started at Ross's house and, as if by magic, her car ended in her driveway. She managed to pull herself from her vehicle and grabbed her backpack. She trudged across each surface she came into contact with: first the pavement, then hardwood floors, and, lastly, carpet. She had walked this path a million times, but it never felt as long as it did today. In her bedroom, her backpack was dropped in a lump at the foot of her bed before she fell into the mattress face first.

When she thought about Ross's offer and the promises he made, she wanted to weep until the green-and-blue comforter beneath her was soaked through with salty tears. The bed made a poor substitute for the warm body of her mother to cry against. What did a bed know about the complexity of life? Its single contribution in this was performing the role of sponge for Mia's sorrow.

It wasn't as if Ross's offer wasn't tempting. She'd never received a more attractive proposition in her life. She could almost imagine herself living a quiet life. One where Ross would spend his days making jewelry, and she would be busy inside the special darkroom he made for her. They'd spend their evenings making dinner and laughing together before ending the day in each other's arms. It was a romantic vision of the future, but that's all it was.

Mia was quite familiar with ridiculous fantasies. She had them all the time, ever since she was a kid. She envisioned herself being a star tutor to Ross. She envisioned being a top advisor in the political world. And, not too long ago, a foolish Mia envisioned getting together with some random handsome man in a red-and-black plaid shirt in Pony Expresso. But not one of these had come true. All this proved was that she wasn't great at knowing what her life was going to be. It was safe to say she was horrible at it.

Her wishful thinking was no more real than her dreams at night. Here she was, once again, envisioning the most charming and splendid life she could have with Ross. How wrong could she be in this? Mia's future might be one where she moved from one failed project to the next, never finding the one job she was successful and happy with until Ross grew tired of pulling her along. She would become nothing but an anchor around his increasingly unhappy neck. In the end, she may become a bigger disappointment than even she imagined. The thought landed inside her stomach with the gravity of a black hole, sucking every other hopeful thought into oblivion.

At this moment, Ross was probably regretting all of it. His promise. His commitment. His love. She had gotten this special gift. Not being able to grasp it with both hands shattered her heart. These same shards were now stabbing her from the inside.

Ross had been wrong about her. Mia wasn't strong

enough. Whenever there was a sure, safe thing, Mia reached for it every time. And though she spent a week ignoring it, she had a sure thing in her hand even at this moment. Wishful thinking be damned, she was as predictable and as much of a coward as she feared. She knew what her ultimate decision would be. Why was she pretending it could be anything else? A maze didn't have multiple paths to the end. It had only one. Ross deserved someone stronger than her. Someone who could accept his gifts without putting them through a debate or writing out a pros and cons chart.

With her fate accepted, the last thing remaining was to escape Placerville as fast as she could. She didn't want to be reminded of what she didn't choose and how much courage she lacked. She headed to her closet to begin the process of packing.

"Mia?" her father said, his eyes scanning the dismantled state of her bedroom, before meeting her scattered gaze. He frowned, the lines in his face retreating deeper.

"Dad, do you think you can pick me up a few boxes from the hardware store? I can't really go out right now, and my suitcase is already full. Probably most of this stuff can be stored in the garage or, you know what, just donate all of it. I don't care."

"What the hell is going on? What happened?"

Mia threw her hands in frustration as if the answer was obvious. "I'm moving. I got into a program. The sooner you can get me those boxes, the better." She retreated inside her closet and grabbed another handful of garments.

"What? Where?"

She let the bundle of clothes fall to the floor in a sloppy

heap and slogged to her dresser, fetching her phone. Through a new curtain of waterworks and short, shallow breaths, she scrolled through the screen until she found the relevant email. With the message displayed, her cellphone was pressed into her father's chest until he claimed it for himself. He held the device at arm's length, his aging eyes squinting at it. "University of Houston?"

"That's right. I'm moving to Texas," she stated before breaking into tears again. "And it's so far away." The pitch of her voice took on a high whine at the end, but Mia no longer cared if she was acting like a cranky child. At the moment, she didn't care about much of anything.

Her father gave her a puzzled look. "Why do you need to leave right at this moment? You have time. And why are you crying?"

"Because I need to figure out what my living situation is going to be and get settled in and learn my way around town. What if I get lost when I'm there or don't know where the best laundromats are? I need to figure everything out. You don't understand."

Her father's bushy gray eyebrows furrowed together. "Do you not want to go to Texas?"

"I don't know," Mia replied.

"Okay, well, you don't have to rush into this." He took a seat at the end of her bed. "My god, honey, you need to relax. You're making me nervous. How about you wait until you hear back from other schools and then make a decision."

"It doesn't matter."

"What do you mean, it doesn't matter? Of course, it matters. Can you please stop? Just stop. Come over here and tell me what's going on."

Mia carried her hunched, sobbing form to the bed, dropping onto the edge of the mattress beside him. Her father rubbed the area between her shoulder blades in slow, soothing motions, until she collapsed against him, becoming a sopping mess of tears.

"What's wrong? Did something happen on your camping trip?"

"No, nothing." It was doubtful tears made her answer convincing, but nothing had happened on the camping trip. Her statement was correct based on a technicality.

"Tell me what's wrong," her father tried again, his voice becoming gruff with impatience.

Mia took a deep, jagged breath before pushing ahead. "Ross asked me to move in with him."

His body stiffened. "What?"

"Well, obviously, I'm not moving in with Ross, because I'm moving to Texas."

"I don't want you crying over anyone, and I especially don't want you crying over him."

She pulled away. "You can't tell me who to cry over! I can cry over Ross if I want to."

"That kid is not worth your tears—"

"Stop calling him a kid. And you think you know him, but you don't know him at all." Her cheeks flushed hot while she pushed her hair behind her ears and slid a hand across her nose.

"I know he's not worth all this. You can, and will, do so much better than him."

"I don't think I'll ever run into someone like Ross. He's

special," she said.

"Mia, you are going to go far and meet lots of people who will be worth your attention and love. He is still going to be here. You will do better, and I'm not just saying this because you're my daughter and I love you, even though both these things are true."

Her father was doing his best at providing the comfort he thought she needed, but it had the opposite effect. The spark inside her was given a healthy dose of oxygen as if someone opened a window, and it flared into full-blown defensiveness. She shot up, returning to her task at emptying the closet. "I already told you I was leaving. I'm doing exactly what you want. Why can't you just be happy and leave it alone?" she replied, not hiding the anger in her voice. Her shoulders slumped again as she leaned against the closet door frame. "I have to burst that lovely bubble, and I can't love him, but at least the judge gets what he wants."

"What do you mean what *I* want? Isn't this what *you* want?"

"I don't know!"

Her father sighed. "Mia, you need to settle down. You're getting way too worked up and emotional over this."

"When *am* I allowed to get emotional about stuff? I'm genuinely curious when this will ever be allowed. I have feelings, and I should be allowed to feel them."

"Do you not want to go? Is that what you're trying to tell me? You want to stay here and live with him? Doing what? Working in a coffee shop? Will that make you happy?"

Her eyes dropped to the handful of hangers in her hands. "What if…what if going to this university isn't going to make me happy?"

"How do you know? You haven't even done it yet. You have to give it a chance."

Mia released a long breath, sinking to the floor. She took in all the chaos created inside her bedroom, both in terms of the physical and emotional. Her chin settled into a hand, staring at nothing in particular. "I told Mom once that I didn't want to continue with my studies, but I was too scared to tell you, so I just kept going through with it anyway."

After some quiet moments passed, he asked, "Why would you be scared to tell me?"

"I knew it would make you upset."

"Of course, I would be upset. Do you know how much money we've put into this? But you should have told me. We would have figured something else out. It's still not too late and you can go to law school. You know that's what I wanted for you all along. You can follow in the footsteps of your old man."

"Dad." The word slipped from her lips, but there wasn't anything there to follow it. She wanted nothing more than to crawl into a cave and live in her own solitary existence for a spell, to savor one period of no disappointments or expectations.

"Okay, so you don't want to do that either. What exactly are you looking for, Mia? If you think I'm going to sit by and say nothing while you ruin your life, I'm telling you right now, I won't be able to do that. And you know your mom wanted more for you, too. We both did. Maybe in five years you'll realize staying here, working in a coffee shop, was also a mistake and you're still unhappy. At least give yourself the chance of living up to your potential. I'd like to think I raised someone who could do more than flip burgers or serve coffee."

It was those final words when everything stopped for Mia, and her view of the world became a flat straight plane of inevitability.

She blinked away the emotions, and began gathering her clothes again. "Anyway, it doesn't matter. I'm going to Texas. Can you pick up some boxes for me whenever you go out?"

There wasn't anything left to do but pack her things.

Chapter Thirty-Four

SHE HAD LEFT.
Ross knew she had left because of the single text message she sent him. The same one he had yet to respond to. In the weeks following Mia leaving, Ross retreated into his workshop. The bitterness, from once again being deemed unworthy, seeped into his bones. He was left with the familiar pain caused by everything he didn't have and would never have.

Life was a fucking tapeworm.

He had almost forgotten it was latched onto his body like a backpack. That was his fault really. His fault for thinking it could ever be anything different. His fault for allowing himself to fall for some of Mia's optimism, to believe he could capture and hold onto some of that light. He wasn't meant to have any of it.

Conversations with Luna didn't help. Sales made by Aanya didn't help. Hermes being in relatively good health didn't help. He sat at the office computer, his jaw locked and hardened into place, and attempted to lose himself in his work, to force himself to care about another online sale to fulfill, to not think about *her*.

When his chair rolled backwards as he bent to retrieve

something from a bottom drawer, it collided with one of the box towers surrounding his desk, almost setting off a domino effect inside his office. Quick reflexes grabbed the cardboard, but the top box toppled to the floor, spilling its contents of ancient paperwork.

"Goddammit!" Another string of curses fell from his mouth as he roughly shoved the items back in the box. He was sick of it. Sick of the boxes. Sick of this office. Sick of all of it. There was a temptation to fling the box across the office and shred everything with his bare hands, to release every frustration he had ever felt in his life.

"Shit!" An angry red slash appeared on his thumb. Like going through everything wasn't enough, he had to suffer a papercut on top of it.

There was a soft knock. "Is everything okay in there?" Aanya asked through the closed door.

"Yeah. Just a small accident." He lifted the page as he sucked the pain from his thumb. The printout was off-white from age but there was the familiar fuzzy green caterpillar sticker in the corner. *Perfect Attendance for First Grade. Awarded to Ross Manasse.*

Good job, buddy, his teacher had said. Yeah. Good job at being able to occupy a desk for one hundred and eighty days. Not that he had much of a choice. His grandfather didn't accept many excuses when it came to missing school. Even then, it was an award for the bare minimum and one more item belonging in the trash. He was about to turn to the small shredder beside him, but something else captured his attention.

He overturned an old photograph, one taken on Victor's

digital camera. He hadn't remembered seeing it before or maybe he'd forgotten it. A brittle piece of tape was stuck at the top, as though it had at one point been hung on the office wall. The image had been snapped inside the workshop. His grandfather was in the center, framed by seven-year old Ross and four-year-old Luna. Young Ross held up his perfect attendance certificate with one scrawny arm, his bright smile was gapped and toothy. His little naïve mind had been completely unaware of the academic frustrations awaiting him in the future.

But the smile on his grandpa's face somehow also took him aback. He was beaming and had his arms around each grandchild while in his favorite place in the world, the workshop. His grandfather looked like a man who had everything he ever wanted. It didn't make much sense. Victor Lanza had experienced his own devastating losses in life: a wife who died of cancer, a daughter and son-in-law whose lives were cut short due to an accident, and another daughter who moved across the country to embrace a life without him.

He also didn't look as old as Ross remembered. The man, who appeared to be in his early fifties, still had most of his dark hair, his back was still relatively straight. He was just a man who kept them going the best he could. And he sat on the stool in his workshop, wearing the leather apron and beaming at the camera.

Ross remembered, after he'd refused to ever go back to school again, how Victor had dragged him to El Dorado Jewelry day after day.

"Do you know who Archimedes is?" his grandfather had asked. "Ross?"

"What?" Ross answered moodily.

"Not going to school doesn't mean you're still not going to do something, even if you have to listen to me and learn a trade."

Ross remained stubbornly sullen, sitting on a workshop stool as he used one of the tools to pick at the corner of a table.

His grandfather frowned at him before shifting tact. "What do you want?"

"For lunch? How about a sandwich?"

Victor threw a rag at him, hitting him in the chest.

"Stop," Ross grumbled, retrieving it from the floor. "You're going to pull a muscle, old man."

"What do you want?" his grandfather asked again.

"I don't know. Maybe I don't want anything."

His grandfather scoffed.

"I know that I don't want to be here." Ross laid his head into the crook of one arm. Maybe if he was sleeping, Victor would give up trying to have this meaningless conversation with him.

"Why? What's wrong with here?"

Ross groaned. The old man was incredibly annoying. "What's the point? Why would I want to make jewelry? It's completely useless. It's for people who like to show off how rich they are. I hate people like that."

"Wrong."

Ross gave his grandfather a dirty look. "No, I'm not."

"Jewelry has meaning."

He rolled his eyes. "Yeah, okay."

His grandfather glanced at him over the magnifier glasses. "We take natural elements from the Earth, and transform them into a single piece that has meaning for us. Then someone buys the jewelry and attaches their own special meaning to it. Maybe love or a celebration of something. Jewelry has a way of reminding us. Your grandmother could remember where every single piece of her jewelry came from."

The only significant jewelry Ross remembered from his grandmother was the vintage crane brooch. It was a red enamel bird perched on a branch, its wings dotted with clear rhinestones. She had worn it while dating Victor, and his grandfather continued keeping it on his nightstand. Luna had always been fascinated with it and eventually claimed it for herself.

Even then, Ross hadn't been convinced. "I'm not making jewelry."

"Why?"

"Because I can't. I can't do anything. I'm a lost cause."

The metal feet of Victor's stool scraped across the concrete flooring until it was in front of Ross. Victor grabbed his hand.

"Hey. What are you do—"

"You have my hands." His grandfather held him in tight grip. "You're a Lanza. If you don't want to do it, okay. But it's not because you can't. I have not given up. I will never give up on you."

Ross was so taken aback by the fierce light, the pure determination in his grandfather's eyes, he wasn't sure how to react. "Okay," was his response.

His grandfather gave his hand a pat before returning his stool to the workbench. "Good. Now I'll ask you again. Do you know who Archimedes is?"

ROSS LODGED THE photo onto the inside corner of the bulletin board which hung on the wall.

His grandfather had been right. Ross could do it. And it turned into something he enjoyed and was good at. The workshop had become his own solitude, a place of comfort, just as it had been for his grandfather.

Ross had been so focused on all the things he didn't have, he didn't realize what he actually did have. A grandfather who *never* gave up on him. Who trusted him with the family legacy. Who saw and encouraged his talent. He also had Luna, a cousin who was like a sister, and who kept him connected to the world, pushing him out of the dark holes he sometimes found himself in.

And then there was Mia. A woman who was smart and warm and everything he wanted. Even during their last conversation, when he was succumbing to anger and dejection, instead of swiping back, she was still trying to lift him up. For all those times he thought connecting with her would be a mistake, in the end, it wasn't. But even if it was, it was a mistake he'd be willing to make again and again.

Ross pulled out his phone. Her last text message was still there. "*I know you don't want me to apologize, but I am sorry.*

You are a Renaissance man. Any girl would be incredibly lucky to share a world with you. I wish it could have been me." Mia always had a way with words.

While Victor knew of Mia from Ross's tutoring sessions, he hadn't known her. This was a shame. There was no doubt his grandfather would have really liked her. He would have liked her way with words, her way with people, her way with Ross.

Mia was still imprinted on his life. Her images hung on the walls in his store. Sales came in daily through the Etsy shop she set up. The flowers she put in the planters outside El Dorado Jewelry were still blooming. Her mark had been made and, despite everything, Ross didn't want to lose this. As hard as things had been in his life, loving Mia had been as easy as breathing. His life was always so much better when she was in it.

When he thought about it, he had more than half the year with her. He had been blessed. Mia could have just worked at the coffee shop and spent her time counting the days until she left Placerville. Instead, she chose to spend most of her free time with him, giving him her affection and smiles and attention. She let him experience a world with butterflies. Ross would do anything for her, even if it took her away from him.

He stood and re-tied the straps of the leather apron, the same one his grandpa had given him when he was too ill to continue working. When he handed it to him, Victor had taken Ross's hand once more, the grip not as tight this time. His dark eyes were unwavering as they pierced Ross's soul. *You'll always be where you're meant to be, and you'll become the man I know you can be.*

Chapter Thirty-Five

MIA'S EYES MADE contact with the bright blue gaze of a ruggedly handsome man. He stood in front of Rio Grande Coffee & Tea Company in a red buttoned-down shirt which stretched across his muscled physique and long torso. Throw in a pair of cowboy boots, and he was a modern-day Marlboro man. His name was probably Jake or Cody or something ridiculous like Ransom. He flicked the ash from his cigarette with a nonchalant grace before returning his attention to the phone in his hand. She proceeded into the shop.

Mia was a formerly-down-on-her-luck, twenty-six-year-old single gal. At least, she was almost sure she was *formerly*. She had at least picked a path and was on her way. It was time to update her bio. Mia Russo: up-and-coming, knew-what-she-wanted, grown-ass lady. Except if she was all of these things, wouldn't she be happier, more confident? How come when she was down-on-her-luck, it didn't necessarily feel that way?

She took a sip of what was becoming her favorite drink since arriving in Texas, an iced hibiscus tea, before returning to her study of the man outside the shop. On second thought, Marlboro and her were never going to work. He was too blond, too blue-eyed, too muscly. The man was *too* everything. Plus, he stared at his phone a lot, was a smoker, didn't nuzzle into her neck in the morning—the point was, it wasn't going to happen.

The revelation wasn't very shocking. Come to think of it, she had a similar experience when it came to finding a new apartment. They were either too dark, too bland, too full of bad vibes. And none came with a three-legged, one-eyed dog, a refrigerator covered in old photos, or a good-looking guy who made her paella. None of the places embodied what she imagined a home to be. In the meantime, she and her suitcases remained hunkered inside the Airbnb studio she chose without much deliberation. It provided a safe bed and privacy. That was good enough for her.

Besides, it wasn't a bad idea for her to spend as much time as possible inside the studio. Mia was convinced she was coming down with something. She walked around in a constant state of feverish exhaustion and nausea. It was a mystery virus that seemed to have migrated with her from Placerville.

This trip to the coffee shop was a quick stop while she waited on the three weeks' worth of laundry to finish their cycle at the nearby laundromat. Three weeks was the same period she had been a resident of Texas. It was also how long it took her to do something other than apartment hunting and Netflix binge watching, which in itself was simply a distraction from crying.

"Is it okay if I share your table? The other ones are taken," a man with a deep drawl said. She lifted her eyes to the sky blue ones of Marlboro.

"Sure." Mia offered a smile, setting her phone aside.

"I don't want to interrupt anything important. Business comes first." He gave a lazy nod toward her phone, his eyes crinkling at the corners.

"Oh. No. I was just...texting with a friend. No business going on here." Mia had downloaded an app to try her hand at learning Spanish again and was keeping in contact with Natalie as a way to practice what she learned. It never got very far before Natalie started teasing her or Mia got frustrated trying to express herself with a limited vocabulary. She was trying though and was determined to reclaim her Mexican heritage by learning the language.

"I'm Jake, by the way."

Point one for Mia. She finally got something right. Sure, it was only his name, but these days she had to take points where she could.

"Mia."

"I like your glasses. You look like the kind of girl who knows how to keep a guy on his toes. I like that."

"Oh. Thank you." An awkward pause drifted between them. Mia cleared her throat. "So, Jake, do you work here in the city?"

"I'm finishing up med school. In fact, I just got my residency."

"Nice. Congratulations. That's a big accomplishment."

"Yeah, thanks. I'm still getting used to it. I guess this means I should finally kick the habit of smoking." He shrugged. "No one wants a doctor who smokes. I was top of my class, but it's a completely different ballgame when you're actually living it inside a real hospital. I'll probably stick with it for a few years. But I really want to get into regenerative medicine and study stem cell therapy. That's the new area of sexy medicine. At least that's what the money tells me." He waggled his eyebrows.

God. Was this how Mia sounded when talking about her plans?

He took a self-assured sip from his cup as he leaned against his chair. "What do you do?"

"I—" Mia's standard answer froze on her tongue. "I'm still figuring it out."

"Aw, a free spirit. I wish I could be like that. Free spiriting isn't going to pay the bills, though. That's life."

She checked the time on her phone. "Sorry, I actually have to go. It was nice talking with you, Jake."

"Yeah, you too—I'm sorry, what was your name again? I'm horrible with names."

"Mia."

Jake did a finger gun in her direction. "Right. Mia. You haven't finished your drink yet. I'll stop talking your ear off. No reason to rush off."

"I'm done. Really. I have to pick up my laundry, and I kind of want to get home to lie down. I'm not feeling that great. But it was nice to meet you." She actually couldn't wait for the comfort and security of the studio.

That's life, Jake had said. But was it? And did it have to be? She wasn't sure which type of life she was embracing. And Mia liked the life she had with Ross. That felt more like living than what she was doing now.

That night, after eating microwave popcorn for dinner, Mia laid restlessly in bed while debating whether or not she had to puke. It was hard to know because of the constant lump in her throat and nervous buzzing in her stomach. What she wanted to do was cry while eating a carton of ice cream. But she didn't have a gallon of ice cream, just a box of generic ice cream sandwiches. And no one nursed a heartache over ice cream sandwiches without looking ridiculous.

Her eyes drew to the cell phone on the nightstand and her thoughts went to Ross. Mia untethered her phone from its charging cable and squinted at the bright screen after unlocking it. She found the last text she sent. It was still unanswered. She wanted to reach out to him again, to reassure him she would never give up on him, she'd always care for him, but Mia had no faith in her ability to find the magical collection of words which would make everything better between them.

Instead, she returned the phone to the nightstand. It was late. Plus, Ross probably hated her for real this time.

Her phone vibrated. Mia wondered if she suddenly possessed the capability to force her will upon the universe. On second thought, it had to be Natalie. She grabbed her phone, and unlocked it.

"Hi."

Ross. She stared at it, not quite believing it was real.

An additional text popped up a second later. *"How's Texas?"*

A spark lit within her. It was him, and he didn't hate her. Mia's desire to assure him *things were great* and *everything was good* was automatic. But a distaste for any iteration of a lie or pleasant platitude caused her nausea to grow worse.

She'd give him the truth.

"I'm managing, I guess. Been feeling anxious. How are you doing?"

"Managing." The dots below this message continued to blink, teasing Mia with the possibility of more. *"You'll do great. Already a success. Nothing can change that."*

The lump in her throat grew larger. Mia blinked away tears in the dark and typed, *"What are you doing up this late?"*

"Couldn't sleep. Trying to read Odyssey."

"Again? You're such an overachiever, Rosso."

"I like Greek tragedies—maybe because my life has kind of felt like one. But I like Odyssey because it reminds me of you."

Mia smiled at this. *"Do you think of me as an irresistible siren, tempting men to their doom?"*

"Ha. No. If anything you are Odysseus going out to find your glory and I'm Penelope waiting at home."

"So does this mean you'll soon be busy fighting off beautiful suitors?"

"Yes. I had to fight you off," Ross responded.

For the first time in weeks, Mia laughed. She missed this. All of it. Her heart almost felt like it wasn't missing a piece. *"You might have to again. I'm going to come back someday. I need to buy my favorite ring when I finally have some real money."*

"When? Need to make sure it's in stock."

"Maybe when I get tenure...so ten years on the fast track."

There was a long pause. Mia worried this was the end, and she kicked herself for allowing a sliver of reality to invade their otherwise fun conversation. A stab of disappointment struck through her.

Her phone vibrated again.

"Are you still doing your photo quilt?" Ross asked.

"I haven't taken any new photos lately. Besides, it's not like I'm going to mail my photo marigold to Pony Expresso. I guess I should forget about that project for now."

"Don't lose your gleam. Take pictures."

"Ok," she replied, feeling weepy again.

"And don't forget me this time, Mia."

The device dropped to her chest as the remaining part of her heart fractured into pieces. *"Never. You're stuck on my mind forever."*

"If you need me, you can call me."

"Ok."

Mia laid in bed for a long time after. She recognized her illness for what it was: absolute dread.

Mia had made a mistake.

What her cousin, Lizzy, had said during their coffee meetup was right. Dream kissers weren't found around every corner. But more than this, dream partners and true friends were an even rarer find. Mia had chosen the path she thought would guarantee a successful and satisfying outcome, but she was doing it alone and her life never seemed so empty. She'd allowed herself to become trapped.

Upon closer inspection her goals were less shiny than when they first appeared. She used to believe her education was her only security. But this wasn't true anymore. Even from a distance, Ross was still supporting her, wanting her to be happy even when they both knew she was miserable. Natalie had become like a sister to her. And she wanted to be able to connect more with her mom's family in Sacramento, to no longer be on the outside. Her time in Placerville, though not perfect, had been full of discovery and love, and maybe that's what she'd needed the whole time.

And now all Mia wanted was passage back to where she was before.

Chapter Thirty-Six

"ARE YOU WAITING for a phone call?"

"What?" Ross turned to Aanya, who was watching him from the office doorway.

"You've been staring at your phone for the last five minutes."

"I—No. I mean, maybe. I thought... maybe Luna might... I didn't sleep well last night. I'm just tired." Ross wasn't sure if he pulled off the lie or not, but Aanya left him alone so maybe he was more sly than he thought. He talked to Luna the previous day and she informed him she didn't know when she'd be coming home during the summer. She had a new boyfriend, and they were going to spend a few weeks at some resort in Mexico.

Ross wasn't even mad because he was so damn tired. He dragged a hand across his face, his palm running along the overgrown whiskers populating the landscape of his jawline. He was exhausted, not strictly from last night but from all the nights prior, every night since Mia had been gone.

He wasn't sure if their conversation last night meant anything, but it meant something to him. It filled his heart with impossible possibilities and perhaps this wasn't an end for them yet. Whatever their relationship was, it would always be on Mia. She would have to be the one to make the move.

Taking a break from tackling the boxes in his office, which were finally being sent to storage, Ross went into the store to check on Aanya.

"There was something I wanted to talk to you about," she said when he appeared.

"Okay." He worried Aanya was retiring for good, and he wasn't sure he could take any more losses at the moment. He'd become attached to the older woman. Maybe he should have commended her more instead of immersing himself in work all the time.

"You know, at my old job, I used to do the jewelry displays in the window."

"Did you?" She may have told him before, but these days Ross wasn't doing too well remembering. He was at least relieved the topic of conversation wasn't about leaving.

"What do you think if I do some nice displays for you? I have some ideas on themes we can do now that summer is here."

Ross studied the current window display and could admit it wasn't impressive.

"You make beautiful pieces. You should show it off more," Aanya said.

He leaned against one of the glass display cases as he considered it. He could almost feel Mia's elbow poking into his ribs. Being smart was knowing when to use talent better than his own.

"Okay," he said.

Aanya provided a warm smile. "Good. I can start now. Do you want me to tell you my ideas?"

"No, it's fine. I trust you." Ross scratched his jawline. "You know, I've been thinking about a new line of jewelry. What do you think of a small bird's nest with a gem in the middle? I can make rings, necklaces, brooches."

"Yes. I like that. We can do a lovely display with blossoms and branches."

He smiled. "Yeah, that would be great. I'm calling it my Penelope jewelry."

"Penelope?" Aanya scrunched her face in amusement. "We can come up with a better name later. First, you need to make it."

"Yeah, I guess you're right." Both he and Hermes moved toward the workshop door, a boost of energy sweeping through him. Making something new might take his mind off other more depressing topics. Plus, when he finished, he could share an image with Mia for her opinion. He liked the idea of being able to talk to her again.

Ross stopped at the threshold. "Thanks, Aanya. I've…uh…really liked having you here at the store."

She patted his arm. "You're a good boss. Now go make your Penelope jewelry."

Chapter Thirty-Seven

MIA SAT AT her mother's sewing machine table, flipping through the pile of quilt blocks as though they were a deck of cards. The muscles in her stomach were tense, but, for the first time, there was the knowledge she was finally doing something right.

The door downstairs opened and shut. There was a moment of silence before her father called out, "Mia?" He couldn't have missed her car in the driveway.

"I'm in the craft room."

Her father's footsteps bounded the staircase before his form filled the doorway, concern etched in the lines on his face. "What's wrong? Why are you home? Did something happen in Texas?"

"Nope." Mia took a deep breath. "I've decided Texas is not for me."

"Okay," her father replied in a measured tone. "Do you know where you want to go?"

"I'm not going to any of them."

"What do you mean?"

"I want to explore other options."

"Do you have a plan?"

"So far my plan was only to come back here."

The muscles along his jaw tightened. "Does your plan have something to do with Ross?"

"Well, only in that the plan relates to my life and I would like him in it, so yes."

The judge shook his head. "This sounds like you're giving up your dreams for a boy. I don't like that and I know your mother wouldn't have approved."

She thought about this while running her fingers across her mother's quilt squares. "Mom never finished her quilt."

"I was saving it for you. I thought maybe someday you'd like to finish it."

Mia released a bitter laugh. "Do you remember when she tried to teach me?"

"I remembered there was a bunch of complaining. But I think your mom would have loved it if you finished her quilt."

"This might be disappointing to hear, but I don't think I'm going to be a quilter or a lawyer." She looked past the window to the old oak tree that stood in the front yard. She was part of both her parents but also neither one. She was simply Mia and she finally understood what her mom had meant that one time in the craft room. "I remember she told me that I needed to make my own quilt, because no one could do that for me. I don't see it as giving up my dreams as much as it's giving up someone I'm not, and embracing the possibility of seeing what a different quilt could look like, one that is truly me."

"Mia, I don't think giving up is a smart idea."

She shrugged. "Possibly. But I think I'm going to be okay."

"Ross isn't—"

"You made a mistake, Dad."

"What?"

"You screwed up with Ross. You failed in your job, at least that one day. Who knows how many others?"

"Mia, it was a long time ago. You need to understand—"

"What if I wasn't your daughter? What if I was just some poor, biracial kid who made a mistake? How would I have been treated in your courtroom? I used to think I knew the answer to that question, but I don't. At least if you could actually admit to making a mistake…I don't know. It feels like it would be something."

"Look, I don't remember the particulars—"

"I've been killing myself my whole life, afraid to make any missteps, to live up to your standards—"

"Okay, maybe the sentencing was a little harsh."

"You made a mistake."

"You are my daughter and all I want to do is protect you. That's all I ever want to do, because I love you."

Tears burned in her eyes, and she nibbled on her bottom lip trying to hold it together. "I know. And I love you. And I love and miss Mom. But I've lived my whole life, looking up to you, so afraid of disappointing you. But, the truth is, you've disappointed me, and that hurts even more."

The color drained from her father's face. "Mia, I…"

Mia got everything out she needed to say. It was hard and gut wrenching and she didn't know where it left them exactly. Even so, her spine straightened with strength. She hadn't crumbled. "Well, I think I'm going to grab a few of my boxes from the garage."

"I'm not perfect. I've made mistakes."

While this was what Mia thought she wanted, she never thought she'd actually get it from her stubborn, hard-edged father. One side of her mouth pulled in a slight smile. "Thank you. Now what are you going to do about it?"

Chapter Thirty-Eight

A GIGGLE ESCAPED Mia's lips. She didn't consider herself a giggler, but at this moment, she couldn't deny being one. The ridiculousness of her current idea gave her an unending desire to giggle nonstop. The plan: housebreaking. It wasn't enough to stop by El Dorado Jewelry or call him or wait on his doorstep. She wanted to surprise Ross in the best way. Unfortunately, her plan also depended on the door being unlocked. Testing the doorknob proved he wasn't going to make it easy for her. *Drat!* Plan A was already thwarted. *Don't people trust people not to break into their houses anymore?*

Time to switch to Plan B: testing the windows. She found success in a window beside the patio. The lack of screen made pushing the window effortless, but climbing through it was another matter. She was soon fighting against Venetian blinds. If this was his idea of a deterrent against thieves, it wasn't a bad one. The blinds managed to catch her hair as she shimmied through the window before landing on the carpet in an ungraceful plop. Her break-in bent some of the blinds' edges. Welp, they were old. She could replace them with her barista tips if Natalie took her back…or really she could do anything. A whole world of options had opened up to her. Another carefree giggle escaped her.

With admission into the home established, Mia unlocked the door, providing easy access to her car and the items inside of it. She'd purchased bags of ingredients from the grocery store on the way over. She'd learned her lesson the first time. Tonight's surprise dinner would be simple. A simple French Niçoise salad, a simple paella with chorizo, and simple Mexican Italian wedding cookies with rainbow sprinkles. All Mia had was the Russo's Italian recipe binder, but she wanted to start a new one with recipes from the Diego family. In the meantime, her Aunt Sylvia had emailed Mia a paella recipe as the first entry for the new binder. Mia figured this dinner would be the good start of creating new traditions between Russo and Rosso.

Even with good intentions, it wasn't long until things inside Ross's kitchen got overwhelmingly out of control. The salad came out a little messy with her hard boiled eggs falling apart and none of the ingredients were chopped evenly. The wedding cookies were a bit burned around the edges and she spilled sprinkles all over the counter. And simmering diced tomatoes from her paella sputtered on Mia's hand. "Ow!" The spoon tumbled from her grasp, marking her tank top with a red stain on its journey to the floor. Mia bent to retrieve the utensil.

"What the hell is going on?"

She jumped. *Ross.* Mia was so absorbed in her tasks, she hadn't kept track of the time or heard the rumble of his truck pull into the driveway. Surveying the current stages of a category-five disaster in his kitchen, led her to believe this surprise wouldn't be the happy occasion she had hoped for.

She slowly turned in his direction. "I meant to clean up as I went—" But as their eyes met, she went speechless. Nothing prepared her for the flesh-and-blood reality of what being here meant for her—for them.

The distance between them vanished as Ross rushed to Mia, taking her face in his hands, pressing their foreheads together. "What the hell is going on? Am I dreaming?"

"You'd dream about me making a mess in your kitchen? Would that be a dream or a nightmare?"

"I don't care about the mess. Is everything okay? Did something happen?"

Mia released the breath she'd been holding, hooking her fingers into the belt loops of his pants. "Yes, there was something wrong. I moved out, but I moved to the wrong place."

Ross pulled away, scrutinizing her features. "What?"

"None of the apartments I looked at had the one amenity I really wanted. You."

A slow, beautiful smile spread across his face as he wrapped his arms around her waist. Happiness radiated from his eyes. "You're going to live here?"

Mia nodded in response, her own joy setting her soul aflame.

"With me?"

"Well, unless you're planning on moving out because of what I did to this kitchen. Although Hermes seems okay with managing the cleanup." The small dog's tongue was making quick progress at the mess on the floor.

"What about your plans?"

She slipped her arms around his neck, her fingers drifting

through his hair. "That isn't going anywhere for the time being. And I'm curious about what kind of a life I could have here while I try to figure everything out. I realized I was trying way too hard to convince myself I had only one path. I've been trying *most likely to succeed* without much success, so maybe it's time I try most-likely-to-be-happy. You'll still hold my hand in that dark room, Ross?"

"Always. You'll never be alone. And let's face it, most-likely-to-be-happy will probably turn into success because you've always been an eager beaver overachiever." He dropped delicate kisses along her jawline. "What I want to know is why you insist on filling my stomach with all this food when you know exactly what I want to do to you after."

"Huh. I guess I didn't think this through very well. Maybe while the food simmers, we can do our own simmering." She ran a light finger down the length of his chest.

"You always have all the answers, don't you, nerd-girl? What about your bastard salt-and-pepper shaker soulmate?"

"I've evolved my salt-and-pepper shaker philosophy. Why base it on nothing more than a dimple? Maybe the guy I want is quite different from me, yet complements me perfectly. What else could a salt shaker hope for?"

"Does that make me pepper?"

Mia gave him a bright smile. "You don't mind, do you?"

"No. I'll be your pepper."

They each tightened their arms, bringing themselves closer together, connecting gaze to gaze, the bright, unknown future of possibilities glittering between them like diamonds.

"I love your dimple. I love you. Welcome home, Mia

Russo," he whispered.

"And I love you, Ross Rumpelstiltskin Manasse."

He grinned. "That's not my middle name."

"Dammit," she proclaimed on a breath, before drawing his lips to hers in a deep, loving kiss.

Epilogue

"COME HERE, HERMES," Mia called, trying to capture the dog's attention by waving her hands. Hermes ignored her as he continued to expand his exploratory perimeter around their campsite, his nose glued to the forest floor. She went to him and attached a staked leash to his collar.

"You don't have to worry about him," Ross informed her while setting up the portable grill. "He never wanders far."

"There could be bears. And I don't want anything to happen to him after he's beaten cancer. He really is a lucky-penny, miracle dog." Mia provided Hermes with head scratches as he propped on her knee. His aggressive tongue slathered the underside of her chin as though she bathed earlier in bacon grease. "Yes, you're a good boy, but we don't want you to become a bear appetizer."

Ross gave her an affectionate look. "Alright, finish up with that dog. Maybe I also want to lick you."

Mia laughed. "Quit trying to seduce me, Ross. This isn't just a vacation. I have work to do here. Playtime is going to have to wait until later."

Mia retrieved her backpack from his truck. She located her camera, slipping the strap over her head.

"Mia, we just got here. There's plenty of time to take photos. You can relax first."

"No, you've been asking for these photos for a while, and I feel bad it's taken me so long to get to it. Besides, the sooner I can get these taken care of, the faster I'll be on vacation."

While Mia did take a Pony Expresso shift every once in a while when Natalie needed her, she was mostly busy helping other local businesses. Her main bread-and-butter, these days, came from providing photography for websites. Her latest customer was a family restaurant that needed new images for the menu. On a whim, Mia also put in a bid with the city of Placerville to provide new photos for the overhaul of the city's website. It may have been a long shot, but Mia allowed herself to feel optimistic, as she did with much of her future.

True, it wasn't anywhere near her original plans, but she woke each day living a life full of potential. No two days were ever the same, each one amazing in its own way. Whenever one of them had a bad day, which was inevitable even with great happiness, the other would scoot closer to the center of their metaphorical seesaw and be the one to lean on. With her completed marigold photo collage displayed in the entryway of Ross's house, she had truly found her place.

She retrieved jewelry from a lock box, removing the gold ring with the delicate bird's nest holding a robin blue stone. Mia crouched beside a tree stump, placing the ring in the center of the flat, cut surface. She arranged the ring with mountain rocks and a cutting from a nearby fern.

"Do you want any type of shots in particular?" Mia asked while adjusting the settings on the camera.

"I trust you to work your magic."

She smiled to herself. "Such a teacher's pet. I just want to make sure I get all these images done before you guys do the relaunch with the new brand. I want to impress the big shot owners of Lanza Fine Jewelry, *both* of you."

While Ross and her father's relationship was coolly cordial for the most part, the judge at least helped Ross work through the system to purge his record. It allowed Ross to feel comfortable moving forward and taking his proper place as one of the shop owners.

Once a week, Mia and her father drove together to Sacramento. Lizzy had introduced Mia to her friend, who worked for the California Criminal Justice Reform Organization. Her cousin was right, they did need help in their public outreach. Mia felt a little of that gleam she thought would be there when she first started in politics. Maybe she could make a difference in some new way, and surround herself with people who actually wanted to do good in the world. Plus, she got her father involved. At the beginning, their car rides were filled with awkward silences, but they slowly found a new way to communicate as equals. It wasn't a lot, and would never return to the way it was before, but it was at least something.

Ross took a seat on a log near her with his guitar, plucking the opening chords of "Hotel California." "The relaunch wouldn't have happened without you and your cousin's help."

Mia's finger clicked the shutter button, taking photos of

the jewelry on the tree stump. "What would you possibly do without me, Rosso? You should probably go ahead and marry me. I think living together for almost a year is long enough."

The guitar plucking stopped. "You'd really marry someone like me?"

She flicked through some of the images on the camera's screen. "Ugh, no. That's like asking if I want a cheap impostor. Why would I want to marry a guy like you when I can have exactly you, the real thing?" She looked at him, and grinned.

Ross's eyes remained locked on her.

"I don't suppose you have a special ring on you," she asked, more than ready for the next stage in their relationship.

"A ring?"

"I mean, I can just take this ring right here, but I figured, you of all people would be prepared for such a situation. You do own a jewelry store, after all. Plus, I've noticed you've been carrying something in your pocket for a while. I don't want this to go on forever."

"This is not how I was expecting this to go. I wanted it to be romantic and shit."

She took a seat beside him on the log, wrinkling her nose. "Just a tip, I don't think romance should be mixed with shit."

"Dammit, Mia. You already know I'm not good at this stuff." He ran a frustrated hand through his hair after propping his guitar beside him on the log.

Despite this, she smiled, finding Ross's fluster adorable.

She looped her arm through his as she leaned into him. "You're not much of an angsty bad boy, are you?"

"I'm really not."

"That's okay. I still want to marry you."

Ross released a sigh as he reached into his pocket and pulled out a small, black velvet jewelry box. "I don't know how you know everything."

"I don't know everything, but I do know sometimes you need a little push for your own good. I'm still willing to give you a nice shout-out on my Instagram. I'll even throw in the hashtag *romance and shit*."

Ross's face reflected amusement as he handed the box to her. "I know you have your favorite, but I made this one just for you. This one is yours."

With it in her possession, she popped the lid. Inside was the pearl twig ring she always loved, but this one was hugged by a circle of small diamonds. Despite her apparent bravado, with a ring and the promise it entailed, all the emotion hit her at once.

"Do you love it?"

"Yup." Keeping her response to one-syllable words was the best way to stay in control. She removed the ring from its case, sliding it on her finger. It sparkled in the sunlight filtering through the tree branches.

Ross put his arm around her, his lips pressing against her temple. "I love you. Marry me?"

"Yup."

"Where are all your fancy words now?"

Removing her glasses, Mia buried her face into his chest, allowing a few tears to penetrate the fibers of his shirt. She pulled away and wiped her eyes with a hand. "Yes, I love you, and I will marry you. Even I couldn't have planned something this perfect."

"Does this mean you're giving up being a planner?"

"No, of course not. I can't change who I am. In fact, this is what I have planned right now. I'm going to send my dad a quick text with the good news. Then I'll finish these images, you'll chase me around, I'll let you catch me, and you'll love me up *real good*. And, lastly, s'mores."

"Sounds like you've got it all figured out."

She gave him a warm smile. "It's the secret to my success. A little bit of planning, but flexibility for the occasional surprise. Walking into El Dorado Jewelry that day, becoming acquainted with you again, was probably the best surprise I could have had in my life. And I never saw it coming. How's that for fancy words?"

He answered her question with a kiss.

Eureka, indeed. They had both struck gold.

The End

Want more? Don't miss the next book in the Love in El Dorado series, *A Poinsettia Paradise Christmas*!

Join Tule Publishing's newsletter for more great reads and weekly deals!

Acknowledgments

I started writing this book in 2019 and it's been such a long journey, it's hard to believe that this is actually happening. While I started writing this story alone, it didn't end that way as there have been a lot of people who have helped me, which I'm grateful for.

Special thanks to Ashley Herring Blake, for seeing something special in my manuscript, and Kelly Peterson for continuing to enthusiastically champion me. Being a writer is not for the faint of heart but both of you have always made me feel loved and supported.

All my thanks to my publisher, Tule, for allowing me to be part of the team. I clearly don't know what I'm doing so I'm always grateful to have a wonderful group of people that's willing to hold my hand, from editing to design to marketing. Thanks to my editor, Sinclair Sawhney. Your insight is always valued.

Because I'm not perfect, this story was read and rewritten several times thanks to my critique partners and beta readers. You are all troopers for putting up with my rough, incorrect, and sometimes over-the-top writing. I will never stop but, with your help, I will tone things back a bit. Thanks to Frank Tybush, Leu LLewtnac, Adler Morgan, Starla DeKruyf, Lauren Sprang, Kristine Akenson, and Sarah

Smith.

I must mention Romance Fight Club for listening to my frustrations, panic attacks, and always giving the best advice, turtle gifs, and making me laugh. Denise, Allie, Beth, and Janel—I love you all! Casey Jones is the sexiest! (Now it's in writing so it's officially true.)

Thanks to my Tule family sisters: Stacey, Rebecca, Lisa, Denise, Heather, Mia, Kelly, and Fortune. Your wisdom and experience have been my guiding light. I'm so glad to have met you and been included in your group.

As always, thanks to my friends and family, especially to my husband who didn't even blink when I mentioned out of the blue that I would like to try my hand at writing a book. Now he knows more about publishing than he ever wished to know, and provides inspiration for some of my characters, more than he suspects. No one tell him!

Lastly, to anyone who picked up this book and decided to give this first-time author a chance, thank you! I will never reveal how many tears writing this book generated, but if anyone were touched by my words, then I feel it was all worth it and that is my happy ending.

If you enjoyed *Striking Gold*,
you'll love the next book in the…

Love in El Dorado series

Book 1: *Striking Gold*

Book 2: *A Poinsettia Paradise Christmas*
Coming in October 2023

Available now at your favorite online retailer!

About the Author

Janine Amesta is a California girl who now lives in the high desert of Oregon with her husband and their cat, Hitchcock. She studied screenwriting in college, but her moody thrillers always had way too much flirty banter. She's a master at jigsaw puzzles, skilled at embroidery, and critiques bad movies on Twitter.

Thank you for reading

Striking Gold

If you enjoyed this book, you can find more from all our great authors at TulePublishing.com, or from your favorite online retailer.

Printed in the USA
CPSIA information can be obtained
at www.ICGtesting.com
LVHW091359140923
758139LV00003B/199